SYLVIE'S SALVATION

AMY J. HAWTHORN

WORDS BY NIGHT PUBLISHING

Amy J. Hawthorn/Words by Night Publishing

ISBN: 978-0-9968801-9-0

CHAPTER 1

*N*oah leaned over the table and stared down the crooked cue stick. He lined up his shot, the shaft's smooth wood sliding back and forth through his fingers as he pumped the grip with his other hand. The blue-chalked tip slammed into the white cue ball, and a satisfying thump echoed in his palm. The white sphere shot across the stained green felt, smacked against the eight, which in turn spun across the table. Black and white design a blur, the sphere slammed into the rail. From there, it spun past his opponent's five ball, skimming within less than a centimeter of breathing room. Finally, just like he knew it would, the globe hit the corner pocket and dropped into the hole with a quiet smack. It landed on top of two other balls he'd knocked into the same pocket a few moments prior.

James Holloway crowed from the table's opposite side. "Sweet! Next beer is on me. Gimme a sec. Don't start another round until I get back."

Noah rolled his eyes as his friend left to place his order. When James sauntered to the bar and grinned at Sylvie, the pretty brunette setting drinks on a tray, Noah wondered if like others she only saw the good-looking playboy with a smart mouth and enough charm for ten men.

They never suspected the mouth hid observation skills that could put an eagle's to shame, a drive to work that would embarrass a squirrel preparing for winter, and tactical skills matched by few in the world. James had asked her out a few weeks prior but, surprisingly, she hadn't taken the bait. He hadn't been able to get more than her first name before she put up a wall.

Noah's opponent—an arrogant kid, barely old enough to drink, who had more money than sense—tipped his head. The kid's eyes filled with regret as he silently bid his money farewell. Noah didn't bother to ask if he might be interested in another game. The dawning realization on the kid's face had been clear when the balls started dropping into pockets one after another.

He wished he felt a fraction of the excitement Holloway expressed while watching the game, but he didn't. He could shoot pool. *So, what?* Yeah, the punk earned the ass-whipping, as he'd been full of swagger and boasts, but Noah hadn't enjoyed taking his money.

He took his winnings and wondered what to do with them. He didn't need them any more than he'd needed the stroke to his ego from beating some arrogant kid. None of it sparked his interest or otherwise made him feel anything.

But when a silken, honey and whiskey-drenched voice spoke behind him, his hand froze even as his blood began to simmer. The sultry sound went straight to his groin. "Here you go."

Shit. Down, boy! It was not the time or the place for his body to react in such a primal way. He turned, knowing who to expect. *Sylvie.* The problem? He'd completely underestimated the blow she'd land to his senses when they met face to face.

And he'd expected a Mack truck.

Short black hair, cut in a sexy, flirty style, fell just below her ears. Creamy skin covered delicious curves—just the right size for a man with big hands to hold onto. Full, petal pink lips smiled shyly up at him, and he forgot his name as thoughts of tasting them took over his mind. Those eyes? Big, bright, expressive. He'd never seen anything like them. Light brown irises, flecked with gray and rimmed with a dark chocolate border, they seemed to see straight into his soul.

What does *she see, when she looks at me?*

"Here's your order." Her voice, with its silken grip on his throat, spoke again. He swallowed hard, but she rewarded him with another lovely smile. After a moment, the happy expression dimmed. She tilted her head as if not sure what to think about him.

Damn it. He'd never had a way with words, and he was making a fool of himself.

K.I.S.S. Keep It Simple, Stupid. "Appreciate it, but I didn't order anything."

She held her tray higher, unconsciously placing the bottle of beer right in line with her breasts. She wore a simple black blouse that should have been decent, boring, but she'd tied the tails at her waist. With the top three buttons undone, the shirt revealed a hint of mouthwatering cleavage. A delicate silver chain suspended a moon shaped pendant just above the valley.

"Isn't this what you drink?" When she spoke again, he moved his gaze back to her face, thankful her voice had broken his thrall. "Your friend ordered it, said you were thirsty."

Forced to look down again, he saw that it was indeed his brand. "It is. Thank you." He pulled money out of his pocket to pay her.

"Oh, it's covered. Don't worry about it."

"Well, here. A tip, then." He handed her the first bill that he found, a twenty.

She started to object, but before she could tell him no, he gently cut her off. "Take it. It's a rough crowd. I'm sure you've more than earned it."

Something like sadness flickered in her pretty eyes, making his

3

throat clinch. Then she squared her shoulders. "Thank you." She took the bill and put it in her apron pocket before giving him another shy smile. This twitch of her sexy lips hit him below the belt harder than his cleavage peeping had. Without another word, she turned and walked across the greasy, peanut shell and bottlecap littered floor.

Once he lost sight of her delectable, denim covered ass as it swayed through the other people at the bar, he found Holloway watching him. His friend leaned against the bar between two, mismatched and battered stools and stared, his eyebrows arched high. His mouth moved at ninety miles an hour, as Holloway silently called him every dirty name in the book. Noah ignored all of it except the last four words. *Ask her out, dumbass.*

Hell.

It wasn't like he'd never asked women out before. For some reason, though, meeting this one tied his tongue in knots. With no idea what to say, he stepped forward to stop her. As he was about to tap on her shoulder, she stopped. She turned and looked up with a sheepish grin. "Oops. Your beer."

His beer still rested on her tray, which she offered to him by extending it in his direction.

He didn't take it. Instead, he opened his mouth. Someone at the jukebox by the door fed quarters into the machine. At any moment, they'd make their selection. The music would blast through the room, preventing any sort of semi-civilized conversation. *Now or never.* "Listen, would you like to go out sometime?"

Her mouth parted on a hitch of breath. She licked her lips, and he just managed to stifle his groan. Although his reaction to her was immediate and surprising, he prepared to be shot down. After all, she was working, and he was just some patron at the bar. But she smiled and knocked him for a loop, answering, "Okay? Sure."

He blinked but contained his surprise. "When is your next night off?"

"Tuesday. I work all weekend, because that's when we're busiest."

Four days. He pulled his phone out, ready to save her address. "Where should I pick you up?"

A strange, dark look crossed her face. That expression caused a gnawing sensation in his stomach, and he worried she would change her mind. Not wanting to skew the scales of her decision against him, he waited. Finally, she answered, "Here? Seven o'clock."

She wanted to meet him at the Thirsty Beaver, the trashiest bar in three counties? Maybe she felt more comfortable there, surrounded by her coworkers? He couldn't fault her for being safety conscious.

"Okay. I'll be here seven o'clock Tuesday." After tucking his phone back in his pocket, he took his beer from her tray.

When she smiled up at him, her entire face lit up.

Maybe I should buy Holloway's drinks for the next month.

No. Hell no. That's crazy talk.

I'm such a dork! Instead of bashing her tray against her forehead, like she wanted to, she slapped it onto the battered bar. Her dream giant asked her out, but she hadn't had enough wits to ask his name. She wanted to kick herself. If it were possible—in her totally impractical, yet favorite heeled boots—she would have.

To make matters worse, she'd managed something even worse than not asking for his name.

She'd spoken two little words, sealing her fate.

Okay? Sure. What had she been thinking?

Okay? Clearly, she hadn't been thinking, hence the problem. While dumbfounded by his presence, her mouth spoke of its own volition! She couldn't go out with him. She couldn't go out with *anyone*, let alone him.

But, damn, how she wanted Tom Hardy meets Paul Bunyan. *Dork.* She chided herself for her unintended innuendo. She would be a liar if she pretended she wasn't attracted to the tall, broad specimen. His thick russet hair, with its intriguing mix of brown and dark reds, begged to have her hands in it. Tonight, she'd finally gotten a good look at his eyes—lush, green irises, a color that reminded her of new leaves born in early spring.

And his facial hair? She'd never had a thing for beards, at least until she first noticed this guy, although she wasn't sure his sexy scruff qualified for full beard status. Not much more than a few days of growth on the chiseled perfection of his face, but a neatly trimmed darkness that tempered the line of his jaw. She loved how the softness of his mouth contrasted with the hard, masculine planes of his face, making him appear more approachable. Kissable.

Everything about him called out steady and strong. Rock solid.

When he'd leaned over the pool table to take a shot with a wild angle, he'd also unknowingly put that ass of his on display. It had taken every ounce of her willpower to concentrate on taking Jerry's order. The dusty old farrier noticed her wandering gaze as it landed on her giant's denim covered backside then laughed outright. He'd remarked in his raspy voice, "He's a good one, missy. You could do far worse. Better snatch up that steady man before some other sweet thing does."

Jerry worked with horses, didn't he? How did he know her giant?

She stifled the urge to throw her hands in the air. Even her customers vouched for him.

She was being silly again. There was no way she could know all of these things just from a few minutes of observation in her uncle's bar. Heaven knew, few characters who came to the Thirsty Beaver were model citizens.

She was just letting her imagination run away again. From before daylight to well past sundown, all she did was work. The poor guy had the misfortune to get caught in the crossfire of her childish daydreams.

But, damn it, hadn't she earned a break? It had been over two months since she'd given herself a full day off. She'd still take care of her morning responsibilities, then she could spend one evening with her lumberjack.

If nothing else? Maybe if she went out with him, she'd find out what a dud he was. Once she knew that for certain, she could put him out of her mind and focus on what was important. He didn't appear to be much of a talker, and her tongue grew clumsy anytime she came within eye-contact range of him, so it wasn't a recipe for success to begin with. They'd likely spend a couple of hours shooting each other awkward smiles over a boring dinner and it would be over, no big deal.

She could do that.

Guilt crept in, reminding her she probably should work another shift Tuesday. Her uncle wouldn't care either way, though, because he let her set her own hours. Still, she desperately needed the money. With one ear, she listened to her uncle give her a new order to deliver then loaded her tray up for another waltz around the room.

Ignore your screaming feet. They can cry all they want when you get home and free them from these ridiculous boots. A little over an hour remained of her shift, and she wanted nothing to dim her smile or her tips. *Every penny counts.*

She glanced in the direction of the pool table. Her giant sat in one of the nearby stools, long muscled legs on full display, while his friend played a round against another easy mark. His eyes weren't on the game or his friend. They were on her.

Heat flushed her cheeks as she delivered a tray of beers to a table of barge workers freshly home after being on the river for three weeks.

Tim—sallow-skinned, dark haired and a little creepy—slid his hand up her forearm before gripping her upper arm. "Hey, pretty

Sylvie. Share a dance with a lonely man? I'll treat you to dinner tomorrow night."

"No thanks, Tim. I'll be working." She pulled her arm free then set down their beers. Smiling, she retreated as quickly as she could without offending anyone. There was no point in subjecting herself to constant unwelcome attention if she couldn't rake in the tips.

Once she escaped groping distance, she turned her back on the table. From across the room, a green gaze collided with hers. Full of fury, her giant stood. Tension hardened the lines of his hand-some face, that of an angry bear, ready to charge across the room.

Chin high, she kept her shoulders straight. She didn't need a knight in shining armor. She dealt with this kind of thing every night, so she gave her head a discrete shake.

His mouth turned down with something like doubt and his fists tightened by his sides.

The last thing she needed was trouble. Her uncle warned her before—if her presence caused too much of an uproar, he'd fire her. He'd made it clear he didn't want cops coming in to break up brawls. Though they were a rough bunch, the Thirsty Beaver's customers were often generous to a kind smile.

She mouthed to her giant, *I got this*, then prayed he would take the hint and leave well enough alone. She did have the situation under control. It might be hard as hell, but she'd get through it on her own. As if doubtful, his serious gaze remained locked with hers.

Eventually, somehow, against the odds she found the will to break the nonverbal connection by ducking her head and getting back to work.

CHAPTER 2

*N*oah opened the battered cooler in the corner of the remodeled barn and grabbed a couple of bottled waters. He tossed one to his sane friend, Trent Dawson, who leaned against a sawhorse to take a break. His possibly not-so-sane friend, James Holloway, stood next to the stack of hardwood planks they'd been cutting and installing on the floor. James' hands curved, palms out in front of his chest, as if preparing to catch a fastball.

Wishing he could pitch a wild one at James's head, Noah instead threw a lazy pass directly into his waiting hands.

He snagged a bottle for himself then joined them in the center of what James had dubbed the Glory Hole. James thought the term hilarious, while the rest of the crew mostly ignored him. Noah and Rick had drawn up the plans which they currently used to convert one of Rick's barns into the future headquarters for Dark Horse, Inc. They'd framed out a couple of rooms, updated the wiring then added insulation and drywall. The walls gleamed in bright white while scents of primer and sawdust filled the air.

He never tired of seeing something new come to life beneath his hands as he worked.

Noah's own construction crew could have easily handled the job, but they were booked solid for the next six months. He already debated the pros and cons of paying out overtime in order to try and catch up with demand. He was planning to hire more employees, but it would take time to train them. Regardless, due to the schedule his team currently had ahead of them, it would have been faster and far more convenient to hire the remodel of Rick's barn out to someone else, but Rick wanted to let as few outsiders know about the build as possible. That choice meant they would be doing the bulk of the labor themselves.

Drying his hands on his shirt, he stared down at the mess of papers James spread on one of their makeshift plywood tables. With a sigh, he glared at James. "Are you absolutely certain *this* is the house you want?" He tapped his index finger on the floorplan, an image clearly ripped from a magazine. If Noah counted correctly, this was at least the fifth time they'd been through the same old song and dance.

James joined him in his consideration of the sketch, a sprawling stone and timber home. The design combined traditional craftsman lines with a farmhouse wraparound porch, perfect for rocking chairs and watching sunsets on the lake. Based on the proposed square footage, Noah estimated it would be more than large enough if James ever had a family but not so large that it would ever feel empty or hollow.

Lonely. That was the last thing James needed.

"I'm certain."

Noah's only response was to glare at his friend.

James held both hands up in defense. "I swear. I knew the moment I saw it. This was the one. I really do like the current plan. It's great, but it's not *the one*. This is. How hard will it be to make the adjustments?"

Noah reviewed the dimensions. As much as he hated to admit it, he could see why James wanted the change. Recognizing the whys didn't mean he wasn't obligated to give the guy a hard time.

It felt like they'd known each other since the dawn of time. He'd be doing James a disservice if he didn't make him sweat at least a little. So, he simply shot James a hard look intended to display every ounce of his irritation and then some.

Before he could express his frustrations aloud, James cut him off. "Oh, I should also let you know I ordered a master set of plans and the materials list."

"You didn't think you should've shown them to me to ensure the plan will fit your building site first? Not all homes can be built on any pile of dirt, you know. What if we have to call the excavator to come out a second time? That adds to the overall expense, not to mention additional time." In truth, Noah doubted that would be necessary. He'd ensured James would have a wealth of level yard around his lake home on the first visit from the excavator. Since then, they hadn't done much more than place stakes in the ground to mark where the corners of the house would be.

James bristled. "I'm not a complete moron. We've gone over enough of these plans together. I knew what to look for." He grinned sheepishly before adding, "Mostly."

Noah crossed his arms, shaking his head as if the entire matter was a trial on his patience. "Fine. I'll call to reschedule the concrete pour, and we'll make the changes...on *one* condition."

"Sure. Name it."

"Stop looking at plans. I mean it. Not another single one."

"I can do that." James smirked as he changed the subject. "Your date is tomorrow night. Have you chosen your destination? Selected your outfit? Does your purse match your shoes? I bet Kate has something that might work, if you're still deciding on a purse."

He'd already flipped his friend off twice that day, so Noah decided to ignore his comments. Maybe he could install all the doors in James' house backward. Better yet, he could switch the hot and cold water in the shower taps...

Unbidden, a vision of a curvy, sexy as hell brunette—as she

stepped into the shower he mentally redesigned to prank James—popped in his head. He shook the dream loose. Thoughts of the curvy brunette with her sultry voice wouldn't leave him alone, not that he'd shared any of that with the big mouth. "I'm well aware of what day of the week it is," he replied, proud that his tone remained even despite his imagination.

Trent crushed his empty bottle of water and tossed it in the recycle box. Addie, the young addition to Rick and Leigh's new family, would have their hides if she found recyclables in the trash cans. "Now that you two are finished planning your Barbie Dream Home and the wedding of the century, why don't you tell us what's really got your goat, James?"

James faced Trent as a smile curved his lips. "Eager to get back to your woman or your horses?" he teased.

In response, Trent took his turn glaring. James held his palms out in a gesture of peace. "Okay, okay. I can't say I blame you."

He figured it went without saying. Any man with half a brain wouldn't blame Trent for his eagerness to get back home. His beauty queen was even sweeter in nature than she was easy on the eyes. In addition to the happiness he felt for his friend, Noah felt relief in the knowledge Trent was no longer alone. He'd have someone to turn to when the dark memories of their past came visiting.

James continued, undaunted by their glares. "An old friend contacted me out of the blue. Haven't heard from Wilder McCoy in at least five years, maybe longer. I think I've only seen him once or twice since we met in Bagram."

Trent's head shot back. "Hatfield? Damn, it *has* been a long time. How is he? What is he into?"

Concern darkened James's usually jovial face. "Looked rough, real rough. But...well, this info stays within these walls and these ears, okay? I would've included Rick, but his hands are full this evening."

Trent nodded. "Yeah, Addie's afterschool open house thing. I remember him mentioning he'd promised her he would go."

"I don't blame him. That's exactly where he needs to be. I've made my decision, so I'll just run it by him the next time I see him." James stepped back from the plans for his dream home and began to pace the room.

Noah's brow furrowed when the full meaning of James's words hit home. "What kind of decision?"

"When I said Wilder looked rough? I think it was intentional. I wouldn't have noticed at all, not if I hadn't known him previously. I think the look is part of his new gig. He made me a job offer of sorts. He's joined an off-the-books operation, and he's running deep undercover. They're recruiting. Wilder wouldn't go into much detail or even tell me the name of the outfit. Very hush-hush stuff. I figure he was gauging my interest before divulging anything that might give away..." James shrugged. "Well, anything."

Trent frowned as he considered James and his words. "Damn. Those kinds of jobs can take a man out of the real world for months, even years. What did you tell him?"

"Not interested. I told him I was honored that he, or whoever hired him, thought I had what it takes to be a part of their unit. Honored, but I'm good where I'm at now. I might be seriously intrigued by the mystery side of things, because you know I love a challenge, but not intrigued enough to change my mind. It was an easy choice to make."

The tension coiled in Noah's shoulder eased. Yeah, no question, James would make a great addition to any team he chose to join. That said, Noah would rather have him on *their* team, smart mouth and all. "Do you want to have Pete do some digging?"

James took a long swig from his water then shrugged. "Thought about it briefly. Decided not to. I got the impression they're doing good work. Dirty, maybe even getting filthy in the process, but ultimately for the right reasons." He tilted his head and surveyed Noah from head to toe. "So, prince charming, about that date. Are you going with the shirt that matches your eyes or the belt that goes with...?"

Tuning him out, Noah hefted another board to cut. As he carried it over to the saw, he thought about rigging the doorbell at James' new house to ring every time he opened his shower door and smiled.

The early morning sun reflected off the coffee shop's door in a golden spray that made Sylvie's already tired, bleary eyes wince. The heavy box in her arms left her shoulders pulsing with a dull ache. She tried to shift the weight to one arm, so she could open the door. A customer took pity on her as he exited the café, holding the door wide. She smiled her thanks and hustled inside before she lost her grip.

The homey scent of coffee filled her nostrils making her regret that she'd lost hers somewhere along the way. An espresso maker hissed as the softer light of the café gave her eyes a much-needed break. A line of customers waited at the counter for their turn while others sat at mismatched wooden tables sipping coffee and working on their laptops or reading newspapers.

She blew a wisp of hair from her face. Increased sales of her baked goods and candies were as big of a pain as they were a welcome blessing. As much as she hated to invest desperately needed funds into her business, she might be forced to do just that. If the uptick in orders continued, she'd have to rethink her delivery logistics.

Something inside her niggled. She wondered if she wasn't selling herself short by delivering goodies by the box load to coffee shops and gas stations daily. Something bigger lurked, waiting for a chance to take that first breath. She knew it in her very bones. Yet, the worry that she might have killed an opportunity before it manifested haunted her daily.

God, I was so gullible! Stupid!

"Sylvie! Come on back and set that down." Marcy, the shop owner, waved her toward the back as she held the swinging door open.

"The fudge weighs a ton. Toting muffins and cookies isn't too bad, but the candy is hard on a gal. Your customers are trying to kill me. Maybe we should charge them more." It was an empty joke, as she knew that wasn't the case. She'd done her homework, researching prices at larger coffee chains and other businesses similar to those where her goods were sold. She'd painstakingly calculated the costs of her ingredients and knew down to the penny how much each recipe cost her. Before she and a shop owner agreed on a tailored menu and delivery schedule, she even took gas and mileage into consideration.

She carefully placed her load on a table before rolling her neck to ease the ache. Opening the box, she ignored Marcy's sympathetic look. Instead of commenting on it, she unpacked containers of cookies, muffins, scones, and lastly, the three flavors of fudge. She then handed Marcy a copy of her order.

Marcy barely gave the paper a glance before putting one hand on her hip and focusing on Sylvie. "Hate to tell you this, doll, but this fudge probably won't last more than a day or two. My customers can't get enough of it. As much as I'd hate to lose your goods, you really need to consider opening a storefront somewhere."

Sylvie met the tall, pretty, blond a few years ago. Since that initial meeting with Marcy, they'd come to know each other well. Recently, their friendship felt like as much a curse as it was a blessing. Sylvie didn't have time for well-meaning, lovely, utterly wonderful friends who wanted to help her. Not while she had so much work left ahead of her.

Just one more thing to hold against Calvin.

Sylvie squashed her pain and yearning as deep as she could and murmured a noncommittal, "Maybe someday." The muffins looked particularly tempting, and she cursed herself for sleeping through her first alarm then hitting the snooze button on the second one before finally prying herself out of bed. Skipping breakfast had become routine, and the gnawing in her belly reminded her she might have missed dinner the night before, too.

Marcy barely spared the clear disposable containers of baked goods a look. Her attention didn't waver from Sylvie. When Marcy bit her tongue and stayed silent, though, Sylvie sent her silent thanks skyward. Physically and emotionally exhausted, she couldn't handle the pity, no matter how well meaning.

Marcy picked up two containers—muffins and scones—and stacked them. "Do you have a minute? Can you have a quick cup of coffee with me?"

"Thanks, but no, I can't. I've got a large order to drop off at the floral shop and some samples for the diner before I get to the office."

Marcy's mouth opened, as if she wanted to say more, but she kept it simple. "Well, at least take a cup with you for the road."

"That would be great." She had no idea where she'd lost hers. Hopefully, it waited, cold and lonely, on the counter at home. Knowing her luck, it had been on the roof of her car as she pulled out. Chances were good that she'd lost her last and favorite travel mug. She followed Marcy out to the front of her shop and watched her friend fill an extra-large disposable cup. She carefully added cream and sugar, remembering just how Sylvie took her coffee without asking. Before handing it over, Marcy spared a glance to her employee, who bustled to keep up with orders. When a blueberry bagel dropped out of the conveyer belt toaster, Marcy grabbed it without missing a beat. She set Sylvie's coffee down, promptly split a fresh bagel, and dropped it into the toaster to replace the one she'd stolen. After spreading cream cheese on the hot bagel, she wrapped it in a white wrapper and picked up the coffee.

When Marcy practically forced both items into her hands, Sylvie's throat clutched. As if noticing the rush of emotion, her friend lost her battle with restraint. "Eat. Drink. And if you need help, then damn it all, *ask* for it. You have friends. Take advantage of them. We want to help you."

Sylvie smiled and prayed she could hold her tears back until she got into her car. "You want me to take advantage of my friends? That sounds like awful advice," she joked.

"Yes." Marcy waved a dismissive hand in the air. "Well, you know what I mean. I'd be happy to come by an evening or two during the week. I could help you bake or even just keep you company and wash dishes. Dad said he's seen you working out at the Beaver in addition to working at the lumberyard—not to mention the baking. You're running yourself ragged, babe. What's going on?"

The urge to spill her painful story to a friend—a sweet, loyal soul who wouldn't pass judgement on her utter stupidity— washed over Sylvie. The soft balm of affection warmed her even as she refused to accept Marcy's offer. She couldn't.

When her stubborn tears refused to hide a moment longer, Sylvie beat a hasty retreat toward the front door. "Your offer means the world to me, but I'm good. Email me this afternoon with tomorrow's order, okay? And thanks for the coffee and bagel."

Marcy pursed her lips for a moment before she shook her head. "Sylvie? I love you. Don't make me play dirty. I will."

"You're one of the best people I know. You don't know the meaning of dirty." Sylvie's backside finally contacted the door. She pushed it partway open with her hip.

"Oh yeah?" Marcy crossed her arms over her chest, her smile a little devious. "Try me. If you don't take a break and tell me what's got you working yourself into an early grave, I might not order any more goods for the rest of the week. Maybe my customers will suddenly grow tired of your lemon blueberry muffins and cherry scones. Same thing will happen over at Morrison's. You won't have a choice but to take a break for a couple of days."

Sylvie sucked in a surprised breath and the door thwacked her in the behind. Marcy's stepsister managed the three local gas stations—Sylvie's second largest retailer, since Marcy's coffee shop held first place. "You wouldn't."

"Marcy! That's sacrilege." The young man working behind the counter's eyes widened with shock. "The customers will revolt. Don't do it."

Marcy didn't spare him a glance, as her gaze never left Sylvie. "Some things are more important than money and baked goods. You know, little things like friendship and health."

An elderly man seated at a nearby table snapped his folded newspaper and glared at Sylvie. "Woman, you do whatever Miss Marcy tells you. I need my daily scone."

Sylvie's insides quaked and shriveled. Panic slicked her hands with sweat. She couldn't tell Marcy about the mess caused by her ex—she just couldn't. Reflexively, she found herself saying, "I am resting. Promise. Tonight, actually. No shift at the Beaver."

If possible, Marcy's glare grew darker.

Sylvie blurted more words, still trying to salvage the situation without admitting the reasons behind it. "It's true. I have a date, actually." She inwardly cursed herself when interest and a speculative light replaced Marcy's glower. Still, her mouth kept flapping, as she dug herself a deeper grave. "He's supposed to be a good guy, from what I've heard."

Marcy's forehead wrinkled. "Well, I would hope so. That's the only kind worth dating. You owe me some girl time, regardless. We'll set something up when you deliver tomorrow's order. Otherwise I *will* hunt you down for an interrogation you won't forget."

Sylvie managed a fake smile then turned, pushed the door the rest of the way open, and beat a hasty retreat. Once she made it to the safety of her car, she sighed. She almost wished she could be proud she'd battled her tears back. Instead of victorious, though, she simply felt defeated.

CHAPTER 3

*F*eeling like a fool, Noah sat at the bar and held his still half-full, single beer. He wondered if he should concede defeat and throw in the towel. He'd never been stood up before. Granted, he wasn't a dating machine like Holloway, but he'd had a fair share without a single one ghosting him.

There was a chance she was the type to be habitually late. Some people were. It wasn't one of his favorite traits, but it wasn't necessarily a deal breaker, either.

Willie, the bar's owner and drink slinger, thunked a bottle on the bar's opposite end, Noah spared him a glance then watched as Willie made his way toward him. The man wiped the battered surface of the old bar with a ragged towel along the way, his motions easy with familiarity. Noah lifted his bottle when Willie approached, so the barkeep could continue his path with the towel. Instead, Willie stopped mid-swipe. "What's got you so down? Something wrong with your beer?"

Noah rubbed a finger over the label, the texture cool and a bit wet under his touch. "Beer's fine." He hadn't even tasted it, really. "I think I've been stood up, Will."

The bartender flipped the towel over his shoulder then scratched his gray beard. "Stood up? By who?"

"Your waitress, Sylvie. The pretty one with bright eyes and great smile. She's got short dark hair, light brown eyes with flecks of gray…"

Willie's eyes crinkled, his dull gray irises getting lost in mounds of wrinkles. "You have a date with Sylvie? Bout damn time the girl went out with a real man. That last one of hers, he was a piece of work. She almost married the sumbitch." The old man visibly shuddered. "He had this fake smile and shiny shoes." Willie's tone made it sound as if wearing nice clothes was the equivalent of kicking puppies.

Noah was starting to think she hadn't been as interested in their date as he'd hoped. When he'd stared into those deep, milk chocolate irises, he'd thought she'd felt the same pull of attraction he did. Her breath caught, in what he thought was the good way.

Maybe he'd misread her signals, like Holloway suggested. At least none of his friends could see his misery.

He set down his beer and shook his head. "Looks like I *had* a date with her. She's almost twenty minutes late. Oh, well. Maybe she still has a thing for Mr. Shiny Shoes." He pulled out his wallet, resigned to her not showing up.

Willie looked genuinely surprised. "Nah. That was almost a year ago, right before she started working here. Even though she never said anything outright, I think he gave her some trouble. The one time I mentioned him I thought she was going to hit me over the head with her tray. Never saw that gal so angry, even when she was little."

Noah sat in silence as he processed Willie's words. Seemingly baffled, the old man continued. "She's never late. Sylvie is one of those annoying types, always ten minutes early for everything. Too damn responsible, if you ask me." He pulled his rag down and clenched it in his fist as he frowned. "Hmm. Maybe she got cold feet or somethin'?"

"How well do you know Sylvie? Do you think something could be wrong?" Even as he said the words, the hair at the back of Noah's neck stood up on end. His instincts clamored to life, and he trusted his gut.

Willie seemed to weigh his words carefully. Noah didn't miss the omission as he skipped over the first question. "Nah. She's probably just tired. She's been working an awful lot lately. She'd work every damn day, if I let her. She even offered to work off the clock, for tips only, if I couldn't afford the overtime. Probably she's just bone tired. Sorry about your luck, man."

Noah didn't like the way the old barkeep's eyes shifted away, and the feeling in his gut hadn't abated. "Willie, seriously, how well do you know Sylvie? What's going on?"

"Nothing. Besides, I don't know her all that well. Swear. I got a policy to uphold, you know."

When his eyes slid away again, Noah lost his patience. "I just want to make sure she's okay, especially if this isn't normal for her. Tell me her last name."

The barkeep grumbled then used his washcloth and wiped circles in the same spot. "You really don't know it? You were goin' on a date with her and you didn't even know her whole name?"

Noah set his nearly full beer on the bar with a loud smack and stood. "Your noisy bar isn't exactly conducive to meaningful conversation. Her full name, Willie."

"I don't like people asking about my waitresses. I gotta protect their privacy and all."

Flat out of patience, the niggling in his gut worsening by the minute, Noah slapped a twenty on the bar to cover his single beer. "I don't want to argue about a policy that you've probably scribbled on an old napkin. Give me her name or I'll call the sheriff to discuss the 'shine you're selling out of the backroom."

Willie's creased face went pale. "Shit. You're playin' hardball.

"Yup. I swear, I only want to make sure she's safe."

Willie's shoulders slumped, and he braced both hands on the bar. "She's my late sister-in-law's girl, Sylvia Grace Smith."

Noah turned his back on Willie. He stormed out to his truck, thinking he should go home and forget Sylvie. It might be the first time he'd been stood up, but it was her prerogative to decide not to come once she'd agreed. He knew that logically.

Still, even if there could be a reasonable explanation why she hadn't shown up, his gut instincts railed at him to get moving.

Something was wrong.

Over the past few months, trouble hounded a few of his friends something fierce. He didn't begrudge them the help he'd given one little bit, but he wasn't ready to sign on for more. He wanted a date—not a new tangle of danger and intrigue, not more problems.

No. No way. He would go home, find a game on TV, and forget this terrible idea.

His hands acted of their own volition. He picked up his phone and sent a quick text. Hopefully Pete was busy helping his wife with their two young daughters, bath or story time probably. He wouldn't get an answer until morning and, by then, it would be too late to act.

Need an address for Sylvia Grace Smith. He set his phone in the cupholder and turned the ignition. The engine had barely grumbled to life before his phone chimed. The hair on the back of his neck stood a little straighter.

With a sinking feeling in his gut, he picked up the phone and read the message.

Only an address? Child's play, big man. Just finished something for the boss. Gimme a sec.

Urgent, anxious dread tightened Noah's muscles. It had to be a result of his frustration over getting stood up. Nothing was wrong.

Yet, years ago, when he'd been stationed in Afghanistan, he'd learned to trust his gut. In the war-torn desert, anything less equaled suicide.

Willie's words replayed in his head. *She's never late. Sylvie is one of those annoying types, always ten minutes early for everything.*

His phone dinged with a new message. *3467 State Route 713.*

He knew the road well, but not the actual house number. He typed it into his GPS app then backed out of his parking spot. A quick drive by, nothing more. In thirty-minutes, he'd be at home watching that game he'd promised himself.

Rushing, Sylvie pulled the top she'd temporarily named "Blouse A" off the hanger and slipped it on. *When in doubt always go with your first pick, right?* She'd hang Top B and Dress C up in her closet when she got home.

No way around it, she would be late. Calvin showed up at the end of her shift at the lumberyard with a bouquet of flowers and a sob story. He babbled about how he wanted her to take him back, and she'd worried he'd get her in trouble by showing up at her workplace.

Some nerve. After all he'd done to her, taken from her…she still could not believe his audacity! Them getting back together?

Not in this lifetime or the next hundred, buddy. And why had he shown up after all this time?

She didn't have time to wonder about Calvin's oddities right then. *Late*, she reminded herself. Her fingers raced across the buttons as she slipped on her heels. She wanted to look nice but feared going overboard. She'd look like a fool if her giant showed up to meet her dressed in jeans and a T-shirt, like he wore last time she's seen him.

Not that she had anything against his clothing choices. The man filled out his long-sleeved shirt like it had been tailored just for him. He'd pushed up the sleeves close to his elbows, the action giving her a peek at his muscled forearms.

But she also didn't want to show up dressed to the nines if they were going to a steakhouse or something casual. *What if he pulls out all the stops?*

Gah! Stop being such a dork! He isn't prince charming come to rescue the fair maiden. He's just a hot guy you met at a bar. High hopes would get her nowhere. They'd only set her up for heartbreak.

As she hurried out of her bedroom, she turned off lights then checked her watch and cursed. She'd planned on getting to the bar a few minutes early, a buffer to give her a time to settle her nerves. She'd have to settle for being ten minutes late. *Hopefully.*

Grabbing her purse off the upstairs hall table, she double-checked to make sure she had everything. Closing the snap, she paused when a loud creak broke the silence. In her haste to get ready, she hadn't even turned on her radio, so that didn't explain the noise. She never had time for TV, so the remote for the set was likely making friends with her dust bunnies.

But that creak? It sounded exactly like the front door when it opened, especially on a humid evening like this one. She paused, listened, and tried to convince herself she'd been wrong.

One inhale. One exhale.

Okay, Sylvie, you just need a vacation. That's all. You're imagining things.

She gripped her purse with both hands, determined to get past the cloying fear keeping her immobile when she was already late. But then the front door creaked again, signaling it had been closed, and her heart jumped, lodging in her throat. Her house was old, no doubt, but she knew it as well as she knew herself. She knew what she'd heard, and she wasn't expecting anyone to stop by. Besides, no one came and went in her home without knocking or announcing themselves somehow.

Shit. What should she do? Ears hyper-alert for the faintest sound, she opened her purse and dug for her cell phone. She backtracked down the hall to her bedroom then touched the doorknob. Her door had a quiet squeak in one of the hinges, its volume nothing compared to the obnoxious front door, but in the oppressive silence, she worried it could possibly be heard down in the entryway.

By whomever was inside… alone with her.

She'd just decided to forego the extra security of a closed door when the mysterious someone stepped on one of the wooden planks near the bottom of the stairs. She knew the exact board. Her uninvited guest had stopped near the bottom of the staircase. From there, they had two options—one of two directions—up to the second floor and down the hall toward her and her bedroom or past the steps to her living room. Heart pounding, fighting panic, she chanced a glance over her shoulder as she entered her room. A small light flickered from in the living room, near her grandmother's roll top desk. One of the ancient drawers screeched as someone opened it.

The small light continued to flicker, clearly coming from the corner where the desk sat.

"Anything?" The quiet male voice spoke from near the front door, and she nearly jumped out of her skin.

"No. Nothing. Start in the kitchen. We'll go over the downstairs before heading up."

Heavy, quiet footsteps moved in the opposite direction of what she guessed was a flashlight and toward the kitchen. She slipped off her shoes and nudged them under the table. Then finally, finally, her feet moved, taking her through the bedroom and to the small attached bathroom.

On the way to close the door behind her, she stopped. She should probably make it look like no one was home. Wouldn't a closed bathroom door look odd? She also wanted to be able to hear anything if they came into her room. She settled for leaving the door half open.

With shaky whispers, she put in a quick call to 911 but faced the very real possibility that no one would arrive in time to help her. She lived out in the country. Unless a deputy just happened to be in the area, it could be fifteen to twenty minutes before anyone showed. When the operator instructed her to stay on the line, she closed her eyes and disconnected the call, not wanting there to be any noise if the intruders came upstairs to her room. She then put her phone on silent and waited for what seemed like an eternity.

Looking for something deadly or at least heavy, she carefully grabbed the toilet tank cover, stepped into the shower, and hid behind the half-closed curtain.

What were they looking for? She didn't have anything of real value, at least not anything easily pawned. She lived alone and didn't have many electronics. Her only working TV was at least five years old, and it hadn't been anything special when she'd purchased it. She had a few pieces of heirloom furniture, but their value was more sentimental. They weren't anything that could be easily hauled off and sold, and certainly not worth robbing her.

Calvin. Damn him. It had to be something related to her ex. He'd probably been running his mouth. He'd always had a horrible habit of exaggerating. When they'd first met, his exaggerations had been so subtle, she'd barely noticed them. He'd just seem excited. It had been so easy to ignore them when he'd been so good to her. *Perfect.*

She should have known better. No human was *that* perfect.

Sometimes his elaborations headed straight into lies. She'd bet her last dollar that he'd made some asshole think she had a house full of valuables or he'd gotten himself into even deeper trouble than she'd imagined.

And over the past year, with his lies, he'd given her imagination enough fuel to create some terrible possibilities. He hadn't been that way when they'd gotten together, at least not that she'd realized. He'd been so sweet and supportive of her dreams, or at least that's what she believed.

In addition to his storytelling capabilities, he'd also been an excellent actor and conman. If she never saw his too perfect, too pretty smile or heard his name again, it would be too soon. As it was, if she was lucky, she might be able to climb out of the hole he'd dug for her before she turned old and gray.

On top of everything else, he'd sent thieves to her home. Even if he hadn't done it intentionally, he'd likely been responsible.

What should she do? What did they want? How long would it take the police to get there?

She wondered if the intruders had left before bothering to come upstairs when she heard footsteps in her bedroom. Her palms grew slick, making the heavy lid slippery. She could hear someone opening and closing her dresser. The tall and narrow chest had eight medium sized drawers, and she silently counted them off as the intruder went through each one, taking long seconds before moving onto the next. When the last drawer shut, she waited. A moment later, she heard the asshole search her nightstand. The old frame of her bed creaked, so someone sat on it or...maybe they looked under it? Something that sounded like shoeboxes being shifted around and looked through drifted through her increasing panic. In the heavy silence, each of the quiet noises hit her like thunder.

Only her closet and the bathroom remained. Her stomach pitched. A bead of sweat ran down her temple. Sure enough, the clothes hangers ticked against each other as someone riffled through her wardrobe.

She closed her eyes and released a shuddering breath. Back pressed as tight as she could into the corner of the shower, she hefted the lid over her shoulder and waited.

The closet noises stopped. A few seconds later, one of the wooden planks just outside the bathroom door groaned. Having lived in the house her entire life, she could picture the exact board. Third from the last, where the flooring changed over to tile, it had a small hot pink streak from when she'd tripped and smeared wet nail polish when she'd been in her teens.

She couldn't imagine living anywhere else but...would she ever feel safe in her own home again?

That is, if I make it out of this in one piece.

The door opened all the way, blocking most of the nightlight's glow. Almost immediately, the drawer closest to the door opened followed by the sound of the subsequent riffling. That drawer shut and the process repeated on the other side of her vanity.

Please don't look in the shower. Please don't look in the shower. They wouldn't, right?

No one kept valuables in the shower. She'd be safe as long as she stayed silent.

Someone moved things around in the cabinet under the sink. A scary thought hit her. Wouldn't it look odd for the toilet to not have a lid on the tank? Hopefully, they'd think it was broken and never replaced or something. Heaven knew, the house needed more than its fair share of repairs.

When the intruder's elbow caught the shower curtain as he stood, making it swing in a way that would surely reveal her at any second, she had to bite her lip hard to keep from screaming. *Don't look behind you. Don't look behind you.* She held her breath, afraid to do so much as blink. Her heart beat against her sternum so fast, it could give a hummingbird a run for its money. A bead of sweat ran down her temple.

A voice called out from downstairs, "I'm almost finished down here. Do you need a hand when I finish the kitchen?"

The curtain fell back into place with a whisper of sound as the intruder headed back to the doorway. The volume of his voice dimmed as he left the bathroom. "I'm just about finished up here."

She was just about to gulp in much needed air when a vicious cramp seized her hand. The pain raced up to her shoulder, making her arm seize. The sweat slickened lid slipped from her hold, falling to the bottom of her ancient, metal bathtub. The clang echoed through the room like a gunshot.

"What the fuck?" someone shouted from outside the room.

From downstairs came the reply, "Man, this was supposed to be a stealthy op. Clumsy much?"

"That wasn't me." Caution and something deadly laced the voice just outside her hideout.

"Seriously? Shit!"

Footsteps returned into the room. A second set of footsteps thundered up the stairs and down the hall.

From somewhere in the cluttered depths of memory, she heard her brother's voice.

Sis, don't be a sitting duck. Those assholes aren't there to make nice. Surprise is your best bet. Fight hard. Remember the things I showed you.

If she could trust any one person on the planet, it was her brother. She might not know where he was or when she'd get to see him again, but she'd be stupid to ignore his words—even if they were imaginary.

Shit. Shit! She hastily retrieved the lid. Feet spread, she readied her stance. A moment later, the pink smeared board outside the bathroom groaned. She counted off three seconds, then unleashed all her pent-up adrenaline and threw her body at the door.

She collided with something in a solid thud. Someone grunted in shock. The door bounced back, but she'd known he would be there and had prepared.

She turned her upper half, caught the door with her shoulder, and barreled through, ready to take out anything in her way. A thump and curse erupted from between the door and the wall. In the darkness, she couldn't make out much more than a shadowy, man-shaped form in her periphery.

So very thankful she could navigate her home blindfolded, she ran, but someone else stood just inside her bedroom doorway. In the darkness, she wasn't able to catch more than a glimpse of shock-filled eyes behind a black mask. The figure held a pistol in one hand.

"Holy shit!" he exclaimed. His arm raised, and the weapon swiveled to point in her direction.

She swung the lid at his head with all her might. Startled, he dodged, and her makeshift weapon connected with his shoulder. It was enough of a blow for her to get past him and through the doorway. Something caught her neck, pulling at her, but she poured everything she had into her sprint. Material ripping sounded harsh in the charged air as she broke free from capture.

Not giving a second's thought to her blouse, she lunged for the stairs.

She all but jumped down them as a large beam of white light swept through the front windows. Probably the police—she wanted to weep with relief—but she didn't have time to verify. She threw open the door as one of the intruders cursed behind her.

Thunder rolled over the stairs as they stormed down behind her, giving chase. "Someone's here. Out the backdoor, go!"

"Is it the cops?"

"No flashing lights but I don't know. Move. Move!"

She paid little attention to their fading voices, focused on not tripping as she bolted onto the porch and down the steps toward the truck that had just rolled to a stop. Had one of the deputies come in their personal vehicle? She didn't care. Someone arrived, and just in the nick of time.

The truck door opened and, bigger than life, her giant stepped out.

Since she'd first laid eyes on him, there'd been something solid and steady that drew her to him. In that moment, she tossed all doubt to the wind. Fueled with fear-laced adrenaline and without a thought beyond reaching safety, she launched herself into his arms. He caught her without hesitation, but when she wanted nothing more than to burrow into his strength, he gently gripped her upper arms and pulled her back.

Searching her face, he spoke. "Sweetheart, what's wrong?"

"Two strange men just ran out the back door. They broke in

while I was getting ready. At least one of them had a gun. I'm sorry I was late. I hid in the shower and—"

Grabbing her by the waist, he picked her up and set her in the cab of his truck. He then reached under the seat. A little box popped out and he placed his palm on its lid. She heard a click as a drawer opened and he pulled out a gun. With his other hand, he slapped keys into her palm. "Stay down. Lock yourself in." He handed her his phone. "Go to my call log. Look for someone named *My Fantastic Hero* near the top of the list. Call him. He lives a few miles away. Tell him what happened. Now." He shut her inside the vehicle and turned, long, muscled legs quickly eating up the distance. In seconds, he'd entered the house.

What in the world?

The moment he disappeared from view, she fumbled with the phone. Eager to get help, she did as he'd instructed and went to his contacts. Surely, she hadn't heard him correctly?

But, no, right there among all the seemingly normal names was one labeled *My Fantastic Hero*. "I guess this isn't any stranger than the rest of my night." Without any idea what to say, she placed the call.

Two rings later, a male voice answered with a lazy, amused drawl. "Date over already? What's your word count for the night? Six?"

"Um." What should she say? She thunked her forehead on the window and closed her eyes. "Is this My Fantastic Hero?" *Oh man. This is ridiculous.*

"Sylvie? What's wrong?" The lazy amusement had vanished from the man's tone.

The view of her house gave her no clues as to what might be happening behind its walls or in the backyard and beyond. "Well, I was late for my date because two strange men broke into my house. It's a long story, but my date showed up in the nick of time and ran after them. He—uh, the big guy, my date?—put me in his truck. He told me to lock myself in and call someone named *My Fantastic Hero* because they lived nearby. Uh…is that you?"

"What's your address? I'm heading out my door now." In a flash, the man on the phone had gone from amused to concerned to stone cold serious.

Remembering her giant's instructions, Sylvie pressed the lock button on the door and slouched low in the seat as she recited her address.

"Is that near the old Smith farm?"

"Actually, it *is* the Smith farm. I live in the white two-story."

"Have you called the police?" A car engine rumbled to life through the phone.

"Yes. It seems like it's been forever since I called them, but I'm so far out in the country. Still, they should be here anytime."

"Good. Stay put and don't open the door for anyone you don't recognize. I'm on my way. I'll be there in just a few minutes." On a squeal of tires, the phone call disconnected.

CHAPTER 4

*A*t the back door, Noah turned off the porch light before turning the knob. The intruders likely got away while they could, but he didn't intend to make himself a sitting duck. He stepped out the door and surveyed the dark backyard. A car sat parked with its bumper a few feet from the bottom step. Maybe for unloading groceries? Beyond the car, in the light of a half moon, he could make out an old barn or garage with a pair of crooked doors, a large barren garden, and a couple of acres of shaggy lawn.

Not surprisingly, his quick but thorough search of the old farmhouse came up empty. If the intruders had half a brain between them, they'd fled fast and far, but he wouldn't be able to rest until he knew the area was clear. In the dim house, anyone would have been able to see his headlights as he pulled in. And the way Sylvie had been moving, they would have heard her.

He stepped down onto pebbled pavers that led to the garage.

Sylvie.

When he'd seen the fear on her face, as she'd flown toward him like a raven in flight, his heart had stopped cold. She'd all but jumped into his arms, and the stunned organ kick-started, jumping into overdrive. Her touch filled him with the drive to discover what scared her so badly. His protective instincts roared to life and he'd wanted, needed, to slay her dragons.

If only he could find the bastards. He didn't doubt her story. The stark fear on her face had been far too real. Unfortunately, he was no stranger to the sight of terror in another's eyes.

He pushed memories of fear filled eyes away. Unbidden, they'd revisit him soon enough.

Smashing the distraction away, he decided he would be damned if he would rest until she was safe.

Had she said there were two men? What were they looking for? On his quick search of the house, he hadn't seen any obvious signs of theft. While it didn't appear that Sylvie had many valuables, all the cabinets and drawers were shut. The locks on her doors appeared clean, no evidence to suggest tampering.

Anger spilled into his blood and spread like wildfire. What would have happened to her if he hadn't arrived when he had? The frightening possibilities were endless.

Those eyes...

He cursed himself for getting lost in the past and trained his focus on the present as he headed to the garage. Ankle-high grass whispered around his boots as he made a quick, silent circuit around the building. Although the structure showed disrepair, he saved his concerns for the state of its soundness for a later date. When he returned to the door, he checked the inside. He found a single light bulb with a string pull switch and turned it on. Light flooded the room, revealing a mostly open, empty space. An old riding lawn mower, gardening tools, and a few random boxes occupied the corners. He turned off the light and left the way he'd come.

In the distance, a finely tuned muscle car growled low and mean, signaling Holloway's imminent arrival. Knowing backup was near, he took a closer look at the landscape.

Heading at an angle toward the east, a barely visible path of what could be recently tamped down footsteps could be found in the damp grass. The depressions were several feet apart, as if their maker—or makers—ran with long strides toward the tree line. The trail disappeared into the dense and dark woods.

If his memory of the area served, Sylvie's home lay nestled in a crescent-shaped curve along the road. He estimated the intruders would only have to cover a few acres of land before coming to the property's border at the edge of the road.

As he debated whether it would be worth the effort to follow the trail, a car started in the distance from the same direction the faint tracks led. There was no way he'd reach them in time to see anything useful. By the time he made it back to his truck, even at a full run, they'd be long gone.

The purr of Holloway's car neared and then shut off. The tension in Noah's neck and shoulders eased. Suspecting it was a wasted effort, he walked a path beside the prints leading to the forest. It wasn't remotely likely, but he wouldn't leave anything to chance. If they'd dropped something or left a clue behind, he'd find it. With the knowledge that Sylvie had someone he trusted at her side, he could devote his complete attention to his search.

It wasn't long before he called his search quits at the edge of the woods. Only the weak light of the moon illuminated his path, so he wouldn't be able to see much farther than beyond his own hand under the dark canopy. With more frustrating questions than answers, he jogged to Holloway's car, parked next to his truck. In a deceptively casual pose, his friend leaned against the passenger side of his classic Chevelle and chatted Sylvie up. Sylvie had remained in his truck, but she'd rolled down the window to talk to his friend.

Just as his feet met the gravel of her driveway, a police cruiser with flashing lights pulled in and parked behind his truck.

"Sylvie? You in there?" the young deputy called as he walked between the cars.

Noah saw a flicker of movement in his truck then she stuck

her head a few inches out the window. "Yeah, Tom. It's me. I'm okay. I called and updated dispatch."

James nodded his greeting to the deputy as the uniformed man approached them.

"Sylvie, why don't you come on out and tell me what happened?" Tom asked. Noah noted that the deputy kept his focus on Sylvie instead of scanning the surrounding area.

"I can talk to you from here, Tom."

As the officer neared Noah's truck, Noah detected a fine tremor in her voice. Adrenaline shakes? Fear? Though it wasn't a fun experience, he hoped it was the former and not the latter. Even with her safely in his line of sight, the thought of Sylvie's fear made his blood run cold.

He found he'd do anything to prevent it. He came around the hood of his truck and joined the gathering.

Sylvie's eyes flashed to him, full of questions. "Anything?"

"No, nothing other than a possible trail leading through the backyard into the trees. Sorry, sweetheart."

She unlocked the door and he eased it open then held his hand out for her. When she slid her palm into his and stepped closer, he resisted the urge to pull her tight against his side.

The deputy, who couldn't have been more than a year or two past his first legal beer, looked him up and down. He gave Holloway the same treatment. "Sylvie, who are these guys? Are you sure someone was in your home? Sometimes sounds can be deceptive in an old house, especially to a woman alone."

"Yes. I know what I heard and saw. There were at least two men inside my house. I hid in the bathroom while they looked through everything."

"*Two* men?" Again, the young deputy looked from him to Holloway and back as if trying to draw a conclusion from something that was a coincidence. Noah was fast losing his patience when Sylvie shifted. In reaction, he placed his hand on her back and felt smooth, warm skin beneath his palm.

He glanced down and swore. The back of her blouse was ripped. A large tear revealed a gaping hole which displayed the area between her shoulders down to just below her bra strap. "What happened to your shirt?" Maybe she caught it on something as she fled through the house?

"They tried to stop me. One of them grabbed for me and caught my shirt. I'm okay."

The deputy asked, "They got that close to you?"

"Yes. I was cornered in the shower and had to run past them to get out. I—"

The deputy's weak patience evaporated. "Sylvie. Who. Are. These. Guys?"

She threw her hands up in the air as her frustration boiled over. "Why does it matter? This is my date for the night. I... I don't know his name, but he's a friend. And—" She pointed to James, who stood straight as she waved in his direction. "That's *My Fantastic Hero.*"

She leaned her backside against his truck and covered her face with her hands.

James, who'd been watching Sylvie in concern and the deputy with annoyance, looked to Noah and burst into laughter. With a heavy sigh, all Noah could do was pull Sylvie against his chest. When her adrenaline rush crashed, a long shuddering breath blew against the base of his throat, breaking his heart.

A low, deliciously rough whisper rumbled close to her ear and strong arms enveloped her. "It's Noah. Noah Ramsey. I'll make it okay. I won't leave until we guarantee your safety."

I'll make it okay. His sure words whispered through her, filling her with the secure warmth of a lover's arms. He didn't ask her if she *was* okay. She'd always hated the empty platitudes and conversation fillers people used when they didn't know what else to say, finding them as pointless as they were polite.

Instead of asking if she *was* okay, he let her know that he would *make* everything okay. As a woman accustomed to doing everything herself, something about his soft, simple words spoke to her.

She allowed herself a moment of solace. She'd lived through a hell of a scare, and no one would blame her for taking a second or two to settle her nerves. If that opportunity happened to occur while cocooned in the heavy arms of a male who smelled like sin and whose solid brawn felt even more decadent, then who was she to complain?

She pressed her forehead to Noah's chest and closed her eyes. Inhaled a slow deep breath then released it.

Noah.

Repeating her deep breaths, she vowed to give herself a break and get some rest as soon as she got through sharing her story.

As ready to face the world as she would ever be, she braced her clenched fists against the muscled wall beneath her and pushed back. When she turned to face Tom, Noah shifted and stayed right with her. One of Noah's hands lightly held her waist and his warmth whispered against her bare back. While she could handle the situation on her own, she sure as hell didn't mind having someone at her side.

"Don't get all badass on me, Thomas Michael Price. I babysat you and won't hesitate to tell your momma you were rude when I deliver her order tomorrow."

"Now, Sylvie don't get all riled up. I—"

She crossed her arms over her chest and gave him the same stare down she'd given him when she'd been a sixteen-year-old babysitter and he'd been five.

He put his hands up, placating her. "Okay, okay. Just tell me what happened."

She told them everything. Tension she hadn't even been aware existed evolved into something much darker and angrier. Charged with outrage, even. Tiny hairs at the base of her neck tingled as they stood up straight. The oppressive air morphed into something gloomier. She wouldn't have been surprised if she turned and found an enormous green hulk behind her instead of the rock-solid teddy bear she'd imagined Noah to be.

She finished her tale, eager to put her terrible night to an end. Unfortunately, that wasn't how things worked out. Tom turned his attention to Noah and...the man who'd answered to the name or title My Fantastic Hero. "And you guys are?"

Thankful he'd shared his name, she placed her hand on Noah's chest and opened her mouth to introduce him. Damn, she didn't really know anything about him other than his name, and she hadn't known that for more than a few seconds.

Fortunately, he handled the matter for her. "I'm Noah Ramsey." He remained stone still, with her half-tucked into his side.

Not quite able to pull it off thanks to his four-inch height deficit, Tom then tried to look down his nose at Noah's friend. Scorn laced his voice. "And you're *My Fantastic Hero?*"

"Name is James Holloway. The name is a joke. I only live a couple of miles down the road, on the lake's southeast side. Noah knew it wouldn't take more than a few minutes for me to arrive. He told her to call me, so she wouldn't be alone while he checked things over."

Noah spoke next, making her feel as though she'd slipped farther down the rabbit hole. "What did you bribe Kylie with? Candy? Money? A stray reptile?" His questions were so random and out of context.

James grinned. "Two dollars. Giving a six-year-old girl candy seemed a little creepy. I couldn't have Papa MacDonald coming after me. He's still got a mountain of work on his plate with the Riley Creek mess."

She couldn't stand it any longer. "What in the world are you talking about?"

"Sorry. James and I have known each other for a long time. Apparently yesterday, when I wasn't looking, he paid the daughter of a mutual friend to sucker me into handing my phone over. She said she wanted to take a picture of her puppy. I don't think there's a man alive capable of denying that little girl anything. I'm guessing that when I gave my phone to her, she took it to James, so he could change his name in my contacts. He was probably waiting until he thought we were well into our date before he called me to share his little ha-ha moment. I just happened to notice the name in my call log when I made our dinner reservation earlier. I've been too busy to change it back."

"Does this happen a lot?"

His heavy shoulders heaved a sigh. "I'd be lying if I said no." Then he grinned sheepishly. "You won't hold it against me when my friend acts like he's still a frat boy, will you?"

"Hey, now." James spoke up. "I graduated with honors." He winked at her.

At a loss for words, she dropped her head to rest against Noah's bicep. While she was there, she sampled his scent once more. *God, this man has turned me into a hussy!* She knew nothing about him, yet and she clung to him as if he was the only life preserver on a quickly sinking ship. This was *so* not her!

After Tom finished talking to Noah and James, he left them to take his own look through the house and at the tracks in the backyard.

Once he'd vanished into the house, James asked Noah, "Do you need anything?"

"No. I'll be fine. I'll check in tomorrow and update you."

"Sylvie? Noah will make sure you have my number. You ever need anything, you know who to call."

She couldn't help it. She smiled at him before teasing, "My Fantastic Hero?"

He grinned and then looked to Noah. "I like this gal. Can we keep her?"

She couldn't prove it, but she caught movement out of the corner of her eye that made her think that maybe Noah gave James the middle finger.

James's grin took on an even more mischievous air. His gaze sobered when he faced her again. "Seriously, sweetheart, I don't think it'll be necessary…" His gaze flickered in the direction of Noah. "But if for some reason, he's not here, or you can't get a hold of him for whatever reason, you can call me if you need anything."

He stepped closer, kissed the top of her head, then headed for his car. The monster roared to life before he backed out, leaving her alone with Noah.

She made herself pull away from his touch. "Thank you for stopping by to check on me. I don't know why you did or how you found my address, but…thank you."

"I had a bad feeling, plus Willie said you're not the type to be late. So, following my gut, I thought I'd check on you before driving home."

"I don't even want to think about what might have happened if you hadn't. Do you want a raincheck on the date? Or did I scare you away?" She forced a smile, even though the question matter more than it should.

"Nope. Can I get my keys?"

His reply stumped her. Did that mean he didn't want to try again? She couldn't say she blamed him, considering the break-in and her panic. Still, the thought that he had enough of her stung far more than she cared to admit.

"Sure. I forgot I had them." She'd kept them clutched tight in her palm since she'd climbed out of his truck, so she handed them over easily. "Um, they might be a little sweaty. Sorry. Nerves." *Okay…Where do I go from here?* She wasn't sure she could make a bigger fool of herself.

"All right, Sylvie." She jumped as Tom walked up to them. She'd forgotten that he was still there. How, she wasn't sure, because his cruiser sat parked behind the truck in plain view. "It's all clear. Call if you have any more trouble."

"Bye, Tommy." She waved and he got in his car. Delaying the inevitable return to awkwardness, she watched him leave.

The sound of Noah's truck door opening registered vaguely as Tom's taillights disappeared around the curvy road through the woods.

One more goodbye then I'm home free. Though, unlike when the other two men left, she felt achy and lonely at the thought of telling Noah goodbye. Sad.

It is better this way, she told herself. She didn't have time for distractions; her life was already far too complicated.

She dug up a bright smile from deep inside in preparation to send Noah on his way. His truck door thumped closed, and she turned just in time to see him stuff his keys into his pocket.

His extended hand was an invitation for her to take, if she wanted. Her traitorous palm met his sure hold before her brain registered the need to make a decision.

Without a word, he drew her with him toward her house. Dumbfounded, she followed him into her kitchen where he closed all the blinds and her curtains. After he turned on a light, he opened her fridge.

Finally, her mouth engaged, and she was able to speak. "What are you doing?"

"I'm starving. Was really looking forward to dinner, but it's too late to go back out." He rummaged through her fridge then set half of the contents on her counter.

"You're cooking?"

"Yes. Do you mind? You've got to be hungry, too. I'll make enough for both of us."

"Wait, you can't use the eggs. Or those sticks of butter. I need those for something."

43

"Okay." He examined the pile of ingredients as if rethinking his plan. "Do you have bread? I can make grilled ham and cheese sandwiches. It's not fancy, but it should do." He sorted this from that and put her eggs back into the fridge. "Skillet?"

She shook the haze of shock away and retrieved a large skillet from the cabinet closest to the stove. "Can I do anything to help?"

"Nope. Have a seat."

She looked at the small, battered breakfast table against the wall where she normally packed her orders. She couldn't just *sit*. Her body thrummed with unspent energy. She knew a crash would eventually hit her like a train, but as kind as his gesture was, she couldn't *not* do something.

It was supposed to be their date. They'd prepare the meal together and make the best of it. If nothing else, the familiar task of making food might distract her from thoughts of masked men searching through her beloved home.

She had been home alone, with nothing but a piece of ceramic to defend herself, which made it worse somehow. Her brother would have a fit, if he knew. *Damn, how I miss him.*

She pushed her constant worry for Brody away and focused on the present.

From the mudroom she used as a storeroom for her baking supplies, she found a can of soup. Returning to the kitchen, she fished a can opener out of the drawer, opened the soup, then handed him a saucepan. Next, she got a saucer out of the cabinet and placed three random votive candles on it in the center of the table. Setting the table with her nicest plates should have seemed frivolous when they were only having grilled cheese sandwiches, but it didn't. It felt right. She pulled out cloth napkins and her favorite soup mugs. Lastly, she filled two tall glasses with ice and set them on the table. "Is tea okay? I'm afraid I don't have any beer stocked." She'd taken a cleaver to her budget, cutting back on anything that wasn't an absolute necessity—though she wouldn't be gauche and volunteer that tidbit.

"Tea is perfect. Thanks."

She poured their drinks and returned the pitcher to the fridge as the sizzle of a buttered skillet awakened her stomach. The scent of warm, toasted bread made her mouth water.

Seamlessly, they put together dinner in a natural way that felt almost practiced. Routine? Yet, it wasn't in a tired, stale way. Working together was comfortable. He turned off both burners and carried the pan of soup over to the bowls. While he served the soup, she carried the plates to the stove and dished up the sandwiches.

Once they sat across from each other, they dug in. "You make a pretty tasty sandwich, Mr. Ramsey. Do you cook often?"

He wiped his mouth before answering. *Nice.* She'd always appreciated a man with manners. "A little bit. Nothing fancy, but it was either learn to feed myself or live off fast food, cold sandwiches, and freezer meals. I've never been fond of cheap, greasy cheeseburgers. I mean, they'll do in a pinch, but every day? Forget it."

"I prefer to eat healthier meals when I can, but I stay busy, so it's hard." She paused, stopping awkwardly. *Gah!* Where did they go from there? He'd likely planned a nice evening out for them, and it had been ruined because of her. Well, it wasn't at all her fault, but still. Guilt poured through her. "I'm sorry our date was ruined. I was looking forward to it, but...well, thank you for coming by to check on me or whatever."

"Not a problem. It bothered me when Willie complained about how responsible you are. He said it wasn't like you to be late or not show at all. I was looking forward to our evening, too. Listen, I wish we had been able to go out on that traditional boy meets girl evening and talk about all sorts of normal topics, but we need to discuss what happened."

She wiped her fingers on a napkin. "Yeah. I know. Freaky, huh? What are the chances?"

His grave eyes met hers, candlelight flickering over the green irises. "Slim to none. That's why we have to talk about it."

"I was afraid you were going to say something along those lines." Nervous energy flittered through her. Facing the memories of what happened, she suddenly wasn't so eager to be left alone for the night. She stood, taking a moment to brace herself for the upcoming questions. With the excuse of carrying their empty dishes to the sink, she steadied herself with a few deep breaths. After picking a clean plate, she filled it with cookies that were odd shaped or otherwise hadn't quite met the muster to be delivered to her customers from the glass jar near the sink.

Once she had them arranged, she placed them on the table and considered the tiny flames from her impromptu centerpiece. They subtly flickered to and fro, and their light chased shadows across the worn tabletop. She and her brother spent countless afternoons doing homework there, after they'd scarfed down whatever afterschool treat their mother made for them. For years, she'd wanted to strip the chipped white paint and refresh it with some pretty stain or a fresh, fun paint color.

Too many things waited on her "someday list," yet she didn't have enough time in each day to keep up with her "must-do" list.

A low, pleasured groan rumbled from across the table and interrupted her thoughts. "Good god, woman. Where did you get these?" Noah held a chocolate chip cookie midair, the perfect sugar and chocolate laden circle marred by a missing man-sized bite. He looked at it as if he had the Holy Grail in his possession.

"I made them last night." She smiled and broke a piece off one of the three peanut butter cookies she'd put with the three chocolate chip treats on the plate.

"You're shitting me." He waved the cookie in the air before taking another bite, then closed his eyes as he savored it. She couldn't see them, but she was pretty sure his eyes rolled back in his head.

Watching his reaction made the hit to her sales she'd take when she wasn't able to deliver more with the next day's order almost worth it. She usually made the cookies the night before. After a few hours of sleep, she'd get up and start on the muffins and scones. She wouldn't have time to make a fresh round, not after the break in and dinner with Noah. "I have a few more. I'll send them home with you. Heaven knows, I don't need the calories."

His gaze snapped to attention then narrowed. "Two things. One? I hope that's not a comment about your weight. I know we don't know each other well, and our first date didn't go as planned, but I see no reason to play games. My crew says when I bother to open my mouth, I can be a little too blunt at times. Maybe they're right, but I don't understand the need for bullshit or to dress up the truth to try to make it prettier. There is nothing wrong with your figure. Not a single thing. I liked what I saw the first time I laid eyes on you, and my appreciation only grew with each sighting."

She couldn't breathe. The air in her lungs seized somewhere behind her sternum. When he kept talking, her heart stopped beating.

"The second thing? As much as I love these cookies, there is no need to pack them up. I'll happily eat them, but I'll be eating them here. I'm not going anywhere until we have a better idea of what happened tonight and determine if there's any possibility you could still be in danger."

Surely, she hadn't heard right? It sounded as if he intended to stay the night? Thank goodness she was sitting, otherwise her ass might have hit the floor when her legs wobbled. "No one would come back to the scene of the crime on the same night. I'll be fine. I'll lock up after you go."

"That's great. I don't like that fact that the intruders made a very methodical search of your home. Thieves, even if they think they have all the time in the world, aren't likely to search the cabinets under your bathroom sink. Something stinks so I'm still bunking on your couch tonight."

An image of long, heavily muscled legs and arms hanging off her small, lumpy couch smacked her. *Good lord.* He had to be close to six-four. His feet would hang off at the knees. "Thank you, but it's really not necessary. I'll be fine."

"I'm sure you will, but I'm staying here tonight. I'll stay out of your way. I'm quiet. You won't even know I'm here." He winked, drawing attention to his green eyes. Her hand, holding her glass, stopped mid-air as her belly slipped to the floor.

Not even know he is here? It wouldn't matter if he didn't say another single word. The knowledge that her giant—Noah—was in the house would stay first and foremost in her thoughts all night. Not trusting herself to swallow without choking, she set her drink on the table. She opened her mouth to respond but nothing came out. Words failed her.

Thoughts battled for supremacy as she watched him eat a third cookie. Should she make him go? *Could* she make him leave? She suspected not. Did she even want him to go? She'd be lying if she pretended she could sleep easy that night. Even as exhausted as she was, she would lay awake more than likely. She'd stare at the ceiling and wonder what the intruders had been looking for. Had they been opportunists looking for a quick buck? Or had Calvin dragged her into some sort of mess? They wouldn't come back, would they? Would they wait? Or was there something they needed desperately?

Desperate criminals equaled trouble, dangerous trouble.

Already, her head grew dizzy with the questions. If it were possible to make Noah leave—and she wasn't going to fool herself into thinking it would be—she'd spend a long night fraught with uneasiness when he left. If he stayed, she'd spend an equally sleepless night thinking about him.

Her decision came easy, even if she suspected she ventured

into slippery territory. "At least take one of the guest bedrooms. You won't fit on the couch."

"I appreciate that, but that's where I'll be. It'll put me closer to both the front and back doors. I promise you, I've slept in far worse beds. During my time in the Guard, I was happy to find a safe place to rest, even if it was on the desert ground. Your small couch will work fine."

Something squeezed her heart when he didn't go into more detail. She tried not to react to the sorrow she'd glimpsed in his eyes before he closed them behind a slow blink. His quiet confidence and mannerisms reminded her of her brother, Brody. She'd often suspected he might have joined the military, and she worried about the unknown dangers he'd faced while away. The thought Noah of in similar situations tugged at something deep inside her.

"Noah…" What could she say? She should say something, but she couldn't come up with anything.

He winked and, somehow, she knew he intended the corny gesture to lighten the heavy mood. Then he stood and held out a hand. "Now, have pity on a single man and get me out of this treasure laden kitchen."

CHAPTER 5

*N*oah scrubbed a hand over his face. An alarm clock screeched somewhere from the second floor. A glance at his watch showed it was just shy of four a.m. Almost as quickly as it started, the obnoxious sound ended. Moments later, from the kitchen, he heard the gurgle of a coffee pot coming to life. An ancient faucet squeaked somewhere above him, then the sound of running water.

He stretched, shoving his arms over his head and pushing his legs straight out over one side of the couch. Something in his neck cracked and one knee popped. The little couch groaned, the ordinary sound like a clap of thunder in the silence. He instantly drew his limbs in, hoping to prevent a furniture catastrophe.

He debated whether he should get up, pour a cup of coffee, and start breakfast but decided against it. He'd stay put and observe. After everything was said and done, it had been nearly midnight when they'd parted ways and gone to bed. Why did she need to be up so early? When they'd discussed the break-in the night before, Sylvie told him that—in addition to waiting tables at the Beaver—she worked in the office of a logging company. Surely that didn't require waking up well before sunrise? She couldn't have gotten more than a few hours of sleep.

After dinner, she'd seemed frustrated when he insisted on helping with cleanup. Even after all the already neat space was spotless, she'd still tried to kick him out, as if he'd invaded her territory. Watching her battle the need to be polite against her desire to force him out amused him to no end. Still, he'd seen past his enjoyment and focused on her needs. It had been late, and she'd had a rough night. He hadn't guessed it then, but if she always started her day so damn early, then she had to have been utterly wiped. He was even more thankful that he'd let her be. He hadn't gotten all the answers he wanted, but he had time. He'd get them.

It wasn't long before Sylvie came down the stairs, her footsteps quiet. No matter how light her footfalls, the creaks of an old home gave her away. Her shadowed form crossed past him, spreading a clean and sweet scent that made his mouth water. She continued through an arched doorway and straight to the kitchen. A dim light snapped on, filling the entryway. Its pale-yellow glow displayed her curvy silhouette just inside the arch, hands on her hips. From beneath his hooded lids, he watched her look from his direction and back to the kitchen. She repeated the routine and sighed. Another brighter light came on, and she moved out of his line of sight. The refrigerator door opened, and it sounded like she sat some things on the counter. A cabinet door quietly creaked open and then another followed suit.

Was she already cooking breakfast? Why? She worked two jobs. Sylvie needed rest more than she needed to cook for either of them. Maybe she was a habitual early riser? He'd give her a little time to herself before going in to greet her.

Time to ponder the puzzle that was Sylvia Grace Smith.

It didn't take long before the random kitchen noises grew in frequency and volume.

Soon, a mouthwatering aroma wafted into the living room.

His stomach growled in annoyance, letting him know he was an idiot for playing opossum on the couch when something magical was happening just a short distance away.

～

Sylvie cracked another egg into the second triple batch of muffin batter. She'd love to be able to expand her operation with another oven. She could double her goods and decrease her bake time, but that wouldn't happen in the foreseeable future. Not for the first time, and likely not for the last, grief snuck up on her.

Damn him. Damn him! Damn Calvin all to hell. She knew the power of her words, yet she still couldn't make herself regret them. He'd taken so much from her, and he'd done it knowingly.

She'd work her fingers to the bone before giving up. That's what her great-grandparents had done when they'd bought the property nearly a hundred years ago. She couldn't let all their hard work be in vain.

Hot tears blazed down her cheeks. She'd die first. It'd be hard but she'd figure it out.

"Hey, something smells amazing. What are you making?" A sleep rough, deep male voice spoke quietly from beside her. *Noah.* She'd been so lost in her thoughts that she hadn't heard him come in. Startled, she looked up, not giving a thought to the tears running down her face.

Caught off guard she rambled. "Hey. The first batch of muffins is almost ready to come out, but, they're off limits." As silly as it sounded, she had to make every last one count.

"Sylvie? What's wrong?" He reached up to wipe her cheek with the calloused pad of his finger. Then he cupped her face in both hands and swept his thumbs tenderly over her cheeks. Her legs turned to jelly and her insides followed suit, melting into a warm puddle.

Oh shit. "Nothing." She forced a weak smile.

His concern morphed into a dark glower, which somehow didn't detract from his beauty. Beauty might have been an odd description to associate with such an overpoweringly handsome man, but that's how she saw it, or him.

And he saw right through her bullshit. Knowing it was a wasted effort, she tried one more time to make light of her tears. "Baking just brings back memories of my mom and grandmother. It happens now and then. Nothing to worry about."

He frowned, but after a long beat of silence, he let it go. "Why are you baking enough to feed an army at four in the morning, if *not* to feed me?" He smirked but continued to cup her cheeks in his palms.

"I'll fix you something, but the muffins and scones are spoken for." She swallowed as the heat of his body enveloped her. The reality of their proximity hit home. Something was happening, something big that she had no idea how to handle.

Then he stepped back. A breath she hadn't known she'd been holding escaped in a long rush. He smiled. *Damn it.*

"It looks like you have your hands full here. Why don't I make us something to eat? I'll stay out of your way." He went to the cabinet where she kept her skillets and pulled one out as if he'd been doing it all his life.

The oven timer buzzed, and she picked up a potholder. "Noah. I have a routine. Although I appreciate everything you've done, I'm good. You can go on home and get some real rest. You couldn't have slept well on the couch."

He acted as though he hadn't heard her and went to the fridge. He peered inside, then pulled out her bacon. "Are you sure you can't spare any eggs?"

She could, but then she'd have to add a trip to the store for another dozen before she could make the next day's goods. "I suppose I could share a few." She pulled what she needed out of the carton and set them on a towel. "It's the least I can do, after everything you've done."

"Sweet!" When he kissed her cheek, her belly pitched. "We need protein."

She swallowed and placed a bracing hand on the counter. The world threatened to tilt around her as he prepared to fix breakfast like it was just any normal morning. "We do?"

"Long day, right? It's not even five and you have a shift at the Beaver tonight. I suspect you've got more on your plate that you haven't shared with me, so I figure you need something a little more substantial than a muffin. Even if they taste as good as they smell, the best muffin in the world won't set you up for the day like bacon, eggs, and toast."

He was taking care of her. Damn, how long had it been since someone cooked for her? He'd done it twice in the span of eight hours and, as far as she could tell, he didn't expect anything in return.

Her heart melted into a pile of lovely, warm goo. He was too good for his own well-being.

The temptation to dive into his arms and vomit all her problems onto his broad shoulders surged to life. God, how lovely would that be? To share her burden, even if for a short time? Somehow, she felt as though he'd willingly take it from her. He was just too...decent not to.

That would be so very unfair to him. Noah didn't deserve her kind of headache. He stepped behind her, placed a hand on her hip, then reached over her shoulder to pull a plate from the overhead cabinet. Without a word, he then turned away.

While his back was turned, she placed her forehead on the door and closed her eyes in an utterly futile attempt to shut out her regret.

～

With only inches to spare, both door to door and bumper to bumper, Noah parked inside Sylvie's sad excuse for a garage. He opened his door and squeezed himself through the miniscule space. He slid sideways then closed the door, releasing the breath he'd sucked in while trying to become a paper doll. He made his way through the dimness, sliding sideways down the length of his truck. He grabbed his tool bag out of the bed and headed out into the bright late morning.

Wrestling the garage doors closed, he sent a little prayer heavenward in the hopes that the heap of warped lumber wouldn't collapse like a Jenga game gone bad on his truck. The weak hinges had to be replaced soon. He'd add it to his list of weekend duties, but he couldn't bear to think about the garage's overall stability issues.

He shielded his eyes as he looked across Sylvie's meadow. *What the hell?* Holloway ambled across the distance with...a dog? Attached to a long leash pranced a tan, dopey, short-legged, and long-bodied mutt. That was the only way he could think of to describe the creature. The beast vaguely resembled a basset hound, but it didn't have the acres of loose skin or the long ears. Yet, it was too...stout? Portly? It was simply too big to be a dachshund. Whatever the little guy was, it beamed with pride as it strutted along James' side, tail and tongue both wagging happily.

When the odd couple neared, Noah greeted them with one word. "Kate?"

With a wry grin James adjusted his sunglasses. "You know it. She made me come out to the rescue yesterday evening to meet Doofus. I'm not sure he needs the leash. He follows me everywhere I turn, but she'll scalp me if he runs off. Apparently, Kate worries about me spending too much time alone out by the lake." James shrugged but didn't meet Noah's eyes. Instead, he looked down at his companion. "She pulled him from the county shelter yesterday. They were going to put him down today because he'd been there thirty days. Seems like an awfully undignified way for a man to go down." James shook his head. "It's just not right."

There were a hundred things Noah could have said but he let

55

them all go. Instead, he bent to ruffle the dog's ears. Doofus slobbered on his hand in appreciation.

"I guess Doofus and I are on a trial run."

"You can't call him Doofus. Have Kylie name him if you can't think of something better."

James shook his head. He leaned down to pull the leash from the dog's mouth before straightening. "Believe it or not, that's the name he came with. Pretty sure we can come up with something better. Kate said he's a perfect match for me. How she knows this, considering she couldn't have spent more than a couple of hours with him before I picked him up, I have no idea."

Noah wasn't sure there was a man alive who could deny Trent's woman anything her heart desired. In this case, it had been a home for a lost or neglected pup. He suspected that Kate was just as concerned about James as she had been Doofus. Noah was, he simply had no idea how to broach the subject.

"You're going to let him ride in your car?"

"Oh hell, no. The goodness in my heart has definite limits. It'll be the old truck for this guy. I've been putting too many miles on Beth anyway."

"Cars are meant to be driven. I mean that *is* their purpose." Noah gave James a month before the mutt rode shotgun, tongue lolling as they drove through the countryside in his '67 Chevelle with the windows down, even in the cold.

They walked to the back porch, and he set his tool bag on the top step. Doofus plopped down to rest his tired, short legs.

"Yes, well some cars are better than others. Ashamed to say that's the one area in life where I'm a bigot. I am a total car snob."

"No one's going to argue that point." Noah couldn't resist asking his next question, even though he already knew the answer. James would've contacted him the instant anyone's toe touched the property line. "Did anyone show?"

"Nah, not yet. Though, I agree, it probably won't be long. Something's off. I couldn't put my finger on it last night, and I'm sorry to bring you bad news. This won't help your suspicions any." He pulled a bandana covered bundle from a pocket in his cargo pants. "I didn't have anything on me, so I rummaged around in your girl's garage, found the old rag and then returned to retrieve it. Not sure there's much point in keeping my prints from it though."

Cocking his head Noah looked down as James handed him an old-fashioned folding knife.

"Turn it over."

As the rock in his belly dropped another notch, he did. He took in the engraved letters along the cover hiding the blade. *B. Smith.*

"What are you going to do about it?"

As he turned the knife over, he admitted to himself that he had absolutely no idea what to make of any single part of the entire mess.

"It's too early. We still don't know what they were looking for. Hell, it's even possible this has nothing to do with the break-in. Where did you find it?"

"About two thirds of the way between the tree line and where her property meets the road. What you see, is what you get. I haven't wiped it down. It's possible one of them found it during their search then dropped it on their way out."

Though well-worn with time, the knife wasn't dirty. It had been well cared for. Wouldn't take a rocket scientist to know it hadn't been out in the woods for long at all. "Shit."

"Yup." James cocked his head as he looked down at his new friend. Doofus lay on his side, apparently asleep. James lightly prodded the dog with his shoe as if checking to make certain he was still alive. The mutt opened one eye, peered at his human before returning to his nap. "Do you need a hand with anything?"

"Nah, I'm good, but thanks. Take your boy home for some beauty sleep. He needs it."

Sylvie's shift at Garrison Timber started at 8:30. It had taken a little work, but he'd finally gotten that tidbit of information from her as they'd loaded the mountain of baked goods into her car. She hadn't been happy about his staying through their early breakfast, helping her with the dishes, and then following her out of the driveway.

He'd wanted to pry, to find out why she exhausted herself by working three jobs. He figured—by overstaying his welcome and with what he was getting ready to do—he'd already overstepped.

When she'd reached the town's outskirts, he waved her on and headed to his own place. He'd showered, updated Holloway, then grabbed his tool bag. He'd also packed a bag with clothes and a few things to keep him supplied for a couple of days.

The larger toolbox called his name, begging to ride along and set to work on Sylvie's...well, her everything. His hands itched with the need to tackle the dozen or so projects that needed attention. Squashing the urge to barge in and take over, he reminded himself Sylvie was an independent woman. She would likely take exception to him straightening the doors on her garage, refinishing the antique mantle over her fireplace, or even fixing the wobble in the little table where they'd eaten.

Not to mention her reaction if he tore down the garage and rebuilt it from the ground up. Or restoring either of the two old barns he'd seen on the other side of the property. Or...he forced a stop to the list of projects running through his head. He'd always loved working with his hands, whether it was creating something new or repairing something old, making it beautiful or functional again.

For the moment, he'd have to settle on replacing Sylvie's locks with something far more secure.

And setting a trap.

He had a hunch and James agreed. His friend had been eager to help, but Noah wanted to handle this on his own.

In mere moments, he'd picked the lock on the front door and entered the dim, cool interior. He locked it from the inside, intending to wait until after his visitor appeared before he started changing out the old locks. Until then, he'd work in Sylvie's kitchen. A few of her cabinet doors hung a little crooked, and two of them squeaked loud enough to wake the dead. She might not even notice the minor repairs, but it would give him something quiet to occupy his time while he waited.

He quickly took care of the cabinets, oiling the hinges and tightening screws. Next, he checked the table legs, fixed the one that had loosened over time. Afterward, he investigated the shelves in the mudroom Sylvie used as a pantry. She needed more storage. As he debated the cost—Sylvie's probable annoyance verses the benefit of better organization for her bulk ingredients —he heard the sound he waited for.

A car coming up the driveway.

It slowed and parked beside the house. When the engine cut off, he concentrated, trying to determine which door the asshole would try first. Footfalls sounded on the back porch, so he waited for the visitor in the kitchen doorway.

The backdoor knob jiggled once, and he frowned. A key slid into the lock, shattering the heavy silence. He crossed his arms over his chest, jaw tight in annoyance.

The knob turned, the door opened. It revealed a man who, judging by her uncle's description, must be Sylvie's ex. The blond-haired male was so focused on his task, he didn't even notice Noah as he quickly turned to shut the door behind himself. He then pulled a phone out of his back pocket and placed a call. The moment it started to ring, he held it up to his ear and headed into the kitchen.

"Yeah, man, give me just a bit, and I'll get it to you. Yes, I have it. I'll have it to you in an hou—" Shock froze his face into an openmouthed gape as he realized he wasn't alone.

A barely audible voice spoke from the phone. Whatever it said spurred the fish-mouthed Ken doll into action. "I'll get it to you; you have my word." With his gaze still fixed on Noah, the man fumbled to blindly disconnect the call. A faint trace of uncertainty and maybe even nervousness colored his voice when he asked, "Who are *you?*"

Noah didn't answer. He simply waited to see what the man would do next. What had Sylvie said his name was? Calvin?

Calvin appeared to gather his wits as he straightened his shoulders. "What are you doing in Sylvia's house?"

"Waiting on you to appear. Where's your friend? Why don't you tell him to come on in? We'll settle this, then Sylvie can rest knowing she's safe from intruders."

"What are you talking about? There's no friend. I just came by to say hello to Sylvia, my fiancée." Calvin exaggerated his pronunciation on the last syllable of her name, as if using her legal name made his claim on her that much more important.

"So, you mean to tell me, as her fiancé, you don't know that she's at work?" He'd known her a week, and he knew her schedule better than this idiot? He didn't buy it. If he weren't so pissed at the asshole for trying to steal from Sylvie, he just might laugh at the absurdity.

Pretty boy appeared to think about his answer for before speaking. "We've been busy and had a little spat recently, but that doesn't mean I can't check on things for her."

"Does she know you have a key to her home? Look, I know you're not her fiancé. Cut the bullshit and call your buddy in here so we can get this over with." He had two job sites to check over and wood to buy for some shelves. Plus, he wanted to purchase hinges—big, heavy duty hinges—for the doors on that poor excuse for a garage.

Bafflement marred the perfection of her ex's features. "What are you talking about? I don't have a friend out there."

"Then wherever your B and E partner from last night is, you be sure to relay every single word of this message. Sylvie's not alone. If I see the flicker of a shadow or hear the faintest whisper of footsteps on any of her property, I'll take action first and ask questions after."

Calvin's head snapped back and his face paled. "I wasn't here last night. Someone else broke into Sylvia's house?" Noah was nearly as concerned about the smooth talker's accidental admission as he was the pallor of his skin. "More than one person? Last night? Shit. I...I gotta go." After his final stuttered word, he practically ran out the door.

Before Noah could debate the merits of catching Calvin and shaking him until he confessed everything versus calling Holloway to follow him, he'd turned his car around in the yard and sent a plume of gravel dust trailing down the driveway.

The sinking feeling in Noah's gut grew into a yawning pit. He'd have to start Pete on an intel search before he got to work on the locks.

Sylvie walked in her front door and sighed. Her feet were already tired and the thought of trading out her work shoes for a pair of heels made her want to cry. She looked at the clock on the mantle. *Should I be good, and start a load of laundry, or be bad and lay down for a quick nap before getting ready to go to the Beaver?*

She kicked off her shoes and slid them over to the corner then wiggled her toes. While she waited on laundry, she could inventory her baking supplies. She needed to make a list of groceries, since she knew eggs were a priority.

Her belly growled, directing her feet to the kitchen. On second thought, a sandwich with a tall glass of tea and then the desperately needed nap sounded like heaven. Once she opened the cabinet, she paused. Something wasn't right. She couldn't put her finger on it, but the hair on the back of her neck stood straight.

When she closed the cabinet, it hit her. That door had squeaked for as long as she could remember. But that was silly, right? Unable to shake the feeling something had changed, she stepped to her right and opened the cabinet two doors over. No squeak. A thump sounded from the pantry room off her kitchen, just on the other side of the wall a few feet away from her.

Heart in her throat, she jumped. Then something hammered in a steady *thump-thump-thump*.

Shocked as she was, even with her heart pounding like the hooves of a racehorse, she wasn't scared.

Just because, she went to the cabinet where she kept her cast iron. Selecting the largest skillet from her collection, she smiled. Her mother had used the large pan to fry chicken for many special birthday dinners.

She'd also hefted it over her shoulder in a two-handed grip when an overbearing salesman forced his way into the house and refused to leave. Sylvie had only been nine years old at the time, but the memory stuck.

Sylvie walked through the doorway, not the least bit surprised to see Noah, tool belt around his hips, reaching up to give a nail one last blow. He pulled a second nail from between his totally kissable lips, placed it, then gave it two small taps.

She waited until he gave it two more, much harder blows before speaking. "Hey there. What were you going to do if I didn't want new shelves?"

Startled, Noah jerked and smacked his head on a new shelf above the one he was getting ready to install. He put his hammer away then glared. "Are you trying to give me a heart attack?"

"Me? You don't think I might be a little alarmed to come home to find a stranger doing construction in my pantry?"

He focused on the nail and gave it two more hard smacks, driving it home. "I'm not a stranger."

She set the skillet on the counter's corner and put her hands on her hips. "I barely know you. Close enough to a stranger, I'd say." Trim hips, muscled thighs and that utterly delectable ass drew her gaze. No way around it, the man knew how to fill out a pair of jeans. She could spend days admiring the view.

She almost missed the meaning of his next words, since he spoke in his quiet, matter of fact way. "I spent the night in your home last night." When they finally registered, she snapped her out of her lust-filled stupor. She looked to his mouth as he spoke, disappointed to find that even when he annoyed her, that portion of his anatomy wasn't any harder on the eyes.

"Only because you're too stubborn for words. I told you I'd be fine. No one came back last night. If they came here because Calvin spun some crazy tale about his ex-fiancée's big, rich, farm, they've seen I don't have anything of value. I'm sure they won't be back."

"Think again. We need to talk. He came by today. Did you know that he has a key?"

Her heart skidded to a halt. "For here? No. He never asked, and I never thought to give him one."

"He has one. He let himself in earlier."

She didn't know whether to continue to be annoyed at Noah for his stubborn intrusion or relieved that he'd been here to stop Calvin. "When did he stop by? How did you just happen to be here? What happened?" She leaned her shoulder against the doorframe and hoped he could shed some light on the craziness consuming her life.

Noah unfastened his tool belt and set it aside. "I had a hunch."

She blinked. "A hunch?"

"I learned to trust them a long time ago." He crossed his arms over his broad chest. "I went home to shower and change, then attended to a couple of business matters. I came back here and hid my truck out of sight. Then...I waited."

"How did you know he would show?"

"I didn't know that Calvin specifically would come by, but I suspected that whoever broke in last night might come back."

"They got caught in the act. Why would they come back?"

"They didn't get what they wanted. For some unknown reason, whatever it is, they think you have it. Where did they get that idea? Who gave it to them?"

"You really don't think it's done."

He didn't even blink before he replied, "No, I don't." The seriousness of his tone hung in the room, far too heavy and foreboding to be ignored.

Damn. Trouble's found me again.

Hadn't she had enough already? More importantly, how much more could she take? She felt her breaking point hurtling toward her like a runaway freight train. She took a deep breath and readied the silent pep talk she gave herself nearly every day. Before she released that same breath, Noah was there. He eased her into the warm security of his chest. Closing her eyes, she inhaled his scent and wished with all her might that she could find some happiness.

It'd been so long, she'd almost forgotten what it felt like.

CHAPTER 6

Noah packed the balls tightly into the chipped rack. Satisfied they were grouped as close together as the aged and warped triangle allowed, he lifted the plastic from the felt and straightened. For what wasn't the first time and likely not the last, he scanned the room to check on Sylvie.

He figured it had been less than a minute since he'd last checked, yet she'd already made her way to the other side of the bar. Again. The woman never stopped moving. As she placed mugs of beer on one table, she smiled—sweet and friendly, without being too familiar. When the coal miner's eyes lit with appreciation, she swiftly retreated and moved to the next table to take yet another order. Her long legs drew the gaze of half the customers. Her jean skirt came below mid-thigh, maybe closer to her knees but wasn't any less sexy as she worked her ass off, her every step graceful and smooth. Her generous and sexy hips swayed with each movement, and her high heels only made her already luscious curves sexier.

Sylvie defined unconscious sensuality.

His hands burned with the urge to touch and hold. To take.

Unfortunately, considering the cold shoulder she'd given him on their drive to the Thirsty Beaver, he suspected she wouldn't take too kindly to any touching or holding from him. Over two hours prior, he'd ticked her off. Now she refused to even glance in his direction.

All he'd done was ask if working a third job was truly necessary. Maybe he'd hinted that he would be willing to help her out financially, if she was in a bind. He'd probably gone too far when he'd let his tongue get away from him—he'd all but demanded she tell him why she felt it necessary to work in a trashy bar. Her bright eyes had gone cold and angry, making him instantly regret his words, even if he didn't understand why she continued to work herself into exhaustion day after day.

When he'd insisted on coming along to watch over her, she'd given him a glare that turned his balls into ice cubes.

Open mouth. Insert foot. For a man who spoke few words, he'd managed to make a fine mess of things with just a couple sentences.

Sylvie seemed satisfied everyone was content for the moment, because she made her way behind the bar and grabbed a bottle of water. He watched the long column of her throat work as she swallowed.

The urge to storm across the room, pin her to the bar and run his tongue up the sweet flesh of her neck slammed into him. Hard. Heady. Hot. In the dim light, her eyes glittered dark and deep as their gazes connected. Time stopped in a moment that seemed endless. She licked her lips, and he swore he could feel the succulent flesh beneath his own.

Until she remembered that she was still angry with him. Then the sweet, sultry glow morphed back into her prior glare. She pointedly turned her nose down as she reached for something under the bar, dismissing him as if he was no more than an annoying fly.

She pulled her phone into view and gave it half of her attention. Her uncle said something that made her shake her head with a wry grin. The uncle then slapped his towel on the bar, tossed his head back and laughed, clutching his gut and shaking. Sylvie rolled her eyes and returned her attention to the battered, purple-cased cellphone in her hand. She cocked her head at the display then swiped her thumb across the screen. Focused, she stared at it as if it held the secret meaning to life.

He watched as her curiosity bloomed into excitement. The delight glowing in her beautiful eyes grew so bright, he felt the same in himself. It looked as if every dream she'd ever imagined had come to life, and he couldn't wait to share in her joyous news. He half expected her to literally jump with joy. Without thought, he was halfway across the dim room, ready to join in whatever mystery celebration was sure to occur.

Just as fast as it appeared, her gorgeous glow dimmed, leaving Sylvie looking twice as tired as she had before she picked up her phone.

And hopeless. It kicked him in the gut, and he could imagine whatever the loss was, it hit her a hundred times harder.

It was then he knew he'd give anything to see that happiness return, if only he knew how. He suspected that, if he charged in like a bull in a china shop, she'd only clamp down tighter on her story. His gut said he was running out of time to find out.

When her defeated gaze met his, he denied himself the urge to crush her into his arms. With a slight nod, he veered off toward the restrooms, as if that had been his intention all along. In his periphery, she returned the phone to its place under the bar then picked up another drink laden tray with a defeated sigh.

Pain knotted and convulsed her feet until they felt so swollen, Sylvie wondered if she'd ever be able to get her shoes off. The ballgame ended almost an hour ago, and the crowd thinned out since then, until only a handful of regulars remained.

Can't keep going much longer. I have to take a break.

With fatigue beating her down, the thought of resting for ten minutes seemed akin to giving up on life all together. She poured herself a soda and debated on where to sit. She just couldn't make herself hide in the back room. It wasn't much more than a closet, and it just seemed…rude. Cowardly. Any other night, she would work through her break or sit outside to get some fresh air. If she sat at a booth, there was a fair chance one of the customers would join her. Sometimes they hit on her. Others were genuinely kind and only wanted to keep her company, not understanding that she'd rather be alone.

I definitely haven't been alone tonight.

Not once through the entire evening had she forgotten Noah, nearby and watching her every move. Granted, most of the time when she looked up, he'd been busy shooting pool or watching the game on one of the bar's TVs. Still, the heat of his gaze warmed her throughout the night. She hadn't been the only one to notice. Most of the customers she'd quickly learned to stay on her toes around had behaved themselves.

Not knowing what to do or where to go, she left the decision up to her feet—which dragged her to the closest empty booth. She resisted the urge to cross her arms on the chipped table and drop her weary head. What little pride she had left wouldn't let her. Plus, she feared if she did close her eyes for even a moment, she wouldn't open them for two days.

Instead, she looked for Noah. She'd assumed he would follow and join her as soon as she took a seat. He hadn't. Still on the far side of the room, he chalked up his cue and watched his opponent line up a shot. He hadn't even glanced her way.

What did it matter? It didn't. No matter how hot he made her blood simmer, she simply didn't have time for a man, not even a really good one like Noah.

The thought only made her aching heart bleed more.

Who am I kidding? I'll never get the loan paid off, let alone get enough money saved for my own business.

The urge to pull her phone from her apron pocket and reread the text she'd received from Marcy nagged her. She pulled it out and laid it on the table. Like a forbidden fruit, it lay in front of her promising her both dreams and heartache.

She'd never felt so alone and hopeless. The knowledge that something so simple held so much sway over her heart only magnified her loss.

She stared at the bubbles in her drink and longed for a pillow to shed her tears into. She pictured a pillow the size of a house, because it would take something that large to absorb all her sorrow.

After what felt like ages, but had only been about five minutes, Noah sat across from her. She tried to ignore the worry in his eyes as he greeted her with a simple, "Hey."

Unable to fake a smile, she used her straw to poke at the ice in her soda. "Hey yourself."

A bubble got caught beneath a cluster of cubes and she used her straw to free it. She sensed Noah's silent but hefty sigh. No one with shoulders that broad should be capable of moving so quietly but he did.

Then again, her brother had been able to do that, too. How she missed him.

Noah cleared his throat, then apparently lost his battle with patience. "Sylvie, enough is enough. We'll start with the message on your phone. Spill." His deep voice rumbled, a rough caress washing over her with a comfort she simply didn't have the strength to fight.

"It's silly." And it was. How terrible was it that something as simple as a cookie order had the power to devastate her?

"It's not silly if it caused the pain I witnessed on your face. One moment, you were flying high. The next, you looked as if you had the rug pulled from under your feet. Or worse."

Closing her eyes, she gave in. "I just received an order that could essentially make or break my...dream of owning my own business." She nearly choked on the word dream, but why hide the truth? That's what it was.

Noah stated the obvious. "That's amazing." Then he found a way to break her heart a little more. She thought there wasn't much remaining, but he found a single piece and with a simple sentence, busted it all to hell. "When do we get to work?"

This kind, sexy, hardworking man just offered to help me bake cookies. If he only knew...

"I'd need to bake almost two thousand cookies for the wedding of a celebrity scheduled in just over three weeks. There's a good chance I could get those cookies, or my brand, mentioned on national television, not to mention all the gossip websites clamoring for wedding details."

His face brightened, and she could actually see his determination set in. She might not have known him long, but there was no question—the man loved his projects. "Babe, are you talking about the same cookies I ate last night? You have to do whatever it takes to fill this order. The world needs your cookies. Explain yourself."

She couldn't hold back the mass of emotion any longer. She simply didn't have any more strength. A sob made of equal parts pain and amusement escaped. Two tears followed before she hastily wiped them away. "Marcy, a friend and loyal customer, is the cousin of Karli Skye."

Noah blinked. "Who's Karli Skye?"

She hoped her eyes didn't bug out of her head. Everyone knew Karli, especially in Kentucky. "She was last season's winner on the TV show *Sing On.*"

Nothing registered on Noah's face other than a flicker of impatience as he waited for her to get to the important part.

"Trust me, the show is a big deal. The winner gets a recording contract and a ton of press. Karli is a fan favorite. She's gorgeous —this mix of sultry country girl meets rebel rocker that really works." She released the drink she'd been turning in circles in her palms when Noah reached for it.

He took a swallow of her soda and gave her a look that said *get to the point*, so she did. "In almost three weeks, Karli is getting married here in her hometown. She stopped by Marcy's café to chat, and she had one of my cookies. She wants to order a six-pack for each of her nearly three hundred guests as wedding favors. The cameras will be there. Karli already set her wedding date and plans before she landed a spot on the show, but now the show's producers want to do a follow up special to air in preparation of the new season. Karli insisted on the cookies, and they offered to feature the cookie favors in exchange for a discounted rate."

He threw his hands up in the air, seeming genuinely perplexed. "Again, that's amazing. I don't understand why you aren't jumping up and down or making a shopping list or...whatever it is that kickass bakers do."

Kickass bakers. God, witnessing his confidence in her abilities was a warm balm to her busted heart. Unfortunately, however, it didn't change a damn thing. She couldn't take the job. "Noah, it's an impossible dream. I can't take it."

"Why not?"

"Time. Space. Help. Hell, I'd need another oven. Maybe two."

"I can do that. A few modifications and it shouldn't be too much trouble. How much help would you need?"

She shook her head. "You can't just *get* me an oven. That's crazy."

She could almost watch the wheels turning as he dove in head-first. "I build houses, remember? I'll round something up. Give me a couple of days, and we can extend your island, pull out a couple of cabinets, run some electrical, and put in another oven. With this time crunch it might not be pretty, but we can put something functional together. For help, do you mean more bakers? What if I can round up two or three competent women, easy to get along with, who know their way around a kitchen? They'll listen to your direction and are all-around great company."

She fought to squash down the bright bubble of hope growing inside her. She'd have to relinquish a little bit of control and trust her dream to virtual strangers. She had nothing but Noah's word and blind faith that he could deliver everything he promised.

But, without those two things, I have nothing at all.

"You're sure they can follow directions, and they know how to bake?"

"I promise. They're some of the best women I've ever met, and I think you all will get along well. I wouldn't trust something as important as this to anyone else. I swear." His eyes radiated nothing but earnest determination. So much so, that the crazy idea almost seemed possible. For the first time in what felt like forever, she had someone she could rely on. The realization was as scary as it was exciting. This man held her future in the palm of his big hand.

"You're crazy. I... *Noah*. This is my everything. I can't mess this up."

"*We*. We can't mess it up. And we won't. Now, what do you say we go home so I can get some measurements and you can get some sleep. In the morning, over breakfast, you're going to tell me the rest of your story. I totally get why you want your own business. It is definitely something worth fighting for, but you're a practical woman. You can't expect me to believe that's what's putting the dark shadows under and in your eyes."

"Okay. My shift is over in an hour. Then—"

He cut her off with a firm but gentle denial. "No. Your shift is over now. Your feet are killing you. You're done for the night and the week."

"I'm fine. I can—"

"Sweetheart, I've spent enough time watching your hips sway as they come and go all over this godforsaken heap. I know that walk. You're stiff as a board. I'm going to go tell your uncle that you're finished for the week, then we're going home." He scooted out and headed straight for the bar. Willie shook his head and then grabbed her purse from under the bar. He handed it to Noah and shook his finger at him with a stern frown. Noah held his hand out and when her uncle did the same, they shook. With all the manly rituals out of the way, he returned and offered the same hand to her. "We've got work to do. Let's get out of here."

Something told her she'd be a fool to argue. And her mother hadn't suffered or raised a single fool. He drove them back to her house in no time. She spent most of the ride with her temple laying against the cool glass. She feared that if she gave in and lay her head back against the headrest, she'd fall asleep and not wake for a month.

Plans, questions, ideas swam through her mind in a whirlpool of what ifs. Through it all, one thing stood out. The man beside her. He simply had to be too good to be true, didn't he?

"Noah?" She watched the night pass them by as he competently drove them home.

"Yeah?"

"You sure you're not a devil in disguise?"

"What?" She heard the confusion in his voice as she admired a passing house she'd always loved growing up. Now she just hoped she could save hers.

"Rescuing damsels in distress. Fixing squeaky cabinets. Building shelves. Finding extra ovens. Are you sure you're not a serial killer in disguise?"

He seemed to think about her words. The weighty pause made her imagine she could be onto something. "I can promise you I'm no serial killer."

She smiled weakly. "But that's what all serial killers say."

"Probably. I can assure you that I am not out to turn you into some sort of grisly trophy. I like your body just fine the way it is. Soft and warm. Sexy. I have no desire to do anything that would change that or you."

"I bet you have a lot of scary looking tools."

"No doubt. I do own a *lot* of tools." He glanced her direction, shooting her an easy grin. "None have ever come in contact with anyone's blood."

"That's comforting."

He pulled his truck into her driveway, parking right in front of the porch as if making a statement. *She's not alone tonight, assholes.* "Wait, that's a lie. James borrowed a handsaw once. He denies it, but I'm pretty sure the bandage he was wearing on his hand a few days later didn't come from the raccoon he claims to have found digging through his trash. So, it's possible at least one of them was ceremonially baptized with James' blood. But I have no fault in that, unless there's a law against loaning tools to inept friends."

The image of his friend with a bandaged hand, shrugging in denial, made her smile. She shook her head as she opened the door.

He stopped her before she could set one foot on the ground. "Hang on. Stay here. Let me do a check."

From the entryway, Sylvie surveyed her dark, silent kitchen. As far as she could tell, everything appeared to be in order. Judging by the noises she'd heard the night before, after Noah brought her home from the Thirsty Beaver, she half-expected to find a war zone.

The moment they'd entered the front door, he'd pointed to the stairs and ordered. "Bed. I'll see you in the morning." Any other night, her automatic response would have been to skewer him with a hard look before offering cold refusal to do as she'd been told. Right then, though, she barely had enough steam to carry herself up the stairs to her room. In Noah's truck on the way home, she'd forgotten her pride and removed her shoes, but her feet still hadn't forgiven her.

As she'd changed into an old loose t-shirt, she'd heard the tell-tale screech of an appliance being scooted across the floor. The creaking of floors, a door opening and closing, more creaking and more appliance scooting had soon followed. Seconds after her head hit the pillow, she'd been out for the count.

Looking at the illuminated clock on the stove, she counted how many hours she'd slept. She'd almost made it to four, but not quite. How long had she been doing this? This was ridiculous. She couldn't survive at this pace, and she wasn't making enough progress for it to be worth the strain. *Something has to give.*

When her alarm went off that morning, she'd wanted to cry. In the shower, she'd finally conceded that she didn't really have anything to lose. Yes, her home—the place where she'd been raised which had been in the family for over a hundred years—was on the line. She wanted nothing more than to save it, but her own stupidity put it on the line in the first place. As a result, she'd landed herself on a quickly sinking ship. If she was going to go down, she might as well give this crazy plan her all.

The thought of giving in filled her eyes with tears, but what else could she do?

Nothing. She'd spent countless hours looking for a way out and hadn't come up with anything. If this crazy cookie plan was the best idea she had, then she'd give it every ounce of energy she could muster. She'd been going months on very little sleep. Surely, she could make it just a little longer. After that, good outcome or bad, she'd be done when it was over.

Thankfully her midweek order for Marcy was considerably lighter. She only had to make the muffins. If Marcy ran out of sweets, her loyal customers would just have to make do for a couple of days while she attempted to get her life in order.

No. Scratch that. They will *have to wait while I get my life in order. No attempting, only doing.*

Marcy would understand. The text she'd sent detailing Karli's order the night before had been littered with enough exclamation points and excited emojis to fill a middle school auditorium.

Marci might even be willing to lend a hand. Hell, she'll be mad if I don't include her.

With the knowledge that she had at least one friend to lend a hand, one of the chains holding her back released. Maybe she could meet Marcy for lunch, and together they could brainstorm how to package the cookies? They'd need something cute but not too costly. Karli would likely want a mix of traditional elegance and country fun.

She went into her new and improved pantry area and looked over her space. She hadn't had enough time to do more than daydream a bit while in the shower yesterday about how she'd like to organize things. Ideas. Plans. Hopes. They all converged with an increased intensity, more vivid and...real.

Warm arms wrapped around her middle and heat blanketed her back. "Hey." Deep and a little more sleep-rough than its usual rumble, Noah's voice did funny things to her belly. She couldn't remember the last time she'd felt something so exciting and delicious. A luscious, liquid warmth came to life deep within her.

Desire.

"Morning. What are we baking today?" he asked.

The wobble in her legs had nothing to do with her poor choice in footwear the night before. *Heaven help me. I'm not sure I've ever wanted a man the way I crave Noah.* Although she knew she should fight the attraction, she simply couldn't make herself do so.

She tried and likely failed to hide her skepticism. "You can bake? Have you made muffins before?" It wasn't hard really, but as capable as Noah appeared to be in all other facets of life, she wasn't sure she was ready to turn over the actual baking portion of her world.

"Nope. But I can follow directions. Can't be much different from a set of blueprints."

"That's okay. You've done more than enough. How about you

make us some coffee to get us going? I was too tired to program a pot last night. Going to be a busy day. We have so much to do." *We?* Guilt cut through the soft haze of attraction. He'd given and given and then somehow given her even more. At this rate, she'd bleed him dry in no time.

What had she been thinking?

She pulled away from his hold and the moment she was free, she missed the mix of arousal and comfort. She returned to the kitchen and set to work, removing ingredients from the fridge. "Noah. I can't thank you enough for everything you've done, and are doing for me, but I really don't think you need to play body-guard on top of everything else. I...I'm going to use up all your goodness, and there won't be enough left over for you or for anyone else. I'll be fine." Could he be *that* good?

Memories of another time when she'd been fooled by an attractive, too-perfect male surfaced, but she slammed the door on them. There was no time for old baggage. Her plate was already overflowing.

"You're not trying to kick me out the door before we have our talk, are you? You promised." He stood in the doorway between the pantry and the kitchen with his arms over his broad chest. That wry, lazy grin made an appearance, softening her resolve to lighten his load.

And making her breath catch.

"Honestly, I wish I'd thought of that. It's not a bad plan."

"Well, time's wasting. You bake and talk. I'll handle breakfast." He again made himself at home in her kitchen, working around her as if he'd done so every morning over the last year and not just for the past couple of days.

She'd almost rather talk about her financial issues than think about the implications of the easy intimacy. She'd been such an idiot. What she wouldn't give to go back in time and listen to her instincts. But, no, that wasn't possible.

She set her largest mixing bowl on the counter, focusing on

the activity she loved. "I guess I should start at the beginning, huh?" She measured flour into the bowl then sighed and kept her back to Noah. Cowardly? *Hell yes.* But it just might be the only way to get through the conversation.

A quiet rumble brushed over her ear. "That's usually best." A soft caress lighted on her back then faded away.

"My great-great-grandfather bought about a hundred and twenty acres just before the turn of the century. This house and the largest barn were built shortly after he married my great-great-grandmother. The other buildings were added over the years. I've lived here my entire life. My mom was actually born in this house. We, my brother and me, are all that's left of my family, and I don't know where he is or if he'll ever come back." *Or if he's even alive.* Pain squeezed her heart in its tight grip, but in a long-standing habit, she forced herself to push forward. "So, really, all I have left of them are our home and memories. I've always been the sentimental sort who loves to hold onto things for no reason other than...just because."

Her sad words washed through him like a summer rain. Every time she spoke, her sultry voice filled his head with decadent images and wicked desires but now, hearing yet more heartbreak, it gutted him. Something about this woman went deeper than anyone had before, reaching his deepest core and grabbing hold. Gripping tight.

When she hurt, he hurt.

He set a skillet on the stove when all he wanted to do was pull her into his arms and soothe her pain away. "When was the last time you heard from your brother?" He wanted her to tell him every minute detail, but he mentally added one more thing to his list of things to discuss with James. His list for Pete grew, too, even as he struggled to figure out how much digging was too much.

"Just before his high school graduation, he disappeared. He did well in school, even took a few honors courses. He left mom a note saying he loved us and that he was sorry. We had no idea what he apologized for. I think it broke the last few pieces of Mom's heart when she received his diploma in the mail a few weeks later. Most of his things were left behind. We'd celebrated his eighteenth birthday less than a month prior. Other than one visit and a few sparse letters or birthday cards, I haven't heard a word from him. It's been almost four years since the last one. I don't know why he left or what he's been doing since."

He forced himself to stay at the stove when everything that made him male urged him to go pull her into his arms.

She wiped a cheek before reaching for a measuring cup and a container of berries. He set the package of bacon on the counter and clenched his fists. He forced them open and pressed his palms flat against the counter beside the stove. Her being so alone in the world explained why she had no help, but it didn't explain the bind she was in, or why she was working three jobs.

Her shoulders rose and fell as she took another deep breath. Her words came out slow, halting. "I made a judgment error. Or, I guess, several? I took a loan out against the property with the intent of opening a bakery in town." An egg cracked then her story continued, but something in her tone changed as she rushed to finish her story. "But I didn't spend my money wisely. It's all gone, and if I don't come up with the repayment, I'll lose everything."

As she mixed whatever muffin magic she had going in her bowl with a big wooden spoon, he'd bet his favorite hammer she held something back. "I'm coming to terms with the fact that I made a mistake. No one else is left to care about the farm or maintain it. It's practically falling down around me. As much as I'd like to, I simply can't keep up with it all. My family wouldn't want me to work myself into an early grave to save it. I mean, what's the point of keeping it? I have no one to pass it on to, and I won't have time to enjoy it or even take care of it like it deserves."

He straightened, turning in time to see her shoulders tighten as she put on a brave front for her finale. "Sentimentality is a waste of energy and time. It's for the best. I'll give it one last go, but if this doesn't work, then I'll just...let the house go." Brushing her wrist over her cheek, she turned away from the counter and retrieved a stack of muffin pans from the cabinet. Her head remained down as she spread them out on a tiny butcher block island. With motions so fast her hands blurred, she lined them with little paper cups then lightly sprayed them with something from a red can. With an ice cream scoop, she neatly dropped the batter in. Before he could form a response, round one was in the oven.

She washed her bowl and started again, all the while keeping her face averted. "My boss mentioned buying the property from me more than once, and it was a more than fair offer. They've been eyeing lakefront access for the logging shipments for a while now. If I decide to let it go, it won't take long for me to sell it. I just hate the thought of what might happen to the land after it changes hands. I mean, I love this house, but the actual property? The buyer would make the largest profit if they split it up into smaller parcels for homes or turned it into a lakefront resort. I know they'll strip all the old timber. Grandad planted pecan trees for Nan ages ago, and she loved them so...but they're mature now, and worth a small fortune. At least Nan would be pleased Grandad's gift became so valuable. While he was the dreamer in their relationship, she was the practical one."

Certain she left something important out, but unable to cause her more pain, he placed a hand on her shoulder. "Sylvie..."

She pulled away and opened the fridge. "It's better this way. Definitely." The sadness in her voice belied her words. Her spine stiffened and, after a brief pause, she looked over her shoulder at him. "What are you waiting on, big man? We've got a busy day ahead of us. Get to work."

She wasn't wrong. He just hoped the guys didn't give him too hard a time when he laid out everything he needed.

Ah, hell. They'll rake me over the coals. I'm screwed.

He'd found that, for Sylvie, he'd happily grin and bear it.

CHAPTER 7

*J*uggling her coffee, her tote, and packed lunch, Sylvie reached for the door to the office building where she worked. When her hand was only inches from the handle, the door burst open, nearly smacking her in the face. She cried out as the door whizzed by her nose. If she hadn't shifted to hoist her tote bag over her shoulder at the right moment, she just might have made a greedy plastic surgeon cackle with glee.

"Oh!" She stepped back and placed a hand over her thundering heart.

"Sylvie, love!"

In a flash, her alarm morphed into white-hot anger. She'd know that smooth voice anywhere. Worse yet, she'd recognize sight of the too-perfect smile until the day she died.

"You! Just get out of my way, Calvin. I'm in no mood to deal with you."

"What a coincidence, running into you here." He poured on the charm, making her stomach churn. His too white teeth reminded of her a big donkey. Shaking the vision of a braying beast away, she looked higher and considered his expertly manicured eyebrows. *Jeez, they're shaped better than mine!* Barbie's Ken had nothing on Calvin Richardson in the plastics department.

Stifling the urge to scream, she hissed. "Coincidence? I work here. You know that." A breeze whispered by, spreading the over-powering smell of his cologne. Long gone was the pleasant aroma of Marcy's coffee. *I do not have time for this!* "You just stay away from me."

He stepped back a few inches and raised his hands in front of his chest, palms out. "Sweetheart, is that anyway to talk to your former fiancé?"

"Don't you *sweetheart* me. That was a con, just the same as every other word that came out of your mouth." He opened his mouth to reply, but she cut him off. "Don't you dare waste your breath denying it."

Calvin ran a hand through his impeccably styled light brown hair. "Now, Sylvie, love, don't get all riled up. I was hoping to take you out to dinner tonight and set things straight."

She was surprised her eyes didn't pop out and roll across the ground, thanks to his audacity. "No. *Hell* no. I have a date already, thank you very much. Now, leave me be, or you'll be wearing more than my coffee on your shirt."

Whether because of the threat to his designer button-up or the utter seriousness of her tone, he backed up and let her pass. Without giving him a second to rethink his retreat, she pushed past him and through the office's small, bland reception area.

"A date? With who? With that...handyman?" His derision cut right through her irritation and revealed white-hot anger. She thought of Noah's big calloused palms, and how gently he'd held her smaller hand in his grasp. All the repairs he'd made around the house, simply because it was work that needed doing and that's what one did. Her blood boiled. Noah was so much more and, even still, there was certainly nothing wrong with anyone who worked with their hands. If anything, to her, it was downright sexy. Strong. Capable. Dependable. And yes, possibly one of the most attractive traits on the planet.

She walked behind her desk and set things down calmly. Really, she would've rather pitched her coffee at Calvin's head.

When he closed the door and turned to her with his fake smile in place, she couldn't take it anymore. Without thinking, she stormed back across the small space, heels clicking over the fake hardwood floor. She stopped with the toes of her shoes bare inches from his. She pointed her finger at his nose and let her temper fly. "That's it. I won't tolerate another word from your smarmy mouth. No matter how big you smile, it won't pretty up the lies you spew. I won't listen to you any longer. I—"

"Sylvie? Is everything all right?" Her heart stopped, freezing her tirade midstream and possibly saving her from an assault charge when one of her bosses spoke from behind her. Teddy Garrison, owner of Garrison Timber stepped up to her side. A sweet, little, round man who, with no need for a fake beard, played Santa in the town's annual Christmas parade, came to her aid. Feeling like she should come to *his* aid, not the reverse, she shot Calvin one last death glare, then focused on her boss.

She took a deep breath. "Sorry, Teddy. Calvin was just leaving. He and I have nothing to say to each other." She tried to soften her tone with a smile.

Teddy didn't buy it. His gray, bushy eyebrows turned down as he looked to Calvin. "Boy, I dare say, you best not give my Sylvie any trouble. I won't have it. You go on and don't come back here to bother her again. I mean it." A hard light entered his normally cheery eyes.

Her ex did the strangest thing. He stammered, all traces of persuasion gone from his tone. "Yes, sir. I won't be back."

"That's not good enough. You'll leave Sylvie alone, too. She doesn't want you pestering her. You apologize and then get out of here, so she can start her day on a good note."

Calvin pulled his gaze from Teddy then looked to her. "I'm sorry, Sylvie." Before she could blink, he hurried out the door.

Hooking his thumbs in his belt, Teddy propped his hands on his hips. "Now that he's out of your hair, what treat did you bring for me today?" He smiled warmly as he nodded expectantly to her large tote.

Shifting gears and pushing her confusion aside to process another time, she pulled a wrapped muffin and scone from her bag. "I couldn't decide. Raspberry cheesecake muffin or blueberry scone? Or both." She smiled held one in each hand out to him. "I won't tell Linda. Seems like today might be a good day for a little indulgence."

"Come now, my dear. You can't let him dim that gorgeous smile. It's too pretty a day. Plus, it would give him too much credit. He's not that important to you, is he?" Her boss, who had treated her like a member of his family since the day she'd walked in for her initial interview, peered at her as if trying to find the answer in her eyes.

"No. No he's not, darn it. It started out as a great day, and I want it to stay that way." Teddy was right. She'd spent far too much time focused on the negatives in her life. Unsurprisingly, more often than not, Calvin held the starring role. With a deep breath she focused on the present. As she exhaled, she smiled brightly.

"There now, that's a genuine smile. Much better. What's made you so happy?"

Unable to contain her news any longer, she babbled her story like a creek in the sunshine, sparkling with cheer.

Beaming, sharing her joy, Teddy clasped her hand in his. "That *is* happy news. I know your cookies well. Everyone will be thrilled to receive them as a gift. Isn't that an awful lot of work for you, though?"

"It is, or it will be, but I'm looking forward to it." Beaming, she waved a hand in the air. "Okay. I've sidetracked you enough this morning. Your ears have got to be ringing by now. On to work."

"It's quite all right, sweetheart. I'm just glad to see you so happy. You're glowing. That's well worth a few minutes distraction."

Waving her left hand at him, she pulled out a notepad she used to jot notes to herself. "Have you heard from Charlie? Over the past week, I've left four messages for him, but he hasn't called back. That's not like him. If he doesn't respond soon, we'll fall behind on the logging inspections."

Teddy patted her hand. "I'm sure he's fine. We'll give him a few more days before we get too concerned."

"Sure." She nibbled on her bottom lip. She wondered if she should try calling his home number.

The front door opened and Travis, one of Teddy's sons, stepped in. "Hey, Dad, Sylvie." He stopped and attempted to kick the dirt from his boots. She always appreciated the effort, even though it was wasted. Theirs was a messy business, no way around it. Taking in his fit figure, faded jeans and company polo, she acknowledged he was a good-looking guy and an all-around good man. At one point, shortly after she'd been hired, Teddy had attempted to set them up.

As much as she would have liked to make her boss happy, there was simply nothing there. They'd never even mustered up enough interest for the first date.

"Hey, son. Sylvie and I were just getting caught up on her highs and lows."

"Ah. Yes, I saw Calvin leaving. Had a word with him." He focused on Teddy. "He won't be giving her anymore trouble."

How odd that he seemed more determined to convince his father instead of me...

But men were strange creatures, especially when it came to their territories. No question, Garrison Timber was theirs. Teddy inherited the logging company from his father, and he'd dedicated his life to making sure it became a legacy worth leaving to his two sons. Travis spent most of his time running the financial side while Michael spent his time onsite.

"Sylvie mentioned Charlie hasn't returned any of her calls. Will you let her know if you hear from him? She's worried about keeping us on our toes. Won't let us fall behind, you know."

"The Pollack job will keep us busy for a bit still, but I'll definitely keep you both in the loop. I'm sure he's fine."

~

"Sorry! I'm late!"

Noah winced. James rolled his eyes when Pete slammed the door. The youngest member of their team hurried inside the nearly finished space and pulled a worn backpack off his shoulder. An unidentifiable faded color with frayed ends and edges on the shoulder straps, the bag appeared older than dirt. He'd refused an upgrade multiple times, swearing that it was his lucky pack.

Pete hustled straight to the old table and gently eased a laptop out of the bag as if he handled a priceless artifact. He set it up at his usual place beside the head of the table then ran a hand over his close cropped, rust-colored hair. "Little Bit wrapped her arms around my leg and refused to let go. Biggest crocodile tears a man ever saw." He shook his head as he logged into the computer, his focus shifting gears rapidly from his family to work.

Noah sat in one of the metal folding chairs they'd found in one of the many storage buildings on Rick's new horse farm. Their friend and leader of Dark Horse had only recently purchased the property and was still learning the ins and outs of his new home. Once a thriving thoroughbred facility, it was now the perfect shell for their budding security business and miscellaneous other operations.

They'd nearly completed the work on the mission room. The only things they lacked were proper furniture and the three extra-large monitors for the intel briefings and satellite imagery when needed. While he absolutely did not mind doing the work for Rick, it was a good thing they'd mostly gotten the renovation wrapped up. He suspected a certain brunette bombshell would keep him occupied in the near future.

He asked Pete. "Did you get her settled?"

"Yeah. It took a little longer than I'd hoped, but when I left, she was cuddled on the couch with her favorite blanket and stuffed puppy. Can't figure it out. Most of the time, the girls couldn't care one way or another if I'm home. As soon as they get sick, Crystal throws her hands up and says she's suddenly become chopped liver. They always want me." He shook his head as if it were the oddest notion in the world.

Frowning, Rick took his spot at the head of the ancient table. "I don't think this will take long. We'll get straight to business, so you can get back to her."

"Thanks, but it's okay. Crystal says Anna's teething, cutting her two-year molars. We got some Tylenol in her before I left, and she's due for a nap. It's all good." He looked around the room. James sat to Noah's left and Trent sat on Rick's other side. "Now, where do we start? With group business or...?" He teasingly trailed off and pinned Noah under his laughing gaze. "With the big boy's love life?"

Trent rolled his eyes and answered. "Business first." When his friend's storm grey eyes shifted to meet Noah's, he added, "Then we'll get to the important stuff. For instance, we're all dying for your explanation about why you didn't let us know you had someone who's important to you and that she might be in trouble." Rick might be the leader of Dark Horse, but when Trent spoke, everyone listened.

Noah barely hid his shock as he answered, "Things started out simple and turned serious quick—super quick. It was never my intention to keep any news to myself. Things just happened that way. Pathetic excuse, but that's what it is." He pointed at a monitor

Pete just powered on and attempted to change the subject. "What's that all about? A new mission?"

The corners of Rick's dark eyes crinkled slightly, and Noah knew it wasn't in a jolly Santa Claus way. Nope, that nearly imperceptible tell meant Rick hadn't been fooled. Noah had only bought himself a small reprieve. Their focus would come right back to where it began—Noah and Sylvie.

Rick's knowing stare moved from Noah to the group. "I have homework for you boys."

Tilting his head, James frowned when an image of a couple of battered assault rifles appeared on screen. "What has our fearless leader cooked up for us this time?"

"Nothing official yet, but it never hurts to be aware of what's happening at home. MacDonald ran into Detective Bowie with the state police yesterday. Bowie mentioned that they've recovered three of these over the past month." If the photos came from Joe MacDonald, then Noah, like the rest of the crew, could rest easy knowing the info was reliable. They could find no better ally than the Riley Creek Sheriff's Deputy in the next town over. Like Joe, Detective Jake Bowie with the Kentucky State Police had proved to be a reliable and valuable asset to Dark Horse.

James studied the images with a frown. "Those are Polish, military issue to boot."

Looking at the closeup image, Noah considered the ugly weapons and their possible implications as he read the stamp on the barrel of one of the weapons. It read *NATO 5.56*, indicating the weapons were intended for military use only. "And those were recovered locally?"

"Yes, recent traffic stops and drug searches."

Filled with skepticism, James asked, "How local?"

"Practically in our backyard. Summer Hill."

"That's on the far side of Riley Creek. I expected you to name one of the towns right on the city outskirts, not one that's almost an hour's drive from the slums."

"How did Polish military issue weapons end up in BFE Kentucky?"

And not just one, but *three* nearly identical models? The uneasy feeling brewing in Noah's gut intensified.

James made air quotes with his fingers when he asked, "What are the so-called owners saying?"

"Nothing." Rick gave them the answer they'd all expected. "Not a single word. They didn't even try to fabricate a lie. They clammed up and appear perfectly content to bide their time in jail.

An ugly feeling took root at the base of Noah's neck. A survey of the faces scattered around the table showed similar degrees of dread. "So, there's a good chance that they're afraid of a much bigger fish swimming in our pond?"

Rick gave a single nod. "I figure that's why Bowie shared. If there is something ugly lurking in our neighborhood, the more trustworthy eyes watching, the better, even in an unofficial capacity."

Trent released a frustrated sigh. "There's not anything we can do to help, is there?"

"No, not yet. Joe knows we have his back and can be available at a moment's notice. All he has to do is say the word. I called Bowie and made sure he knew the same. Also, I let them know we'd like to be kept in the loop as much as possible."

James scanned the images on the monitors. "I don't like waiting on the sidelines."

"None of us do. I'm working on something that might help some. I'll update you all as soon as I have something concrete, but I want to get Dark Horse running in an official capacity. Then we can do more than hide in the shadows and help from the sidelines." Rick pinned Noah with his glare. "So, to kill some time while those bureaucratic wheels are squeaking away, why don't you bring us up to date on Sylvie's trouble."

Pete chimed in helpfully. "*Troubles.* Plural." Grinning, he winked at Noah.

He'd yet to decide how much to share. Danger? No question, the more heads on the case the better. But her financial worries toed a line that he debated whether or not to cross. Then again, by bringing Pete in to search for information online, he'd chanced opening that can of worms wide and gaping. He'd start with the obvious and most pressing issue—her safety. "Things have been pretty quiet around her place. Other than a snooping ex, we haven't caught a whiff of trouble since the first night."

Trent crossed his arms over his chest. "What do the police think?"

He frowned in frustration. "They seem content to accept the simplest explanation."

James shook his head. "You mean go with the theory that requires the least amount of work."

Noah tamped down his frustration. "I asked Sylvie to call the Sheriff's Department and check for updates. With the recent increase in drug-related crimes in the area, their department is spread nearly as thin as Riley Creek's so yes, I think without anything concrete to go on, they won't do anything unless the situation changes."

Though the break-in at Sylvie's was no laughing matter, Noah fought back a smile. It always amused him when James's protective instincts surfaced. His friend spent ninety-eight percent of his life as a smart-ass. When someone he'd claimed as a friend was threatened, he became a mother bear.

Noah pursed his lips tighter when James got up to pace the room. "By change, you mean gets worse. Don't you laugh at me, lover boy. You're all but lost for her already. That means she's one of ours. You need to move her into your place. Your security system is a hundred times better."

"Actually, she doesn't know it yet, but she's getting a damn fine system installed. Besides, nothing is making Sylvie budge from her farm. It's been her home all her life. Add in the fact that she doesn't believe there's any true risk, and you'll find a stubborn woman on your hands. Would you like to try to convince her otherwise?"

"No." James stopped and pointed at him. "That's your job. You make her fall in line."

Noah laughed outright. "The only reason you dared to say that is because Cara, Kate, or Leigh aren't here. They'd wipe the floor with you for that comment."

"No doubt. Hell, even if it were you alone, or Trent, I'd tell you to pack a bag and stay at my place or here. It's not only because Sylvie's a woman."

"You don't have a house, remember? You're living in a camp trailer on the lakeshore. What's laughable is not the fact you're concerned about her safety, it's that you think I can tell the woman what to do."

James waved his hand in the air. "Dazzle her with your mojo or whatever. Stupefy her!"

Turning from his friend and his worried meltdown, Noah rolled his eyes. He wouldn't admit it to Holloway, but his gut told him that James had every reason to be worried. "Pete, I'm half-afraid to ask, but what do you have for me so far?" Guilt for intruding on her privacy stood up, demanded notice, but worry, slammed it back to the ground in a chokehold. He would take no chances with Sylvie's life. "Give me everything."

Staring at his computer screen, Pete answered. "No criminal record. One parking ticket three years ago and a speeding ticket eighteen months ago for going fifty-three in a forty-five. Graduated with a two-year-degree in business from the community college. Up until the last year, she paid her few bills on time and lived conservatively. She's worked at her current employer, Garrison Timber, for six years. Appears to be a perfectly responsible woman. Then, almost a year ago, she signed for a forty-thousand-dollar loan using her property as collateral. It appears that within a few months of taking out the loan, her finances fell apart."

Rick frowned. "If her credit was good, and by all accounts she was responsible, why did she put her home on the line? You said it's important to her, correct? She probably could have gotten a loan without collateral. That doesn't make sense."

Frustration beat at Noah as he stood. "No, it doesn't. Her home is probably the most important thing in her life. That doesn't fit. At all." He began pacing.

All traces of humor gone, Pete continued, "It only gets stranger from there. The money sat untouched in her bank account for two weeks. At that time, a check was cashed on the account for a couple thousand dollars. I did a little digging and found a digital copy of the check in the bank's records, written out to a leasing company. On the comment line, it said *down payment* and listed an address. I pulled up the address, and it's a business location that's been sitting empty in the town square for almost two years."

Noah ran a hand through his hair. "Her bakery. She's wanted to own her own business and to do something with her baking for years now. She was going to open a bakery or a café or something along those lines. What happened from there, Pete?" He dreaded the answer as much as he needed to know how she got into the current mess, one that broke her heart a little more each day.

"It looks like she never followed through on the lease. Crystal came in to drag me to bed at this point in my search. Caught me mumbling about the realty company—her cousin works there. She called this morning and gossiped with her, then she traded two days of babysitting for info on Sylvie's deal. The owner and listing agent had paperwork ready to go. All she had to do was come in and sign. Sylvie's agent tried for two weeks to reach Sylvie then gave up, figuring she'd gotten cold feet."

Noah stopped pacing and pinned Pete to his seat with glare. "So, she lost the deposit on the business location, but what happened to the rest of her loan? Don't tell me you've managed to find all this out but don't know what happened next."

James waved a hand in the air, adding his two cents. "Don't stop the info-vomit now."

Pete took a deep breath then blurted the rest as if ripping off a bandage stuck to a crusty wound. "The day after Sylvie had her appointment to sign the paperwork on the lease, she transferred the remaining amount to a bank account in Calvin Richardson's name."

Noah instantly regretted letting Calvin get away. He wished he could go back in time and grab the filthy weasel by the neck as he ran away.

Rick steepled his finger as he put two and two together. "They were engaged right? He conned her. There's no telling why he wanted it, but somehow he conned her out of the money."

"Yeah, about that." Pete continued, "I figured you'd want a deeper look into his dealings, so I started a more thorough search. I'm still working on a few things, but he works at the bank where she took out the loan."

Noah rubbed his hands over his face. "Makes sense, in an ugly way. He didn't seem like her type when he came by. Very polished, and nothing wrong with that, but he was so squeaky clean, it appeared fake. Plastic. I wouldn't be surprised if he played her from day one, possibly even giving her bad advice."

Trent sighed. "Why would he do that? Beyond suckering her out of the loan money, how does making a mess of her finances benefit him? And that doesn't explain why he came by her house when he knew she'd be at work or the break-in."

Noah nodded his agreement. "My guess? He was looking for the same thing that the intruders were. I believe he had no idea they'd been there. I thought he was going to puke on my shoes when I told him to warn his friends not to come by again. He was on the phone, promising to deliver something to someone."

Rick's glare darkened. "So, he's probably in trouble with someone bigger and nastier. Whether it was intentional or accidental, he's pulled Sylvie into his shitstorm."

Pete cracked his knuckles and asked, "Keep digging?"

Rick answered first, saving Pete from Noah's sarcastic and bitter response. "Dig deep. I want his damn T-ball stats."

Trent added his agreement and reassurance. "No question, he's dirty, but we'll figure out what he's up to, so you and Sylvie can rest easy. It sounds like she's a hard worker and a fighter. We'll help get her straightened out."

Noah remembered the other thing he needed help with. "Thanks, truly. We need your help with just one more, little thing."

Trent nodded. "Name it."

"I need Kate." He looked to Rick. "And Leigh, too. I need to borrow your women for a day, maybe the night, too. It's a group thing, and the more women the better." He grinned at the mix of confusion and suspicion looking back at him.

CHAPTER 8

S he opened the bottom drawer to grab her lunch bag and purse. Setting everything on her desk, she shut the drawer with her foot. As she doublechecked to make sure she had everything, from somewhere in the depths of her bag, her cell buzzed with a silent text notification. Her blood heated with irritation. By lunchtime, she'd received six messages from Calvin, each one more apologetic than the prior. Without replying, she'd put her phone away in a futile attempt to block his presence from her thoughts.

He'd become…desperate.

That wasn't like him at all. From day one, he'd always been a smooth operator—never a hair out of place or without his ever-present smile.

What if there really is more to this mess than Calvin looking for another handout?

He had to know, by this point, she wouldn't take him back even if he were the last man alive. Sadly, she probably wasn't even the first woman he'd conned. Though she wouldn't wish him on her worst enemy, finding a new sucker would certainly be easier than trying to squeeze another penny from her. He, more than anyone else on the planet, knew the pitiful shape of her finances.

So, why won't he leave me alone?

Bracing, she dug her phone out and found four unread messages waiting. Should she be relieved that Calvin had only left three of them? She doubted he'd changed his mind. Something had him by the tail. He'd be back.

The fourth text was from Noah. Just the sight of his name sent an altogether different and welcome kind of warmth coursing through her.

A little, happy hitch caught and fluttered behind her heart as she opened the text.

Don't worry about dinner. I've taken care of it. Come on home and get some rest.

No making dinner? No shift at the Beaver? All she had to do was bake the sweets for the next morning's deliveries?

Child's play.

She'd been doing that and more for so long, she didn't know what to do with the prospect of free time.

Living on quick sandwiches and cheap microwaved meals had been her norm for what felt like forever. Juggling three jobs left her with literally no time for...anything.

Mulling over the possibilities took up so much space in her thoughts that, when she pulled in her driveway, she realized she hadn't even turned on her radio. She always listened to music and only turned it off when the morning radio shows got on her nerves. Not turning her music on for the evening ride home was unheard of.

Shaking her head, she debated whether to get a jump on the laundry or to tackle the dusting as she opened her car door.

I might even treat myself to a bath instead of a ten-minute shower.

The delicious scent of something mouthwatering sent all responsibility related thoughts scattering. Her stomach growled. Helpless to do anything other than follow her nose's command, she headed around the side of the house and straight to the source.

Noah and his grill were stationed just outside her backdoor. His. *Grill.* In her yard.

It had to be his. That was the only reasonable explanation. The gleaming stainless-steel beast looked like something spawned straight out of a home improvement show. The only grill she had was small, pitifully rusted, and likely collecting dust in a barn somewhere. She couldn't remember the last time she'd used it.

Still processing the scene, she stopped moving just as he looked up. A lazy, sexy as hell grin spread across his face as his eyes lit. "Hey, gorgeous. Steaks have only been cooking a couple of minutes. How do you like yours?"

She thought she answered him. At the very least, he nodded, telling her to get a drink and relax.

He stood beside the shining beast in faded jeans that molded thick, muscled legs and called attention to a flat abdomen that made her think of things her body had long been without.

Needing to catch her breath and wanting to make sure she didn't have any drool on her chin, she went upstairs to change.

Cursing her need to do laundry, she went for the closet and chose one of the few remaining clean items—a simple sundress. Adding a light sweater, she stopped at the mirror and wasn't ashamed to admit, at least to herself, that she did indeed do a literal drool check. Just because she was there, she swiped on a little bit of lip gloss. Slipping on her beloved flip flops, she refused to admit she might not be able to wear them much longer, as the days grew shorter and the nights cooler. Before life became so busy, she used to live in them until the first snow fell. Lately, she'd had no choice but to wear practical shoes to her day job or uncomfortable heels to wait tables at the Beaver. It was a trivial thing to be bitter about, but she didn't care. Calvin had taken so much from her.

The idea of having someone who gave instead of took seemed

as impossible as a trip to Alice's Wonderland. Yet, down in her backyard, a man prepared a meal for her. That same man was going to great lengths to help her try to obtain her dream.

A little voice, the one still hurting from Calvin's lies, continued to whisper *he's too good to be true.*

She paused at the bottom of the stairs as a thought hit her. What did she have to offer him? Nothing. Absolutely nothing, except herself. Yes, he loved her baking, but even the biggest sweet tooth in the world wasn't enough incentive for a man to go to the lengths Noah had in keeping her safe. He'd gone miles farther than ensuring her safety. He was working hard to help her in a myriad of ways.

And that, she feared, just might be more terrifying than danger.

Pondering the mysteries of women with one sexy as hell curvy brunette standing at the forefront, Noah closed the grill's lid. He needed to discuss several things with Sylvie, but he hadn't decided how best to approach her. The urge to pepper her with questions interrogation-style bit at him, but it didn't take a wise man to know it probably wasn't the smartest or safest path.

He reminded himself their relationship was new. Judging by her history with Calvin, she had every right to be leery of trusting another so soon. But telling himself repeatedly that Sylvie was actually being smart in her caution only made him feel marginally better.

Just because he knew he was a decent guy, it didn't mean she'd had time to figure that out or actually trust in it, and him, yet.

Still his patience waned thin. Very thin.

Knowing she was the one woman he wanted from now until the end of time only made it doubly important for him to find the patience that served him well in nearly every other aspect of life.

The back door opened, gifting him with a glimpse of long curvy legs beneath a swishing skirt. The muted green material caught in the slight breeze, revealing more of her smooth calves. While some men were fond of one particular piece of anatomy or another, he went for the overall package. For him, Sylvie delivered in spades. Unable to control the urge, he swept a long look from her slender ankles, up those lovely calves, past curvy hips to her narrower waist. He envisioned running his palms over every soft inch, lifting her skirt along the way.

"Smells great. It's been ages since I've eaten good food grilled outdoors. I love cooler weather, but this is one of the few things I miss during the winter months. At least I'll get one good meal in before fall ends." She stepped down to the ground and leaned against the end of the stair rail. Unable to stop his survey, he pushed away thoughts of gripping that waist in his hands and skimmed his gaze over her breasts, which were no less tempting. The creamy column of her neck, the soft curve of her cheeks, the promise of her sweet smile. He wanted it all in a way that told him this need wasn't going anywhere anytime soon.

Instead of going over to pull her into his arms so he could kiss the daylights out of her, he set his tongs down and crossed his arms over his chest. "Fall's just getting started. We've got plenty of time yet. Besides, when a good hunk of meat is on the grill, it doesn't care about what month it is. We can grill all year, if you want."

Frowning, she sighed. He wondered how long she'd sit on her suspicion before she tackled it. He wasn't surprised when she didn't make it more than a few seconds. "Noah…" She heaved another sigh. "I can't tell you how much I appreciate everything you've done for me. Truly. But you have to stop."

Knowing she wouldn't buy it, but unable to resist, he feigned innocence. "Stop what?"

She crossed her arms and tilted her head. "Stop being so perfect. It's too much."

He couldn't help it. He laughed. "Honey, I'm not perfect."

She glared making him want to kiss the frustration off her face. When she pointed behind him to the grill, he shrugged his shoulders. "What?"

"What is that doing here? How long is it staying?" Suspicion darkened her eyes.

Even turned on by her sass, and half-brainless with his want for her, he knew better than to voice the real answer to her loaded question.

Forever.

Instead, he said, "I don't know. Until we don't need it, I guess. Do you want to eat inside or out here?"

The corners of her eyes tightened, but she let it go. "I'd love to eat out here. I've got an old tablecloth. I'll throw it over the picnic table. It looks rough, but last time I used it, it was still sturdy. What else do you want me to get?"

"How about drinks and silverware? I'll plate everything up and be right behind you."

As she pulled her mother's old faded tablecloth from the linen cabinet, she was hit with the strangest feeling. Warmth and affection flowed through her in a wash of comfort she'd only experienced once in a long time—in the few seconds she'd spent in Noah's arms the night he'd come to her rescue. The peace she'd felt had been as perfect as it had been far too brief. Maybe it was silly, but all had been right with her world. Of course, the peace fled as fast as it had come. She'd wondered if she'd imagined it.

Yet it was back. She could almost feel her mother there, offering her blessing. Instead of the usual stress of worrying that she was somehow wasting her life and what she'd been given, she felt approval. She knew to the bottom of her soul that her mother would have adored Noah.

Why shouldn't I be happy? I deserve happiness as much as anyone else.

She was a good person who worked hard. The prospect of having a meal prepared *for* her instead of *by* her, an easy evening, and good company sounded like heaven. She'd have to be an idiot or have her head up her ass to not stop and enjoy the moment.

She'd spent far too much time in the latter state.

Not giving a guy like Noah a chance could become a lifelong regret. So, what should she do about it? Pondering her dilemma, she grabbed an old basket, added the tablecloth, a couple of candles, then went back to the kitchen. There, she added matches, glasses, napkins, silverware, and a jug of tea.

She paused when an odd realization struck her. *Happiness. I'm happy. How long has it been?*

No, she wasn't at the same level of delight as a child jumping with glee on Christmas morning because Santa had come. Yet, since she'd received Noah's message, a soft cloak of contentment had enveloped her. She pushed open the backdoor and realized that, with the blush of bliss, came a sense of anticipation.

She wanted more. She *deserved* more. And she wanted a man like Noah in her life. A man who gave instead of took. She chided herself as she went down the steps to make her way across the yard. While having an inner self-help counselling session, she might as well go all the way and admit that it *was* Noah she wanted. She didn't *need* any man. She *wanted* him.

So, what am I going to do about it?

She set the basket on the table's bench. She couldn't very well tackle him to the ground and declare a mad passionate love. That was premature and ridiculous.

But she could make sure she became a woman who gave instead of took, because giving should go both ways.

From the night of their attempted first date, and for nearly every moment since, everything revolved around her. She'd hadn't meant for it to, but she couldn't help but wonder if she'd been selfish. What could she do for him to show her appreciation? Whatever she came up with, it had to go beyond baking cookies.

Oh shit. I know nothing about him. Nothing.

By all appearances, by each word he'd spoken and his every action, he was a good guy. A great guy, even. Noah had prior military experience and currently ran his own construction business. At least one of his close friends were willing to come running at a moment's notice to lend a hand, but he likely had more. A man didn't make the kind of friends who offered aid without hesitation in the middle of the night without being that kind of friend in return.

As she shook out the tablecloth, the memory of a Thirsty Beaver regular surfaced. *He's a good one, missy. You could do far worse. Better snatch up that steady man before some other sweet thing does.* Even Jerry knew more about Noah than she did.

She couldn't start peppering him with questions as soon as they sat down to eat. That was nosy and just seemed...rude.

She couldn't even be sure he desired her with the same level of intensity that she did him. She thought he did. After all, he asked her out in the first place. He'd said he found her sexy, and he wasn't a man to waste words.

Unbidden, doubt closed in again, making her wonder if he might just be the nicest guy on the planet. It was possible he could've been just being kind...or somehow, impossibly, running a bigger con than Calvin.

Instead of going over to bash her head against the nearest tree trunk, she set out the candles and remembered why she hated dating. Doubts set their claws into doors and windows of her mind, trying to barge in.

She shook the image loose. Redirecting her thoughts, she looked for the peace she'd lost yet again.

Noah's palm brushed the small of her back and she nearly jumped from her skin. "You need a screened in porch, so you can enjoy the view more often. Seems a waste to only use this pretty area during the summer." He set down the plates then rubbed a light hand over her back as she stood. "Didn't mean to scare you."

"It's okay. I was just lost in thought. I've wanted a nicer porch for as long as I can remember. I like the rain, so I'd love to be able to relax with a book during a good soaker." The soft stroke of his palm soothed her rattled nerves. She fought the urge to arch into his touch like a purring kitten.

"The leaves will change color any day now. I bet it's a sight."

"It is. I've lived here my entire life, but I've never taken it for granted. I'd like to travel a little, maybe take a real vacation once in a blue moon, yet I can't imagine coming home to any other view." With his hand on her back, she looked across the green meadow leading to a wall of towering trees. "When the leaves fall, you can just make out a glimmer of the lake at sunrise. I love to have my morning coffee and watch for it. If the morning is not clear enough, then the fog hugs the ground and whispers through the tree line. That's nearly as pretty a sight. Deer come up almost to the porch, but I think the turkey families are my favorite to watch. They waddle across the yard, all in a line, the largest leading and the smallest trailing at the end. So adorable, though, it makes me a little sad to see their family shrink as summer turns to fall."

She waved a hand in the air then poured their drinks. "Enough of my sentimentality. No room for melancholy. If dinner tastes half as good as it smells, I'm in for a treat."

He kept his hand on her lower back as she sat at the old table, almost as if he were holding her chair in a fine restaurant. "It should be edible."

She could almost hear the grin in his voice. Then he sat across from her and winked.

Fussing with the table, she set out napkins instead of fanning herself. His roguish smile might be her undoing. In a feeble attempt to distract herself from temptation, she tried to concentrate on the meal, but the mouthwatering aroma had nothing on the man sitting across from her. Giving up the fight, she took in the sight.

Wide, brawny shoulders filled out a long sleeve tee the color of the forest behind him. A couple of days' worth of scruff covered his jaw, yet it appeared neatly trimmed. The masculine shadow only made his full lips so much more captivating. He'd pushed his sleeves up, revealing the tight, muscled forearms of a man who worked hard physically. When his gorgeous green eyes gazed into hers, she knew without a doubt he was more than she could ever hope to handle. His physical strength offered the icing on a sound and well-rounded cake.

Taking a bite, she didn't bother hiding her reaction. Her eyes nearly rolled back into her head from the pleasure. She closed her eyes, savoring as she chewed and swallowed. "Is there anything you *can't* do?"

"Can't bake worth a damn," he admitted before he shot her another devastating grin.

"Surely there's more than that? Even superman has a weakness."

When the light in his eyes dimmed, she immediately wished she could take back her words. "It's okay. I was just teasing." She searched for a subject change. "When did you learn how to grill?"

He looked past her, gazed off into the distance, then shifted his focus back to her. "That's a two-part answer. I think I was around twelve or thirteen the first time I attempted to grill. I was a few years older before I attempted something like steak or produced anything edible."

"Twelve? Did your father let you help him?" The idea of a younger version of Noah proudly helping his dad cook hamburgers made her smile.

He took a long swallow of his tea. "No. It was my bright idea." He absently rubbed a faint scar on the back of his hand.

She felt bad about pressing for more information about his past, but despite her regrets, a heavy silence weighed on them.

Uncertain, she forged on. "Boys will be boys, huh? What in the world made you decide to man a barbeque on your own?"

"My sister had been in the hospital for three or four days over the Fourth of July holiday. She was devastated that we couldn't watch the fireworks in town. When she was given a hot dog on her lunch tray, she pouted because it wasn't a cookout hot dog. Wasn't the same unless it had stripes on it, she said." He smiled wryly. "It's mellowed now, but she always had a flair for drama."

He finished cutting a piece of his steak, and she spoke to give him a moment to take a bite. "You have a sister? Why was she in the hospital? She's okay now, right?" Waiting, she set her fork down because details of his world became more appetizing than their delicious meal.

He wiped his mouth with a napkin. "We're twins, preemies, born six weeks early. She was much smaller and suffered with severe asthma and respiratory troubles off and on throughout most of our childhood. I can't remember exactly what she was sick with that particular time. I spent a lot of time with my uncle when mom stayed in the hospital with Nic. I dug out an old rusted grill from beneath a mountain of junk in the outbuilding behind our house. After I sprayed it off with the hose, I filled it with part of a bag of charcoal I got from my uncle. He was under the impression that Mom planned to help me." Finally, his grin reappeared, bringing her a shocking amount of relief.

"I'm guessing you didn't correct his assumption?" She didn't know whether to put her hand on her hip mom-style or laugh.

"Nope. Whenever I stayed with him, he tried to do his part by teaching me all things manly. He only lived a couple of miles away, so I carried that grill home and hid it in the storage building until Mom brought Sis home. I had a little bit of money from mowing the neighbor's lawn, so I bought the hot dogs, buns, and sparklers. When they got home, I pulled my grill out and set to work. Everything went fine until a bee buzzed me, and I dropped the hot lid on my hand. It burnt the hell out of me, but I didn't want to tell Mom. She'd just gotten home and didn't need another worry." He poked at the remains of his potato.

"How mad was she?" She took his fork from his hand, laid it on his plate, and pushed it all aside.

His gaze wandered into the distance again, looking over her shoulder before he met her eyes. "Not at all, or not at first. She didn't know. She was even more tired than usual, worried about Nic, and touched that I tried to make my sister happy. Three days later, though, the burn got infected. On day four, she came home from work early. She caught me trying to clean it up on my own at the kitchen sink. *Then* she got upset. I'm not sure if she was more mad because I'd hidden it from her or because I had tried to be the man of the house again. I know she carried a lot of guilt when we were growing up."

She pulled a small storage container out of the basket beside her. She popped the lid off and set it in front of Noah. "Why did she feel so much guilt?"

He pulled out a brownie. "She was caught between a rock and a hard place. Single mother, trying to work as much as possible to support us, yet feeling bad about not being able to spend much time with us. She worked herself into exhaustion, yet she still could barely afford to get us clothes for school or any of the things growing kids burn through. Nic was easy. She was so little and a cutie to boot. There were always pretty hand-me-downs, and I think people felt sympathetic because she was sick so often. I was always big, forever outgrowing my clothes. Mom tried to get me something each payday, but before the season ended, my pants were too short or my shoes too tight." He heaved out a sigh before taking a bite of dessert.

She pinched a corner from her brownie as she came to his defense. "You couldn't help that you grew so fast."

He swallowed. "No, but the knowledge didn't stop my guilt. My uncle always joked about how I ate all the food, even before we were born, and that's why Nic was so little at birth. He didn't mean any harm, but it always made me feel a bit guilty. Mom never once complained, though. I tried in little ways to make it up to both her and Sis. When we were around fourteen or fifteen, I knew Mom wanted a new table, but she couldn't afford it, so I repaired the one we had and refinished it. I learned how to replace doorknobs, refinish furniture, and whatever else I could think of to try and ease Mom's burden."

Something about the fondness in his voice when he spoke of his mother warmed her. "But she didn't see you as a burden."

"Not once. Even at the end of sixteen-hour days, she never acted as though we were too much to handle. Every time Nic or I walked in the room, her eyes lit with joy."

"You're lucky to have each other."

"Very much so. And, luckily for her, I can buy my own pants and shoes now."

"Is she...doing okay now?" She wouldn't know Noah's mother if she stood in line next to her at the grocery store, but tenderness for the woman filled her heart all the same.

"Yeah, she's great. I tried to build her a new house in a nicer area, but she refused it. Nic and I finally convinced her to retire about two years ago. We alternate every six months, each sending her on a cruise or whatever vacation she wants."

"Let me guess...you've remodeled the house around her?"

His full smile broke out, slamming her with its beauty—such an intriguing mix of masculine strength and warmth. "Guilty. It's been long enough, now, she's stopped fighting me over it."

She arched a brow. "She lets you have your way with her house?"

"Oh, no. She's full of opinions, and I still receive an occasional eyeroll when she disagrees with my suggestions."

She pushed her dessert away as a mix of emotions whispered through her—the loss and longing for her own family and the warmth for people she hadn't met, but already grew fond of. "I think I'd like her."

"I know you will." He said it in that quietly confident way that both frustrated and warmed her. She'd meant a hypothetical meeting, not a real one. For the time being, Sylvie decided to ignore the assurance behind his words. That was no maybe, Noah meant she *would* meet and like his mother.

Rather than attempt to process how she felt about the assumption, she switched gears. "What about your sister? How is her health?" Even as she said the words, she mentally crossed her fingers that another woman she'd never met was all right.

"Nic's great. Sometime around the start of college, she decided she'd had enough of being the sweet, pitiful, little doll everyone pitied. She wanted to be left alone, not fussed over." When Sylvie arched a brow at his phrasing, he raised a hand palm out and continued. "Her words, not mine. She convinced her doctor she was up for it then started working out with a personal trainer a little bit at a time. Gradually, she worked her way up to some pretty tough endurance training. It wasn't easy, and by no means was it a cure-all. She still has issues crop up from time to time, but she's much happier."

"That's wonderful. I'm happy for her. I bet your mother is super proud of her."

"We both are, but we're not surprised either. She's always been a fighter."

She tilted her head as she peered him. "You still worry about her."

"I do, but not so much about her health. Now, I miss her as much as I worry about her hardheaded determination."

"It's great that you two are still so close. I miss my brother something fierce. Then again, I'd also like to whack him over the head with mom's frying pan."

Noah appeared to consider his words carefully. "How long has it been since you've seen him? What's kept him away?"

Worry and frustration summersaulted in her abdomen as she thought about the last time she'd seen Brody. After his brief visit, she'd watched him walk down the front porch steps to his old, battered truck. He got in, started it, and without a glance, he drove off. He'd seemed so alone. "It's been six years since I've actually *seen* Brody. I received a birthday card and some money from him about four years ago. He said it was to help with the house upkeep. The property was supposed to be split evenly between us when Mom passed away. He refused to take an inch of it. Demanded that the attorney put it all in my name, then he sent me a couple thousand dollars to help maintain it."

She shrugged. "He's always been that way though, loyal to a fault. I haven't heard a single word from him since then."

"Do you think he got into some sort of trouble or that something bad might have happened to him?"

"Brody Allen? Get into trouble? Like drugs or crime? No. Never. Not to mention, I can't bear thinking something terrible might have happened to him." She usually did everything she could to avoid thinking about the situation at all.

When she'd thought about trying to find him on her own, something told her that he didn't want to be found. That she'd be hurting him, if she did search.

"So, he didn't give you a single hint as to where he was all that time or about what he'd been doing?"

She poked the tines of her fork into the brownie's frosting. "No. Something made me think he'd might have been in one branch of the military or another—maybe the way he held himself? So straight and proper. Then there was his super-short haircut, out of place because he'd always worn his hair a little long and shaggy. The change in his appearance was a shock, but he'd never once mentioned wanting to join any branch of the service before he left." Looking to the last wisps of purple light fading behind the trees, she rested her chin in her palm.

Since Noah still hadn't spoken, she continued. "I just hate that our visit was so short and strained. He apologized for not being here when Mom was sick and for not coming for the funeral. He informed me he'd already gone to Mom's attorney to sign his share of our inheritance over to me. The brat even offered to pay me back for her funeral expenses."

She threw her arms up in the air. She still wanted to shake him for that. She'd just wanted *him*. To know where he'd been, how he was. "But after that first hard hug, and talk of Mom, things were so awkward. He wouldn't answer any of my questions. He tried ignoring them and then moved on to changing the subject. Even after I gave up and went along with his tactics, the tension didn't ease much. We'd always been close, so to have things between us turn so uncomfortable? It hurt."

Hoping to contain the threatening tears, she looked to Noah's concerned gaze. "He stayed for dinner and, even though he said little, it seemed as though he quietly savored each bite. Watching him, being within arm's length of him and not knowing how to crack open his hard head to pull out all his secrets, it broke my heart. I had the strongest need to fix...*something* for him, to take away his pain, but he acted as though everything was fine."

She leaned over to blow out the tiny flames flickering atop the candles. "I can't stand secrets, especially dark ones. Calvin and his lies. Brody and his omissions. Even my mother waited until she didn't have any choice before she told me she was sick. She knew for a full two months before she told me her illness was terminal."

She set her fork on her plate with a quiet clink when she would've rather thrown it like a dagger, so hard that it stuck in the nearest wall. She was so damn tired of hurting and being... tired. "I'm sorry to dump on you. This was supposed to be a nice night, yet again I've taken more from you than I've given." She'd strayed from her original path and into dark territory likely to dredge up gloom for them both. She smiled, attempting to lighten the mood, then forced herself to wink at him. "You're too good, Noah. If word gets out that you're Mr. Perfect, you'll have scores of women beating down your door."

~

Damn, if she only knew the things I've seen and, worse, done. And if she knew what I suspect about her brother? A gut punch, her words hit him just below his sternum. Guilt ripped through him. He swallowed. "Sweetheart, I'm no Mr. Perfect. I guarantee it."

Her features softened until she gave him an almost genuine grin. "How's that? Do you have stinky feet? 'Cause that might be a deal breaker. Wait! Don't tell me. You have an obsession for toss pillows, right? Bed has to be made perfectly every morning with all twenty-three floral pillows in their proper places?"

He chuckled as he stacked their plates. Damn, but she was pretty when she was happy. Her eyes were so big, expressive. Fighting temptation, he stood. "Let's go in before the mosquitoes make a meal out of you."

She put a hand up. "I draw the line at six pillows." She grinned then appeared to realize that she was talking about them sharing a bed. Tucking a stray lock of hair behind her ear, she turned to pack up the basket.

Holding out a hand, he waited. "Come on." She surprised him when she turned to him and put her palms on his chest.

Looking up, she met his gaze. "Thank you for everything." She brushed her soft body against his, stretching to touch her lips to his. Unable to deny her, he parted his mouth.

Featherlight and oh so sweet, the kiss put her baked goods to shame. With heavy guilt strangling his emotions, he sampled when he wanted nothing more than to drink her down. Swallow her whole, savoring every drop of the goodness that was Sylvia Grace.

Hungry for her, desperate to explore every inch, he needed to anchor his hands. Intending to stem desire's rising tide, he gripped her waist. Her curves only invited him to explore, tempted him to take everything she offered and more—and she'd offered a starving man bliss. When her palms rested flat against his chest, sliding up to his nape, stars burst on the backs of his closed eyelids.

The scent of her filled his nostrils and went straight to his brain. The potent spell weakened his defenses until he feared that, with one crook of her finger, she could draw him through the gate to Hell. Hints of dessert mingled with Sylvie's heated sensuality, becoming a drug he'd die without.

His tongue met hers, and she smiled beneath his mouth. Fighting to get his bearings, he sucked her bottom lip in a poor attempt at farewell as he pulled back from the kiss. He touched his forehead to hers and struggled to catch his breath. He didn't want to pull away. For the life of him, he couldn't remember why something so very good could be such a bad idea.

They both wanted it, craved it. Their bodies fit together like pieces of dovetail carpentry.

She cupped his jaw in her palms and smiled, all wicked temptress and sweet seduction. She licked her bottom lip, as if preparing to go back for one more taste of him. The subtle blush on her cheeks, combined with her kiss swollen lips, rocked him.

There couldn't possibly be a more beautiful woman on the planet.

He had to have her as his.

He just might die if her didn't get another taste.

Unable to deny either of them, he dipped in for another kiss. Just a quick farewell treat before he put the brakes on this...madness. It was the only word he could come up with to describe the fever burning through his blood, demanding that he take everything she offered—then steal more.

When she moaned into his kiss, a sweet offer, he wanted to roar with primal satisfaction.

Sylvie was his.

No matter who had been in her life previously or what danger lurked, he'd claim her, keep her, as his.

At the briefest thought of Sylvie in danger, it all came back.

The reason he couldn't have her.

He pulled his mouth from hers and gently held her in place as he stepped back. He created a distance he hated nearly as much as he despised the men who'd put them in this situation.

He couldn't have her, because when she discovered what he suspected, she'd likely come to loathe him. And as loyal as she was to Brody, that anger would come both swift and hot.

"Noah?" The soft, questioning tone of her voice and the confusion in her eyes gutted him.

The hollow feeling in his chest was the only reassurance he did the right thing. He picked up the basket and took another step back.

With a puzzled look on her gorgeous face, Sylvie leaned down to blow out the candles. She gathered them up and silently followed him into the house. It was one of the very few times in his life where he detested being the good guy.

CHAPTER 9

Sylvie read the text from Noah. *Don't worry about dinner. Have a big crew coming in to finish work on kitchen, and it will be a mess. We'll figure out something afterward.*

Accustomed to doing everything on her own, Noah's considerate updates, even the smallest ones, continued to catch her off guard. Somehow, having a man, or more accurately having Noah, essentially live in her home hadn't taken her off guard at all. His presence seemed so...natural. He was in her home nearly all the time, but in a quiet, unobtrusive, entirely Noah way. With enough energy for five men, Noah always worked on or tinkered with something, but somehow, he never seemed rushed or anxious. Just quiet and steady. When she suggested he should take a break and watch a ballgame or something, he shrugged and went right back out the door toward the old garage.

Does he ever get angry or irritated?

She didn't think so.

She'd also noticed, with more than a touch of disappointment, how he intentionally kept distance between them, at least physically. They still ate together, got ready for their days together, and even texted each other often, but he wouldn't come within an arm's length of her. *Why the about-face?* She knew he was attracted to her.

More than once, when she'd caught him looking at her, his eyes simmered with a heat like she'd never seen before. That look made her breathless. Achy.

She'd watched, even felt his reluctance when he'd pulled away from their kiss after dinner a few nights prior. His muscled chest heaved beneath her palms, and as he'd pulled his mouth from hers, she could have sworn it was his way of saying goodbye.

If only she knew why. *What changed?*

He'd probably decided that, with the shape her life was in, she would be far more trouble than she could ever be worth. What man would want to take on a woman with a mountain of financial trouble and danger possibly dogging her every step?

Though she didn't care for the one-eighty, she couldn't blame him. She wouldn't want to take on a man with her kind of troubles.

But if that man was the one—a man like Noah...

Her conscience called her a liar.

She tried her best to push her disappointment aside, telling herself it was for the best. She had so many things on her plate, and while it was a Thanksgiving bounty of goodness, it required all of her attention. She'd be a fool to not give the cookie job her all.

She'd just begun looking over the next day's schedule when the door to Teddy's office opened. Accustomed to the usual office traffic she paid no attention to it until she heard her name spoken. "Hey Sylvie, how are you?" She looked up as Michael approached. Despite standing at least four inches taller than his brother, there was no mistaking the Garrison family resemblance in his features.

Out of course of habit, she answered with a generic reply. "Good. You?" She abruptly realized Michael's question went deeper than mere pleasantry. Concern deepened the creases around his eyes.

They'd gone on a couple of dates the year before and, though his father had been ecstatic over the news, their time together had just been...blah. She'd wanted to want Michael but just hadn't. She still couldn't figure out why Michael hadn't appealed to her. A little bit more rugged and fit from his time outdoors running the logging operations, he was more her type than Calvin had been. Ultimately, she turned his next two or three date offers down.

She'd been thankful they'd remained friendly around the office, even after she'd told Michael she just didn't think things would work out. How did one tell someone else that, even though they liked them as a person, you didn't want them?

Like the way she wanted Noah. Craved him with everything she was in a way that put all her old schoolgirl crushes to shame.

Figures. I find the man I can't live without, but he doesn't want me.

He tipped his head down with a knowing look. "Really. So the break-in and Calvin's harassment hasn't cost you a moment of lost sleep? I still wish you would've called me that night. You know I could have been there in no time."

"I know, and I appreciate that. Fortunately, it wasn't necessary. My friend arrived in the nick of time." The thought of what might have happened if Noah hadn't come to check on her at exactly the right moment made her nauseous. She'd avoided thinking about it altogether.

"We've been so busy around here, I haven't had a chance to hear the full story of what happened that night. Do the police have any leads?"

"Not so far. Tom thinks it was an isolated incident. He thinks it was a crime of opportunity, that they won't be back."

Michael's lips curved downward. "Do *you* think it was an isolated incident? I don't see how you're able to sleep. I don't care what Thomas says. He's a good kid, and he means well enough, but he's still wet behind the ears. I don't like you staying out there alone."

"I'm fine. I have so much on my mind in regard to my business,

I don't have room in there for anything else." She tapped a finger on her temple. "Also, I'm not alone, so you don't have to worry about me."

Maybe, that was why she'd never felt anything more than familiar affection for him? He was more like an older brother than a friend. Though always kind and attentive, his tone often held the faintest hint of condescension. As if, simply because he was male, he needed to do all the things for her or give his approval. Even if it was intended as a nice *I want to help the little woman* behavior, it still rankled.

When the corners of his eyes tightened, she wondered where the conversation was going. He didn't look relieved by the news she wasn't alone or afraid. At all. "That's kind of Marcy to drive all the way out there to stay with you, but she's..."

"She's what? Another woman?" She closed her laptop with a snap. "Care to explain what would be wrong with that?"

He sighed. "I'm not saying there is anything wrong with her keeping you company. It's kind of her. I would just feel better if a man, preferably an armed man with some semblance of skill, were there with you. Will you reconsider letting me stay with you? I'll stay in another room."

Noah still sleeps on the couch, so he's closest to the door.

"I'll save the feminism argument for another day, but it's not Marcy staying with me. Another friend is, and *he* more than meets your qualifications."

"Wait, is this the same guy who just happened to appear in the nick of time that night?"

She placed both palms on her desk, hoping the cool wooden surface would calm her rising temper. "Yes, it is."

"Who is this guy?" He paused then added, "Don't you think that's a little bit coincidental?"

"No. We were supposed to meet at a specific time the night of the break in. When I didn't show up, he came by to make sure I was okay." *I almost wasn't...* "Look, I appreciate your concern, but I know Noah is a good guy. We have everything covered. Also, not that it's any of your business, but he's sleeping on my couch, and he installed a security system. Even though it's not necessary, I'm well protected."

He put both hands up. "Okay, I surrender. Just let us know if you need anything. We worry about you out there."

Before her blood heated further, she decided she needed to let his concern go, so she changed the subject. "How are things looking at the job site tomorrow? There's a good chance for rain, I saw."

As the conversation returned to familiar territory, she couldn't help but feel something between them had changed. With so much on her plate, though, she couldn't afford the barest vapor of mental energy to examine it to figure out what.

Even knowing she'd likely find a mess when she arrived home, she found that, as her work day wore on, she looked forward to its end with eagerness.

When she finally pulled into the driveway, there was little space to park. A variety of trucks and SUVs filled the worn gravel path leading to her backyard. She squeezed her car in, ending up parked in the front, next to a large blue pickup. Grabbing her purse, she looked up to see a small face peering at her from between her curtains.

The front door flew open to reveal a little girl, the one from the window, with a crooked ponytail. "Hi! Are you Syl-bie?" Without waiting for an answer, the imp arched her head back to yell into the house, "She's here! Can I let her in, or should I make her stay outside?" She faced Sylvie again and whispered, "It's s'pposed to be a supise."

A petite blonde came to the door. "You must be Sylvie. Come on in." She shook her head. "That sounds terrible. I mean, it's your house, so of course you can come in." Stepping back, the blonde opened the door wider and placed a hand on the little girl's head.

"This is Kylie and drama is her middle name. I'm Cara. We were with Joe when the call came in for extra hands."

"Daddy is a police ocifer. He helps people all the time."

Before Sylvie's imagination got more than two steps into why someone from law enforcement might be in her house, Cara put the brakes on the worst of her worry. "Nothing's wrong. He's friends with Noah. They're just a group of good men who often help one another whenever they're...helping *other* people out." Cara shrugged. "Which they do. All the time."

A little lost and a lot confused, she greeted them. "Nice to meet you. Dare I ask why so many people are in my kitchen?" Sylvie swallowed. Noah proved, again and again, he was more than capable, so why did he need an army? He was only putting in an extra oven and a basic island.

At least that's what he'd told her... Visions of complete kitchen destruction assaulted her, making her belly pitch. She didn't have time for complications. Everything had to be perfect when the time came to make Karli's order. Hard arms of anxiety squeezed around her ribs, forcing the air from her lungs.

"Noah asked James for a hand, and James was out at... Rick's working on something else, so the entire crew came along."

Deeper inside the house, a male voice called someone else an asshole.

"Do they do that often?" She followed the sounds of male voices through her house.

"Yes. Pretty much all the time. They can be a little over-whelming and bossy at times, but they really are a good group of men."

"My daddy's the best! I like Twent, too. He has horses. And he saved Fwank." Kylie looked ready to bolt through the house until Cara gently took hold of her shoulder.

"Slow down, squirt. They're moving around all sorts of heavy things in there. We don't want any more accidents."

Her lungs struggled to draw in short pants of air. She resisted the need to brace herself with a palm on her grandmother's old hutch as they passed by. "*More* accidents?"

"Nothing major. She spilled her kid's meal on your floor when we first arrived, but with this little stinker, it's always better to be safe than sorry. She has enough energy for ten people."

As if to prove Cara's point, Kylie jumped in place. "I just want to tell Noah his Sylbie is here." Kylie looked from Cara to Sylvie. "Noah told daddy that your floor is so clean that it probably wouldn't hurt to eat my nuggets."

Cara sighed, as if she were used to being outnumbered, even if she didn't always like it. Then she shrugged. "I choose my battles."

"Yeah." Sylvie tried to remember the last time the house had been visited by the presence of little people as Kylie twisted to and fro beside Cara. "I can see how that might be wise." Helpless, lost, she looked to the only other person available and threw caution to the wind. "Do I want to know? Like, it's not bad, is it?"

Cara's jaw dropped open as if the thought jarred her. "Noah's work?"

Sylvie shook her head. "I don't mean to sound offensive. My kitchen might not seem like anything special, but right now, especially this week, it's literally my everything."

Cara's face softened, as if in understanding. "You and your kitchen are in good hands. The best, I promise. He explained a tiny bit about your big order and said you might need some help. I'd be more than happy to lend a hand."

Sylvie's first thought was to brush away the kind offer and take on the task herself. She stopped to remind herself she was smarter than that. The bands of pressure around her ribs loosened a fraction. "I'd appreciate it."

"It's exciting. Karli seems like a genuinely sweet young woman. It was exciting to see a local girl, and one who's so kind, do so well. I'm happy for her."

"Noooowah!" Kylie shouted on another hop. "Can we come in? I wanna show Sylbie!"

Sylvie's belly pitched again, harder and deeper than before. She closed her eyes.

She heard Noah's amused voice call from just around the corner, "Come on in, Little Bit. You can show her."

"Yay!" The little girl landed on another excited stomp. "Sylbie?" Kylie asked tentatively. "Let's go see."

A little hand took hold of one of hers to pull her along.

This is silly. She blew out a breath.

"Okay." She smiled down at the sweet face peering up at her in concern. "Show me the way, Kylie."

The little girl gifted her with a huge grin and finished tugging her along, grunting and groaning dramatically even though Sylvie put up no resistance. The moment they entered the adjoining dining room, Kylie dropped her hand and went directly to a man dressed in a Riley Creek Sheriff's Department uniform. "Sylbie's here now. Can we go home? I gotta feed Cookie. She misses me."

He looked down at the child before he answered. "Sure thing, Pickle. You need a bath, too." He stepped toward Sylvie and tipped his head in greeting. "Nice to meet you. I'm Joe MacDonald. We hate to run, but Kylie's puppy is waiting at home. She'll fret until she's fed and played with it. You take care and good luck."

He went to Cara, who placed a hand on his chest and murmured, "Wait one sec."

After the little family passed through the doorway, Sylvie stepped inside the heart of her home. The first thing she saw? A virtual wall of brawny men with sheepish grins. Thankfully, she knew one of them. *My fantastic hero.* He stepped forward and smiled.

The tightness in her chest eased a tiny bit as she greeted him. "James."

He stepped in close. "Hey, love. If anything's not up to spec, let me know and I'll set the big guy straight."

She smiled. "Something tells me you don't have a lot of remodeling experience."

"Nope. Next to none, but I can kick his ass if he screwed something up."

Someone coughed the word "bullshit" in the background. James only grinned wider.

She laughed. "I promise, you'll be the first to know."

He took both of her shoulders in his warm palms and leaned in to kiss her cheek. He whispered, "It's going to be fine. You'll see." Then he quietly left.

A wiry younger man stepped up. "I hope you like it. My wife said, if she can get a sitter for our girls, she'll try to come by and help with the baking extravaganza. She said she could use a break."

"Um, that's great. I appreciate it, but... I'm not sure baking two thousand cookies will be much of a break."

"For her, it would be. She doesn't get much adult time. Our girls could give little Kylie a run for her money in the energy department."

"All right, then. I appreciate your help today." *If I only knew exactly what he helped with...*

"You're family now. Anytime." Without turning, he blindly waved to the guys behind him on his way out.

She blinked and tucked those words away for later examination.

A tall, sandy haired male with gray eyes and a worn ballcap stepped forward. "I'm Trent. Nice to meet you. Good luck." He winked and tipped the frayed bill of his hat to her.

Uncertain of what she should say, she smiled and kept it simple. "Thank you." He shot her a grin of his own then made his way out in a ridiculously sexy, unconscious, long-legged swagger.

The wall of muscle had thinned out enough that she could have seen her kitchen easily enough, but she wasn't above admitting she was chicken. More importantly, she owed each of the men her attention and thanks.

Procrastination is the name of my game this evening.

She focused on the dark headed male dressed in well-fitting crisp jeans and a navy polo. He stepped forward to greet her.

She wondered again, *what could have required so much help?*

"Thank you. I really do appreciate everything."

He leaned in close to whisper, "Nothing is permanent. If there's anything you don't like, we can take care of it after your bake-fest. The big guy really put his heart into this project, so try not to be too hard on him." He kissed her on the cheek then disappeared on silent feet, leaving her alone with Noah.

He sighed then held up both hands, palms out. "Nothing has been painted or stained yet, so the cabinets don't match. In addition to our time crunch, I wasn't sure if you would want to match the new with the old or go for a completely new look."

Tension marred his handsome face, making her soften. He really was worried about whether or not she'd like what he'd done. Right then and there, all of her anxiety disappeared. The man worked hard, called in favors, and who knew what else for her. She realized the details of what he'd done didn't matter nearly as much as the simple fact that he *had* done it.

It was more than anyone had done for her in...forever. Literally.

She smiled. "What would you recommend?"

He tilted his head at her, as if she'd become a mystery he couldn't solve. "You haven't even really looked yet. Are you okay?" Warily, he considered her as if she might burst into hysterics at any moment.

"I'm good. Promise. Why don't you show me around? Something tells me you did more than install an extra oven."

He grinned sheepishly. "It really does make sense to reconfigure it all at once."

Unable to resist, she walked up to cup his jaw. His five o'clock scruff was more pronounced than usual. She wondered if it was because he had so much on his mind that morning. Fatigue deepened the creases and faint wrinkles around his eyes.

For me.

She touched her lips to his. "Thank you."

He accepted her kiss, joining his mouth with hers in a sweet, heated tempest of lips and tongue. When he pulled away, she wanted to shake him.

Clearing his throat, he took her hand in his. "Okay, I guess we'll start with the overall space." He gestured to the room. "Remember, nothing is permanent. I kept everything we pulled out. If you hate it, then we'll figure something else out or undo it all."

She arched a brow, silently telling him to get on with it. Then, finally, she forced herself to focus on the room and the changes he'd made.

Her jaw dropped. It was completely different, yet...still the same.

"I thought, by giving up your eat-in dining area here, we could add both a larger island and storage here. That also gives us room to add a more upper and lower cabinets along the wall, there, plus a little more work space." He pointed to the wall where they'd eaten their first meal. Disbelief stole her voice, made her shaky, until she had to wrap her arms around her middle to steady herself. The space he referred to used to house her little table and an old baker's rack. In their place, he'd installed eight unfinished lower cabinets, creating about six feet of fresh countertop, below eight upper cabinets. She immediately decided it would be the perfect area to setup cooling racks—a safe place to allow the mountains of cookies to cool. She would dust off her rarely used dining room table in the other room, then clean the unused space like a mad woman. It would be a logical place to package everything.

Hope and happiness swelled and rose up like an inflating balloon.

Organizing the kitchen that way would give her the island—a new island with more cabinet space—as a place to set up two mixing stations on the opposite ends. She wished for another stand mixer. Then, an odd thing happened. She reached out for help.

"Cara?" She turned her head to see if the woman had left already.

The other woman came deeper into the kitchen, her smile huge and warm. "Yes?"

"You said you were able to help? Do you have a stand mixer I could borrow? Just for the day." She gestured to the island as she spoke. "I have mine, but what do you think if we set mine up here, and then put another there?"

Cara nodded. "Yes. I think that would work well. You could line up all your ingredients here, between this stove and the sink. Then you would have enough space on the far side of the island for baking sheets." She paused as if catching herself. "Um. If you like, but I think that's what I would do. I do have a mixer, but Leigh's is newer. She's with Rick, the last guy to leave, and he spoils her. She has a beast of a mixer, and I'm sure she'd be happy to loan it to you. She's already said she'd come and bring her daughter Addie to help."

As Cara spoke, Sylvie lost focus because she noticed what Noah had done with the oven—or, more accurately, *ovens*. Her heart skidded to a halt. Just when the world began to grow dim, it stuttered and did a happy little tap-dance. He'd installed a double wall oven and replaced her old stove with a new model, one with two ovens stacked beneath the cooktop as well.

Her gaze snapped to Noah's face. Then she walked right up to him and cupped his scruffy jaw in her palms. "I have four ovens? *Four?*"

She dimly heard Cara laugh quietly, then she said farewell. "Sylvie, we're leaving. Noah has my number. Text me with the details, and we'll be here. One way or another, we'll round up another mixer and anything else you might need."

His eyes softened as he lightly rested his hands at her waist.

"Yes. I hope that's enough to handle the job. I tried to figure out how to fit one more in, but it would've required a great deal more electrical work and you'd lose a lot of counter space. I went over the plans with Cara, and she assured me this was best."

"I have four ovens. *Four.*"

His concern returned to his expression as he replied cautiously, "Yes... Four. Is that okay? We can change it afterward, but I'm afraid we won't have time to do much before the wedding."

Unable to contain the balloon of relief and growing excitement any longer, she laughed. Actually laughed. Without thought or hesitation, she jumped and wrapped her limbs around him. "Thank you."

Stunned, he caught her, holding her by the backs of her thighs. Pressed tight against the warm strength of him, weightless with bliss, she threw herself into the moment and sought his mouth with her own.

He opened, letting her in, answering her kiss with equal passion. Tempting, tasting, seducing, until her head swam with the rightness of it. Heated, delicious and heady, he only made her hunger for more.

He broke the connection and slid her down until she stood. A bubbling cauldron of foreign emotions, she didn't know whether to tackle him to the floor for another kiss or to shake the answers she needed from him.

As she'd moved down the muscled wall of his body, one particular part of his anatomy had called the bluff on his disinterest. It also showed her the promise of what could be, if the hardheaded male could get past whatever held him back.

He'd worked so hard on the remodel for her, and she owed him a lifetime of favors, though. She'd let him have his way.

For the moment.

He cleared his throat. "So, does that mean, you can make this work? Cara seemed to think it would work well."

She tore her gaze from his delectable mouth and surveyed the miracle that was her new kitchen. "She was right. It's so much more than I could've ever hoped for. It's perfect. I'll have to thank her." Instead of planting another kiss on his lips, she walked over to the new cabinets on the wall. Running a finger over the butcherblock countertop, she couldn't help but ask, "Is she really as nice as she seems?"

"Yeah, she is. We've known each other for almost ten years now. There's no one I'd rather have at my back."

Something in his words made her pause. Even though he vouched for Cara, it wasn't in a way she'd expected. "At your back? She looks like a kindergarten teacher. What do you mean?"

"She's a nurse now, but she served with us in Afghanistan a few years back."

Her belly clutched. "Did you guys see a lot of conflict?" She knew that's what soldiers did, but it all seemed so far away. Almost impossible.

"Some." Without missing a beat, he changed the subject. "We went with butcher block countertops because, even if you had something else in mind, I can repurpose them somewhere else."

"No, I love them. I love all of it. I don't know how to thank you."

He paused as if thinking about it. "Well, as long as you save me a few cookies, we'll call it even." She couldn't put her finger on the why, but for some reason, she felt he held something back. "You've only got about a week to get everything ready. Will that be enough time?"

"Are you kidding? With this kitchen, I think I could bake enough for ten weddings."

Unable to resist, she returned to give him a quick kiss.

She just wished the new kitchen didn't feel like a goodbye present.

CHAPTER 10

The world shook as concussive pressure slammed against him in a violent shove. Raising one arm as a shield, he braced against the unknown threat. Horrific screams split the air, piercing his eardrums. He looked across the barren, bland landscape, searching for the source of the shocking force.

Horror hit him harder than the blast when he found Justin lying in the sand broken and...

Noah awoke on a strangled, ragged shout. One moment, he was horizontal on Sylvie's couch. The next, he was vertical as his feet landed with a thump. Running a shaky hand over his face, he struggled to get his wits together. The dark room felt cramped, barring all oxygen from his lungs. His panicked heart fought against his sternum, trying to beat through its bony prison.

He needed...*out*.

He grabbed his zippered sweatshirt from the chair where it had lain for a few days and shrugged it on. Silently, on bare feet, he walked across the cool wood floor to the front door. It opened on a squeak, and he cursed himself for not taking care of the annoyance yet, before he hurried into the night.

When cool, crisp air hit his nose, he inhaled deeply, filling his lungs. His chest rose and fell with tight, heavy breaths as he took in the still darkness. As far as he could see, beneath the moon's pale light, lay acres of grass, trees, and peace.

A complete contrast to the land of his nightmares.

More accurately, his vivid memories of a living, breathing hell.

Those eyes. If he lived a thousand years, he'd never forget the terror in his friend's eyes.

He braced his arms against the porch railing and fought to steady his breathing. When the shakes made his elbows wobble, he jerked his arms back then stuffed his hands in his pockets. The backs of his knuckles felt something hard, and he remembered the knife James had found in the woods.

His frustration rose. The knife reminded him that, sometime soon, he needed to tell Sylvie what he'd found. He hoped to give Pete time to come up with something more concrete, but their resident computer wiz hadn't found anything.

The inability to find anything created a problem nearly as troubling as if Pete had found something incriminating. Pete always found info. Good or bad, he inevitably turned up a trail. But finding nothing at all? Not possible—unless someone had erased the man's past.

He pulled the knife from his pocket and examined it. Such a little thing, yet the old blade held the potential to keep him from the one thing he really wanted.

Sylvie.

He ran his thumb over the inscription, cursing the letters.

The door behind him opened, catching him off guard. As if summoned by his thoughts, she appeared, dressed in a long robe, open and loose, over a short nightgown. In one hand, she held a battered baseball bat. Her slightly tousled hair didn't hide the concern dimming her normally bright features, yet she was simply the most beautiful creature he'd ever seen. She scanned the length of the porch as if searching for a threat. Finding nothing, she leaned the bat against the inside wall, and pulled the door closed behind her.

Eyes soft, head slightly tilted, she quietly greeted him. "Hey. Everything okay?"

He searched for an answer. When it came out, he prayed it sounded true, even if it wasn't. "Yeah. Everything is fine." The simple words came out on a hoarse croak. He swallowed and tried again. "It's chilly. You shouldn't be out here barefoot."

"You don't have a shirt on. Or shoes." She pointedly looked down at his feet. "Do men have a foot-warming secret they're forbidden to share with women?"

He looked down. "No." He grinned. "Smartass. No secret. I didn't plan to be out here for more than a minute. I'm coming in now." He stepped closer to her, with the intention of ushering her inside.

"Why did you come...?" She trailed off then stopped him with a hand on his bare chest. "Noah, you look like you've seen a ghost. What's wrong?"

Her guess was more accurate than she knew. "Nothing's wrong. It was just a bad dream. Let's get you back inside." Driven by his need to get her out of the cold night air, he reached out to open the door.

"What's that?" She asked quietly, lightly touching his wrist.

"Nothing. Just an old knife." He closed his hand around it then jammed it back into his pocket. Silently, he cursed himself for being so distracted. Between the sweet concern in her eyes and his shaken state of mind, he didn't stand a chance.

But she only had eyes for him as she took him at his word. He felt about two feet tall. She opened the door and took his hand in hers. "C'mon, big man."

"You should be in bed. You have so much to prepare for."

"I've taken a couple of vacation days, and I've planned and prepped. At this point, all I see are cookies and ribbons dancing on the backs of my eyelids every time I close my eyes. I couldn't be more prepared if I hired a team of celebrity chefs. I have time to sit with a handsome man in the dark for a few minutes." When her milk chocolate eyes met his, he would have followed her through the gates of Hell and never given their dangerous course a second thought.

She pointed at the couch. "Sit." She shrugged off her robe and laid it in the armchair. Powerless, lost, he did as she instructed. She sat beside him and looked up at him with a considering look. "You're still pale. Hmmm.... doesn't look like you're ready to talk. Do you want to watch a movie or something?"

"Ah...no. The quiet is good." The softness of her warmth beside him was far better. The warm honey and whiskey of her voice soothed the ragged edges of his nerves better than the stiffest of drinks. She grounded him in comfort without even being aware of how powerful her presence was.

"Here. I know. Take this off." Without waiting for him to comply, she grabbed the neck of his sweatshirt and tugged it down off his shoulders.

Feeling ten kinds of awkward, he pulled his arms from her to finish the job. "I can do it." He shook his head. "You sure are bossy."

"Yep. Scooch forward." Somehow, she maneuvered and squeezed herself behind him until her legs were on either side of his hips. Not much more than half of his ass sat on the couch. The moment she was satisfied with their places, she put her hands at the base of his neck. Her thumbs began a soothing, rhythmic massage into the muscles on either side of his spine. "Are you going to complain?"

"Huh?" Between the stress of the flashback and the sweetness of her concern, his brain had become pudding.

"Are you complaining about my bossiness?" Her fingers danced over his shoulders in a light caress.

He stifled a groan. Barely.

"No. Not complaining." He dropped his head and gave up any semblance of control he might have had.

"You're still so tense. I'm sorry." The genuine compassion in her voice wrecked him. No prying. No useless platitudes or empty words.

Just company and warmth.

He made a weak attempt at waving her concern off. "It's passing. I'm okay, really. I'm sorry for waking you up."

Her fingers were no less magical, but her voice contained a harsh bite as she replied. "Sorry? For having a nightmare? That might be the most ridiculous thing I've ever heard."

"I woke you. Judging by the Louisville Slugger leaning against the wall there, I scared you, too. Don't want you afraid." The dark silence offered unconditional anonymity, a safe haven for truth. He looked down at the forearms braced on his thighs. He eased the pressure from his right arm. When his hand proved mostly steady, the last of the bands around his ribs relaxed their hold.

"Think about it—would you expect an apology if I accidently woke you because of a nightmare?"

His response came quick. "No, not at all." He put a little deeper thought into her question, then gave into the night waiting for its truth. Anything else seemed wrong. "I'd hope that you would wake me and...share your fear with me." On his last sentence, each word came out a little slower as he surrendered. "I'd want to be there for you. I'd expect you to wake me." He said it as if they slept every night together, and that he *would* be in bed beside her. Not a room or another town away.

She asked quietly, near his ear, "So why are the rules different for you?" She found the tense area at the base of his neck again, pressing deep with her thumbs then asked, with a tone that he couldn't quite label playful or dangerous. "It's not because you're a man, is it?"

Knowing his answer would get him into trouble, he sighed. "Yeah. It just ...is." He shrugged. "I can't help it."

She pinched his cheek playfully, but he suspected it was to get his attention as well. "So, because I don't have testicles, it's okay— even expected—of me to need your help and care. Of course, since you have a big set of these magical beans, you're not allowed to seek comfort. Is that the way it works, then?"

He shook his head. "You make it sound silly." He fought the urge to crouch, to hide from the bite in her voice. He feared she might pinch and twist his ear at any moment or pull out her frying pan and knock him upside the head.

"It *is* silly. There is zero reason for shame."

"Can't help the way I feel." He wanted to shrug his shoulders like a guilty schoolboy.

He couldn't see her face, but when she spoke, he wouldn't have been surprised if he turned to find her rolling her eyes. "Okay. For the record, that's wrong, and I totally disagree, but if you and your big magical beans refuse to see reason, look at it this way…"

Her hand left his neck, but he only had a moment to mourn the loss. The couch creaked then shifted. Next thing he knew, she sat on the floor directly below him. Cross-legged, in the short nightgown, she revealed acres of pale, sleek, curvy, leg. The thin sleep shirt let him know she wasn't wearing a bra. Full, round breasts with slightly upturned tips tempted him. He swallowed hard. But when her eyes melted with warmth, they stole the show from even her gorgeous body.

His breath fled his lungs again, but for an utterly different reason. "Sylvie."

She shook her head. "Listen, Neanderthal man." She cupped his jaw in both hands. "As much as it hurts me to say this, look at it this way. If a man's job is to protect and provide strength, then the woman's is to provide comfort and love. Correct?"

Fuck. Me. I don't know which is better—her sweet or her fire. He responded with the only answer he could muster, a heavy sigh.

"So… even using your outdated caveman logic, this is what I

was born to do. Why should you feel badly about receiving what I was meant to give?"

He released a short, unhappy laugh. "You undo me."

She paused as if considering his words. After a soft smile, she responded. "You know what? I'm glad. I think you need some undoing." She raised herself until she knelt between his legs. Brushing a thumb over his bottom lip, she whispered, "Why don't you want me, when I *know* you *want* me? I can see it."

Unable to resist, he kissed her thumb. The stubborn, still night wouldn't allow him to speak anything but the truth. "I thought I was doing an okay job at hiding it. I guess not."

"Nope. I can see right through you." At that moment, he believed she could see his every secret. Her fingers threaded through the hair at the base of his neck. Silken wisps of solace, mixed with the warm glow of desire, bathed him in the light of her love. "Noah, let me in." She closed the distance and laid a butterfly light kiss on his lips, tilting his world on its axis.

Broken, weak, hungry, desperate for a taste of her, he surrendered. Returning her kiss, he welcomed her into his arms, wrapping them around her waist. When her fingernails grazed over his nape, he shuddered. A jolt of pure, potent lust raced from his neck to his groin. Electric current awoke all the desire he'd fought to keep banked. Free, it rushed to the surface demanding it's due. *Sylvie.*

She arched into his hold and smiled a kitten's smile of satisfaction.

So be it.

If he was going down a damned man then, for just once in his life, he would be a selfish bastard and take what he wanted. Needed. He released the hands he'd struggled to keep off her. He slid his palms down over her hips, savoring the curved lines of her body.

Needing her even closer, finished with their unequal positions, he gripped her by the backs her thighs, lifted and stood to reposition her. Her firm, silken flesh filled his palms with a sample of heaven and the ecstasy to come.

~

Sylvie gasped as Noah lifted her into the air. Shocked, she gripped his shoulders to hold tight. His hands—a hard, hot brand just below the curves of her ass—pressed her pelvis against his abdomen.

His gaze penetrated hers with a deep intensity that, if she weren't so lust-starved for him, might scare her. She wasn't remotely afraid, though, because she wanted it. Every ounce of him.

When his mouth crash into hers, she met him with matching passion. Hungry, half-worried he might change his mind or regain his sanity and call a halt to this madness, she dove in, glorying in the rush.

His tongue circled hers, teased, and taunted, mimicking an altogether different type of dance.

Her hands raced over the muscled flesh of his chest, exploring with abandon.

The world rocked yet again as he sat them on the couch with her on his lap. Momentarily, he broke from their kiss as her nightgown disappeared in a flash of flying cotton.

Noah's low groan of appreciation reverberated through her as he looked down. "Damn, but you're beautiful. Almost as sexy on the outside as you are beautiful on the inside. I'll never get enough."

He cupped her breasts, lavishing them with attention, somehow tender and hungry all at once.

That heavy, ravenous ache she'd missed bloomed, hot and desperate inside as her body demanded she not wait any longer.

"Sylvie, please tell me you're protected. I have some somewhere, but if I have to release you to find it, you'll see a grown man cry."

She responded between ragged breaths, each word a second taken away from what she wanted. That sexy bottom lip that she'd long lusted over. She dipped in for a quick, nipping sample before taking breath to respond. "On the pill. Clean." She weaved her fingers together behind his neck, holding on. "Non-existent dating life. Now, please." Desperate hunger drove her in for another nip.

"Same. I mean other than the pill. I'm a terrible man and can't even be sorry for the lack of sex right now."

She shifted, reached for the waistband of her panties, fumbling, trying to figure out how of get out of them.

"I got you." Two large hands batted hers out of the way and ripped them down one side. He shifted throwing her against his body as he freed his shaft from his sweatpants. "Good god. Please tell me you're ready."

"Yes. Now."

With an urgency she couldn't comprehend, her mind couldn't keep up with her body's demands. She braced one hand on his shoulder and raised up, helping to align their bodies. Slowly, she lowered herself onto his hard cock.

Sweet, heated pressure filled her, sending waves of delicious sensation through her. She couldn't tell which was more agonized, his groan or her whimper. It didn't matter because it wasn't a competition to see who gave or got more, but a celebration of...their love. Something she'd long given up on finding and something she'd be stupid to give up on.

One way or another, she'd get to the bottom of this man's secrets.

When fully seated on his length, stretched by and full of him, she met his gaze and smiled. There was simply too much goodness. His appearance, the strength in that glorious body, his mouthwatering scent. Big, steady hands roughened by years of hard, honest work. The feel of all that firm male flesh beneath her palms. Those intelligent, attentive green eyes.

And that big, incredibly soft heart.

Puzzled, he looked as if he couldn't quite figure her out. Eventually, she'd let him in on her secret, but not now.

"Let's go, big man."

"Yes, ma'am."

His hands moved to her ass, cupped it firmly and guided her with an easy rocking motion. Pleasure bloomed in her core, growing and spreading through her every cell. Warmed with ecstasy, she smiled as she joined her mouth with his. After a teasing tangled kiss, she asked, "This good for you?"

His muscled arms flexed and bunched with each synchronized motion. "Yes. Perfect." On a deep thrust, he groaned. "Perfect but I want more. Need more." He nuzzled her ear. Kissed her neck.

She agreed, replying on a whimper. "Yes. More." While the pleasure slamming into her with each thrust pushed her higher, it wasn't enough. Their position hampered their movement as much as it helped their closeness. "Let's move to the floor."

"Floor?" He spoke against her neck in a rush of breath.

She ran her palms over his chest. "Bedroom's too far. Floor. Now."

He shook his head. "Don't want to hurt you."

Then it hit her. "You're holding back."

He half-guided, half-lifted her to prepare for another thrust. "Can't hurt you. Won't hurt you."

Her already squishy heart melted into a puddle. Taking his face in her palms, she didn't know whether to choke him or kiss him. "The only way you'll hurt me is if you don't lay me out on the rug and do me hard. Now."

He grinned. "You want me to do you hard?" He arched his hips and pulled her down on the word hard.

When pleasure rolled through her, she arched back. "Quit talking and get it done, big man."

When their bodies disconnected, she wanted to grab him and pull him back inside her. He stood lifting her with one arm wrapped tightly around her waist. He grabbed a pillow from the couch before taking two strides. He tossed the pillow on the floor and lowered them both to the floor. When her head was on the pillow and back was flat against the rug, he joined her. The moment he slid his length inside her, she wrapped her legs tightly around his waist, wishing she could keep him there forever.

Without another word, he kissed her hard then set them on a brutal pace. Each hard thrust of his cock rasped over her hyper-sensitive flesh. Weight on his forearms, he stayed close, his body blanketing hers until his chest brushed against hers. Her breasts ached, throbbing with each body shaking jolt.

Too hungry for each other and too focused on the pleasure of giving and taking, they stopped talking with voices and communicated with their bodies. Moving in time to his near-violent plunges, racked with ecstasy, she gave herself over to the bright joy growing inside her.

Sounds of sex filled the air. Sighs. Heavy breaths. The rhythmic slap of flesh against flesh as Noah plunged his cock into her again and again, each time pushing her closer to that place she desperately needed to be. She put her hands at what had become her favorite place—tangled together at the base of Noah's neck.

She marveled at the strength of all that muscled male body as he worked them both. Her body tightened with delicious torture. Her breasts ached and nipples tingled. The electric joy grew sharper, winding her ever tighter until she could almost taste its magic.

"Sweetheart, please, please tell me you're close." His thrusts quickened.

"Very." She hummed as he licked up the column of her throat coming to a rest at her mouth. Swallowing her response, he drank her in, merging their mouths until every part of them was connected.

The growing tangle of sensation swelled and tightened, further amplifying her pleasure, as her body gripped him tighter. Then, on a deep, hard thrust, that knot of ecstasy exploded, throwing the pieces of her afar. Crying out, her every cell alight with the fiery bliss, she held onto the weight of Noah, knowing he'd keep her whole.

He drove in, pinning her down, anchoring her to this world. His back bowed in a magnificent display of masculinity. With a low growl, he finished with a series of quick, brutal plunges, filling her with liquid heat.

Gasping for air, she held on and closed her eyes, savoring each of his heavy breaths. When hard arms wrapped around and once again lifted her, her eyelids popped open. He was carrying them up the stairs.

"What are you doing?" Though his mood improved, she didn't want her stoic warrior spending any more time alone in the dark that night.

Or ever.

"Bed. Not doing that to you again on the floor, and I'm afraid the couch won't survive what I have planned." He pushed her door all the way open with a shoulder.

Her still racing heart paused. "Again?"

"Good thing you don't work tomorrow. You're going to need to catch up on your sleep after I'm finished."

CHAPTER 11

*a*fter spending most of her morning doing laundry and playing catch up around the house, she decided to go over her pantry and plans one last time. She'd ordered half a dozen new cookie sheets, a few more mixing bowls, and a few other odds and ends that should arrive in the next day or two. She was waiting until the last minute to pick up the refrigerated ingredients. She'd run through the operation countless times yet, no matter how hard she tried or whatever she used to distract herself, she just couldn't settle. Her body hummed with anticipation, excitement and worry.

Cautious hope warred with exhausting doubt.

She heard the thump of a car door shutting and set down her pen. She'd been going over her shopping list to ensure she had everything they'd need for Karli's order and then some. Once they started baking and packaging, she planned to keep everything moving as smoothly as possible. The last thing she wanted was to have to stop and make a store run.

She stretched and straightened her shoulders as she stood. The legs of her old chair squeaked against the wood floor as she pushed it back with her legs.

Wondering who her company was and what sort of news or drama they'd brought with them, she made her way to the front door. When she opened it she found Marcy and Karli. Karli's pixie face appeared hard, possibly even angry. Her trademark red hair had been pulled back into a messy topknot. Her arms were crossed tightly over her abdomen.

Marcy look resigned as they walked closer. "Hey, hon. Karli needs a quiet place to blow off some steam and do some hard thinking. We were going to take a walk by the lake, but the parking area is packed. Looks like someone's having a party or something down there and Karli's not, um...in the mood for polite company."

Karli's smile was anything but friendly. "Or children. I probably shouldn't be around impressionable children. Bad words. Lots of bad words have been spoken. I've dropped more F-bombs in the last few hours than I have my entire life."

Marcy grimaced. "Can we use your access to the lake? Maybe wonder around down by the shore or the creek for a bit?"

"Absolutely. You can have the run of the place. It's just me. I mean, Noah's around here somewhere, too, but he won't care or mind any F-bombs. I think he may be poking around in the barns, but you go and do whatever you please. I'll just go back to the kitchen and leave you be."

Karli had stopped just before the bottom step with her hands on her hips. She turned sideways to take in her surroundings. Her slender shoulders rose and fell on deep breaths. "I'm sorry to barge in on your quiet weekend, Sylvie. I know you don't get much downtime. Just because my world is a hot mess, doesn't mean I have the right to intrude on yours."

"I don't mind. I'm just going over my shopping list. We'll get started on your cookies soon."

Marcy winced and Karli closed her eyes on an exhale as if she was battling for control or fighting back tears. "Ah, about that order..."

Filled with concern, Marcy looked from her cousin to Sylvie and back to Karli. "Sweetheart, we'll figure something out. Don't do anything rash just yet." She faced Sylvie to explain. "We're in crisis mode. The church where they'd scheduled the wedding canceled. We need to find another venue, like yesterday. And the entire thing has become...kind of unpleasant." Marcy tried tactfully.

Karli let out a choked sob. "Kind of unpleasant? Oh, Marce. Cole's father threatened to punch the minister of my mother's church." When Karli covered her face and silently shuddered, Sylvie ached for the young woman.

Marcy rubbed her cousin's shoulder. "So, yeah. We needed to get away from the hordes of angry and well-meaning, but pushy, families to breathe some fresh air."

"Your farm is lovely, Sylvie. Why don't you show us around? Please. If you have time. I just need a break."

Sylvie wasn't sure she would be much of a worthy distraction, but she did have something else that might help a broken heart, or at least numb the pain for a moment or two. "Give me a minute to put on shoes and tell Noah where I'm going." If he came back up to the house and found her missing, he'd track her down. The last thing Karli needed was Noah in raging papa bear mode. She quickly returned to the house, slipped on her old gym shoes, then retrieved her phone and sent Noah a text.

She grabbed three bottled waters from the fridge then loaded a paper bag with wrapped pieces of fudge.

As she loaded her arms with provisions, she saw Noah responded to her message with a thumbs up.

She returned to Marcy and Karli to pass out drinks. "Where to?"

"The lake?" Marcy shrugged.

"Sure. The most direct path is through the two smaller barns and straight down the slope. It's only about a five-minute hike."

Karli exhaled a heavy breath. "Sounds perfect. Marce, what am

I going to do? It's too late to reschedule." They set off at an easy pace and let Karli vent. This was her show, whether she wanted to stew quietly, scream and rage, or talk it out. Karli threw her hands in the air. "The flowers, favors, decorations, food...everything. Not to mention the circus that comes with filming the TV special. Ugh. I wish now that I hadn't agreed to allow them in on our special day. Isn't that what the wedding is supposed to be about?"

Marcy answered. "Absolutely."

When a damp shimmer filled Karli's eyes, Sylvie pushed aside her own worries about possible effects on her virtually nonexistent business and agreed. "Weddings are emotional events, especially when everyone has invested time, expense and energy into the planning. It's easy to forget the reason for them in the first place—the bride and groom. Ultimately, I think you should do what's best for you and Cole. As hard as it may be, don't worry so much about pleasing everyone else. Dare I ask what happened? I'm not trying to be nosy, but I'd like to help."

"You're fine, Sylvie. The minister of my mother's church, who has always been a bit of a judgmental stick in the mud, decided at the last minute that he didn't want his church's name tarnished by a 'reality TV circus.' My brother thinks it's because I beat out his oldest granddaughter for the county beauty pageant four years ago. He overheard her whining about how it's unfair I have a TV show and she doesn't. She's always been a spoiled brat. Wants everything but won't work for a single dime."

Karli shook her head. "Oh, who knows? The why doesn't even matter at this point. He called us in to tell us this morning. My mom was stunned speechless. Cole's mother tried to smooth things over but totally lost her composure. She ended up in angry tears over the mess. When he saw his wife in tears, Cole's father lost his cool and my dad and Cole had to push him outside before he actually did as he'd threatened—deck Pastor Jim. Jim's sister owns the bakery where we ordered the cake and, conveniently, she suddenly has a staffing issue and won't be able to make the cake. Now everyone has some grand idea to fix it, and they're all terrible because our options are really limited. Feelings are all rubbed raw. I feel like if I choose Mom's plan, then Cole's mother will be offended and vice versa."

Sylvie led them through a gap in the trees that would take them down to the lakeshore. Spying a couple of large boulders, Marcy led them over and leaned back against one. She pointedly looked to the bag in Sylvie's hand. "What sort of treat did you pack for us?"

"Just some leftover fudge." Sylvie handed a piece to Marcy and Karli. "It's a temporary bandage, but I figured a little sugar couldn't hurt."

Karli unwrapped her piece and put the wrapper in her jeans pocket. "Oh, wow, is this good!" Looking out over the quiet silvery lake, she exhaled a heavy breath. "Mom is calling the supermarket and the big club stores in nearby cities to see if by some small chance we can find a cake in time, but I worry it's a waste of energy. Even if she *can* find something, it'll be as generic as can be. This was supposed to be the start of mine and Cole's future. While we might be able to laugh about having our wedding at a bingo hall twenty years from now, I had hoped to make the show work for my career. Maybe it's silly, or even greedy..."

Sylvie thought of her desires. Dreams that some days seemed close enough to touch and on others seemed light years away. "It's not silly or greedy. You're going into business and need to make smart decisions." They walked down the shoreline, stepping over fallen branches and around large boulders. "You have a great brand and protecting, even advertising it, is using smart business sense, not greed."

"Thank you for saying that. It's nice to talk to someone who understands. Marcy runs a successful business. She said close to the same thing, and it makes me feel better to talk to women who understand." Karli popped the last bite of her fudge into her mouth. "Damn, woman, is there anything you can't bake?"

Sylvie laughed. "Noah asked me the same thing over breakfast this morning. Though technically, making fudge isn't baking." She led them up a path, away from the lake to an area where the trees were sparser. "Thank you. It's just something I love to do."

"Well, it shows. You should open your own business."

A fist squeezed around her heart at the sincere encouragement behind Karli's words. "I'd hoped to someday. We'll see."

Marcy held her hand out for another piece. "I know you've got more in there. Hand it over.

Shaking, her head, Sylvie handed her the bag.

Karli stopped in her tracks, turned and looked straight to Sylvie. "You're making my cake. I'll pay double. No! I'll pay *triple* your rate, plus add a great big tip for the inconvenience of a last-minute order. I've only used half my allotted budget from the show. I've still got a huge chunk to spend. At least I'll have a fantastic cake at my bingo hall wedding. Maybe the cameras can focus on that and my dress instead of the bingo board on the wall."

Shock made her stumble. "Karli, I'm flattered, but…"

"No buts. I don't need a sample tasting, just keep it simple, yummy, and big. We can take some of the flowers from the florist order, and you can use them to decorate it, instead of wasting your precious time with icing flowers and whatnot." In a clear mood shift, Karli brightened as she waved her hand dismissively over the imaginary icing flowers.

"I…" She'd love nothing more than to help Karli. She hated to think that the young couple's wedding plans were at risk, but she couldn't take on a wedding cake, too.

Could she?

"Which way do we go next?" Karli looked around the mostly cleared field with a babbling creek running through it. "Oh! Look how lovely!"

Sylvie looked at the old stone bridge

"It is pretty isn't it? My great-grandfather had it built for my great-grandmother. He proposed to her there and laid out his hopes and plans for their future." Sylvie blinked back tears as she thought about her family's history—the history she'd once hoped to continue. "He was the romantic while she was the more practical one."

"And the barn! It looks like it's in great shape. I love the faded gray paint. And it's so big!"

"It is. It hasn't been used for anything other than storage in ages. It's dusty and could use some sprucing up, but it's solid."

"Oh! Perfect! I have an idea." Karli whipped her cell phone out of her pocket. In a flash, she had it plastered to her ear with one hand. She gestured happily with the other as she spoke. "Cole? Hey, baby, guess what? I found our venue, and it's gorgeous. I mean it's to-die-for perfect! We'll need to pull together some help, because we can't expect Sylvie to do it all. We'll have to set it up, or maybe hire someone to handle setup. She has to focus on making my cake. Or cakes? Maybe we need more than one? Oh, but it's so pretty and absolutely perfect. I'll take some pictures and send them in a minute. Love you, too, baby." She paused for a brief moment, then laughed. "Well, maybe I'll let the studio executives sweat a little more before I call them, but I'll call my agent from the car."

With wide eyes, Marcy turned to Sylvie. "What just happened?"

Dazed, not quite comprehending, Sylvie just stood there, afraid to do...anything.

Giddy with excitement, Karli was all but skipping down to the little bridge. "I know you won't have time to help with the cleanup and prep. I'll get dad and my brothers to do it. Maybe the studio can bring in some people? Right now, with everything that's happened, Daddy will be relieved to have an end to the wedding madness. At this point, he probably has enough frustration to work off. Oh!" She paused at the bridge's edge and turned to Sylvie. "I didn't think to ask. Is it sturdy? Will we need to make any repairs?"

Sylvie swallowed. "It should be." She started to walk.

When she got close, Karli grasped her hands. "Oh, Sylvie. Does your farm have a name? I need something to put on the announcements. Thank you so much!"

"Um, no, it doesn't really have name, but—"

"Well, we'll have to think of something pretty, then. When everyone watches the show, they'll want to know where the wedding was held. Why, it could become a tourist attraction! Of course, we'll find out what the going rate is for hosting a wedding then we'll double it for the trouble and time crunch. Come on, Marcy. I have a million things to do!" She grabbed Marcy's hand and all but pulled her across the field. "I'm going to come back first thing in the morning with Dad, Cole, and maybe his father, too. Hopefully by then his temper will have cooled. Oh, this will be amazing! So much prettier and, well...more *me* than a church wedding. Tents! We'll need tents and tables! And chairs for the ceremony. I'll put Cole's momma to work on that. She'll be so relieved, and the project will give her something happy to focus on. Oh, and my brothers! A big project like this will keep them occupied and possibly out of jail. Evan and Rusty were ready to bash some heads in when they saw mine and Mama's tears. Sent me a bunch of F-bomb loaded texts, and that's never a good sign."

Marcy looked over her shoulder with a dazed, apologetic grimace. She mouthed *I'll call you.* Not bothering to keep up with the redheaded whirlwind practically dancing across her property, Sylvie wandered down to the bridge. She stood there and listened to the creek. Sounds of nature surrounded her with their timeless comfort. The meadow *was* an absolutely lovely place. It had always been one of her favorites, but recently life had been far too chaotic and stressful for her to give it much thought.

She couldn't let it go.

But she *could* share its magic.

An additional driveway led from the main road straight to the barn—a tad overgrown, but still totally viable. Parking in the North pasture, just beside the road, should work. The meadow really was a great location for weddings. Or what about the large party Marcy had mentioned? This side of the lake only had two small picnic areas. She could cater meals or baked goods, just like she was apparently going to do for Karli and Cole. Or pictures? There were so many places around the property that would make gorgeous backdrops for photos.

In time, maybe she could convert the old cabin into a bed and breakfast. The cozy living area and adjoining kitchen could be a good place for showers or smaller parties. Maybe she could install a commercial grade kitchen into the small barn closest to the house? All the space she'd dreamed of for her baking, yet she wouldn't have to go far from home. Heaven knew, she didn't have the space at the house to do serious catering. She'd talk to Noah, maybe get an estimate on what it would take to do some remodeling. At this point, she couldn't afford even the materials, let alone the labor and design costs, but it wouldn't hurt to explore all her options. She'd have to start small, then take baby steps as she got her finances straight.

I can do this.

She looked out at toward the lake. She could just barely make out the shimmer of silvery green water as the sun began its evening descent.

Recognizing the pattern of his gait, she heard the rustle of grass behind her. A familiar big arm wrapped around her middle in the way she'd come to love. "Everything okay? I saw your friends tear out of here like their tails were on fire."

He *would* come straight to her to make sure she was all right, wouldn't he? She turned from her view to wrap her arms around his middle. There, in what had become her favorite place to be, she smiled. "Everything is good. Fantastic, even."

His brow furrowed in suspicion. "Oh yeah?"

"Yeah. Warning, things are going to be ten kinds of crazy around here for the next two weeks. Hopefully it will be the good kind of crazy this time around. I think I'm going to have to ask my boss for a few more days off before the wedding. I have the vacation hours saved. Apparently, I'm baking Karli Skye's wedding cake...or cakes."

"This is in addition to the cookie madness?"

"It is. She trusts me to do the flavor, design, everything, sight and taste, untried." The words felt almost as crazy on her tongue as the idea did in her mind.

Noah seemed perplexed by her doubt. "Of course, she does. She'd be a fool, not to."

"She offered to pay me triple my regular price. I don't even *have* a regular price. One more thing to figure out. Also, I'll need a name for my farm, or business. They're having the wedding here."

Oh no.

"What's wrong? I could literally see the happiness fade from your eyes." She loved the way she could feel the deep rumble of his voice.

She let her forehead thump against his chest. "I need to ask you for another favor."

She felt his silent chuckle as she rubbed her forehead against the muscled man-wall. "So ask."

"You've already done far too much for me."

With a gentle tug on her chin, he tipped her head up. He stared down at her full of impatience. How could such a quiet male be so expressive?

"Okay, fine. Karli is going to come back tomorrow morning with her family. She wants to show them the big barn. They'll want to clean it up and prep it for the wedding reception. I would feel better if you could oversee things a bit. I don't know them well, and I'm sure they have the best of intentions, but..."

"Consider it done."

"Thank you. I can cross that off my list of worries then." And she really could. Without thought or hesitation, she sought his mouth with her own. He paused for a moment so brief, she almost missed it before he joined her in a kiss capable of melting the coldest of hearts.

CHAPTER 12

*N*oah stood at the barn's entrance with his cell pressed to his ear. Half of his focus was on the flurry of activity all around him, the other half on Pete's one-sided rambling in his ear. Sylvie's barn had been dusted and cleaned within an inch of its life. He would have liked the chance to treat the old oak beams, but for now, a quick dust and shine would have to do. Fortunately for the bride, the powers that be behind the TV special were thrilled with the idea of a rustic country wedding with a lake in the background. The theme had exploded, spreading to include the reception dinner which would be held inside the barn.

Karli's father and her agent had come together in what Sylvie called a rare show of unity and pried every penny they could from the studio. In the end, they'd been able to amass an army of family, friends and hired help. Sylvie's friend Marcy had come over and, together, they'd researched pricing for all manner of wedding related services. It seemed Sylvie, if she could pull it off, had a virtual business dropped in her lap.

He would do everything in his power to make sure the entire event went off without a single hitch. Fortunately for them all,

Karli's family appeared to be a very competent and determined crew. Their one and only priority was Karli's happiness.

He wasn't above making sure Sylvie got the most out of the deal when it came to renovations funded by the TV studio.

As he watched Karli's mother point this way and that, while yet another stand of fairy lights were draped from the old wood beams crisscrossing the cavernous space, he put an end to Pete's story. "Pete. Man, I don't have all day. Did you find anything at all on the brother?"

"No. Not yet. I'm still thinking and digging. Rick said he would put out some feelers, too. Something's definitely off, though."

Frustrated and feeling as though time was running out, Noah ran a hand through his hair. He stepped aside as someone ran an extension cord across the floor. "Fine. Start on the employer."

"The business, owners, or the employees."

Knowing the saw would start screaming any moment as they resumed cutting planks for the floor, Noah turned to step outside. There, he found Sylvie stared at him with a weak smile. "All of them. Find me something, damn it."

A slash of confusion cut through her expression.

"I gotta go, Pete. Talk to you later," he said.

Pete quickly asked, "Do you and Sylvie need a hand with anything?"

"Thanks, but I think everything is under control now. I'll call if something comes up. Thanks again." He disconnected before Pete could continue his chatter. "Hey, how are things coming along inside?"

"Good. At least I think so." When she paused, as if weighing her words closely, his gut tightened. "I need someone willing to sample a couple of things."

He forced a smile and placed a hand on her back to usher her toward the house. "I guess, if no one else is available, I'll just have to take one for the team. What are we tasting today?"

"Cake."

"Again? I'm certainly not complaining, but what was wrong with yesterday's? Pretty sure that one can't be topped."

She stopped then turned to face him. "Noah, what's going on? What was your conversation about?"

He wasn't the least bit surprised by her head-on approach. He even admired it. He just wished it didn't put him in such a tight spot.

"Okay." He blew out a breath. "I'm still not satisfied that the break-in was an isolated incident. My gut says this isn't over yet. They were way too methodical for a quick robbery. Plus, they tried to put their hands on you. Calvin's behavior leads me to believe he may have hidden something in your home. I'm having Pete do a little digging on anything that could have even the slightest chance of being related. Chances are he won't find anything damaging, but I won't rest until I know otherwise."

"Even my brother? Noah, I know he wasn't involved. I'd know his voice anywhere. He'd never in a million years do anything to harm a hair on my head. I... know it sounds funny, but in a way, I think he saved me. I mean, I know he wasn't there, but I knew, like the way I know the sun is going to rise tomorrow, what he would have wanted me to do to get out of that situation. I know you haven't met him, that you only have a loving sister's word to go on, but you're wasting your friend's time. Truly."

"I know that. I hate to upset you over this, but when it comes to your safety, I won't leave any stone unturned. You live too far away from help. Added to that, you have a mountain of work on your plate. I won't leave you alone on that front either. All I can say is that Pete's digging into Calvin's business, too. He'll find something." He gestured to the house waiting in the distance. "Now, cake. I really don't think you could improve on yesterday's bliss, but I am more than willing to sacrifice my taste buds for your culinary needs."

Somehow, even with the barrage of noises coming from the

barn, the evening settled in quiet and cool as they walked across her property.

When they neared her house, she peered up at him with suspicion. "You're pretty smooth, you know that?"

"Me? Nah. James has all the moves and sweet words. I'm just the quiet brawn." He winked, hoping to lighten the mood.

She shook her head. "As if! Beware. I'm onto you Mr. Ramsey."

"Point taken. Now onto the really important issue." He paused when she just looked up with an arched brow like she wasn't fooled. For the moment, though, she seemed content to let him have his way. He'd have to settle for that small reprieve. "Baked goods."

"Well, big man, that I have. By the way, you took the wind out of my sails."

"How did I do that?" He hated to think he'd made her unhappy. Knowing that it had only been a matter of time didn't lessen the sting. He opened the door and held it for her.

"I was prepared to send you home after I abused your taste buds."

Stepping in behind her, he paused. "Excuse me."

"I hate that you've given up so much for me. There haven't been any signs of trouble since Calvin's visit. I think you scared him, or them, away. I feel like I'm taking advantage of your kindness. So...you can go home now. I'll be fine."

He didn't bother replying. He just went to his spot at the new island and sat. He figured his look said it all when she sighed and put her hands on her hips.

"Cake me." Of course, when she did, he found she had indeed somehow improved on the previous day's decadence.

Fresh out of the shower, Sylvie just finished dressing for the day when a knock sounded at her door. She glanced at the clock and verified it was almost an hour sooner than she told everyone to come. Curious, she made her way down to the front door to find a bleary-eyed Marcy waiting with a large paper bag. "Morning."

"What are you doing here so early?" She opened the door and stepped back to let her friend inside.

"Here. Breakfast. Didn't know what the big guy likes, so there's a variety of sandwiches in there. I knew you'd be up before the chickens, so I figured I'd swing by the drive-thru then lend a hand with...whatever." She shrugged. "At least until the crowd gets here in a bit."

Sylvie accepted the bag and led the way back to the kitchen. "Thanks. I was getting ready to throw something quick together for breakfast then I intended to gather my thoughts." She set the bag on the bar.

"Liar. At best, you would have settled for a piece of toast. At worst, only a large coffee. That's why I'm here." Marcy pointed to the bag. "It might not be the healthiest, or even the warmest, of offerings but it will be more substantial than hot caffeine."

"Okay. You're probably right except for one thing." She grabbed a paper wrapped sandwich out of the bag and put it in the microwave.

"What's that?"

Noah chose that moment to make his appearance. He headed straight for her. He leaned in for a slow, heated kiss before he answered Marcy. "Me." The moment his lips touched hers, she forgot all about Marcy's presence. He released her with a low grumble. "I wouldn't have let her get by with that. I planned to stay in her way until she ate something, then I would have helped her clean up before getting scarce." His eyes glittered with promises of wicked things to come later as he moved toward the coffee.

"I'd hoped to let you sleep in this morning. There's really no need for you to be up already." As she'd slipped out of her warm, very full, and far too comfortable bed, she'd mourned the loss of his big arm holding her close. He'd looked so handsome and… peaceful as the moonlight spilled across his face. In a flight of fancy, she'd wished she could keep him that way forever.

"I was cursed with early-riser genes. Being in the military, even part time, didn't help." He brushed a quicker, lighter kiss over her mouth. "I like the pre-dawn quiet."

"Well, I hate to burst your serene little bubble, but there won't be much of that around here today." She grinned wryly.

"Good."

Marcy looked at Noah, considering, before looking back to Sylvie. "Does this guy have a brother?" She slid the bag in his direction. "Help yourself to a lukewarm, greasy breakfast. There should be enough for a football team in there."

Sylvie pulled her sandwich from the microwave and traded places with Noah at the coffee pot. "I really appreciate breakfast, and no, he doesn't have a brother."

Marcy put her hands on her hips and shook her head at Noah as if she were annoyed by the idea.

He pulled two sandwiches out of the bag then shrugged. "Sorry. I only have a sister."

Marcy's shoulders sagged. "Damn."

Noah grinned. "Thanks for the breakfast." He nodded to Marcy. "I'll leave you ladies to your magic making. I'm going to see if they need any last-minute help at the barn. Some of the bride's brothers and cousins planned to pull an all-nighter. Someone came up with an idea for a giant bar involving old whiskey barrels and pallets. They decided they could complete it if they worked through the night." He paused, leaning against the mudroom entryway.

"Do you really think they can pull it off?" She hoped they could, for Karli's sake. Heaven knew, they were giving it their all.

"Yeah, they will. Her family really came together for her. It probably hasn't hurt that the TV special is involved and they're a competitive bunch. Losing the church wedding only made them want to ensure the new location is at least twice as better. Doesn't hurt any that they want to show that *better* off to the world." He stuffed one wrapped sandwich in his sweatshirt. Juggling a coffee tumbler and the other sandwich, he exited, through the early morning dark to lend a hand to virtual strangers.

Marcy waited about a full ten seconds after the door shut before she said, "So, I noticed no signs of anyone living in the front room when I came through the house. Is he that tidy or has his sleeping arrangement changed?"

Sylvie loved that wasn't a single hint of cattiness in her tone. Just honest, friendly curiosity.

Out of respect for that, she didn't even try to be coy. "Both. He really is that neat, and he's been sleeping in my bed for a couple nights now."

Marcy glanced at the clock on the microwave. "Gimme the details, quick, then we'll go over your plans for the day."

Giving in a little, Sylvie smiled as she shared a few details. She hugged the rest close.

In the late afternoon, Noah sent Karli's family home. As promised, they'd finished the bar and done a fine job of it. Not content with simply topping the barrels with sheets of plywood, her two oldest brothers constructed an eight-foot-long piece of art. The barrels hadn't given them the height they wanted, so those has been converted to tables for people to set their drinks on which would be spread throughout the room after the catered dinner. Karli's sister-in-law proclaimed the finished bar amazing. The men all beamed until she came up with an idea to go with it. She proclaimed they need a matching, smaller bar for the kids. It would be a self-serve hot chocolate, coffee, and cider bar. They'd been willing, but exhausted. Due to that, Noah sent them home and called James. While he made a run to the hardware store,

James made a pizza run for the women. A quick text to Sylvie and she'd confirmed that operation cookie magic was going well, but they hadn't taken time for a break or to eat.

He arrived back to Sylvie's house minutes after James and heard the voices from the front porch. As he opened the door, Addie's voice chimed from the living room. "*My* favorite! No one ever orders my favorite toppings. Thanks!"

James answered and Noah heard the smile in his voice as he walked through the door. "Wish I could take credit, kiddo, but Noah called the order in. I'm only the delivery boy today."

She stood first in line behind the sofa, where they'd made room for the boxes of pizza on an old couch table. Beaming, she found him at the door. He loved the way her face lit up whenever she saw any of them. He'd been there the day she'd gotten away from them in the woods and a few weeks later on the day they'd found her. He marveled how this young girl became so important to so many so quickly. "Eat up. There should be plenty for everyone. I'm sure you've earned it."

Marcy, it seemed had taken the young girl under her wing and vouched for her, as she gently ran a hand down Addie's blonde ponytail. "She *has* earned it. I've lost track of how many ribbons we've cut and boxes we've assembled."

"And the tags!" Addie chimed in. "They're pretty, even for pink, but, man. We've got tags everywhere."

"Yep. But you've done good. All the ribbon is cut and most of the boxes have been unfolded. We're over halfway done. We'll start boxing the cookies soon." A hint of sadness washed over Marcy's, suggesting Addie probably revealed part of her past.

"Are you going to have any pizza, Noah?" Addie took her plate and sat in an armchair by the fireplace.

"In a minute. I want to check on Sylvie first." He tried to stay out of the way. Since he'd left that morning, he resisted the urge to peek in. He knew she was capable and determined to make this work. He also knew he'd sent her the best help imaginable.

In addition to Kate, Leigh, and Cara, he called in his secret weapon.

At the kitchen, he bypassed the counter laden with cookies and went straight for the first woman he'd ever loved. "Hey, Mom." He leaned down to kiss her cheek. "You doing okay?"

With an ice cream scoop full of cookie dough in one hand, she reached up to pat his cheek with the other. "I'm wonderful." She raised up on tiptoe to whisper in his ear. "I really like her. Good choice. Now, step back before you get sawdust in the batter." She shooed him away.

Kate measured something into the gleaming bowl at one end of the island while Leigh did the same at the opposite end. Cara washed another bowl at the sink. "Really, I think you should go ahead and start. We've got this licked. Take a break, get a bite to eat and then dig in. I'm excited to see it. Please, make sure you get plenty of pictures after it's assembled tomorrow. I really want to see it all put together. Oh! You'll want to have some for your portfolio or website, too! Probably should set up something pretty to photograph the finished cookie boxes, too."

Sylvie worried her bottom lip between her teeth by the fridge, her hands propped on her hips. "I think I'll go ahead. The florist delivered the flowers for me to work with this morning, and they're lovely. Navy, sage, pale pink and just a hint of plum. It's a gorgeous combination."

He stepped in. "Nope. No starting another project yet. I want you to get a piece of pizza and sit for fifteen minutes. Then you can start on whatever has got you worrying a hole in your lip."

When the only argument he received was an annoyed look before she turned to actually do as he wanted, he was surprised.

Cara answered before he could ask. "She's worried about the cake. She knows Karli said simple was perfectly fine, so long as it tasted good, but everyone knows the wedding cake is a big deal. It has to be something special, especially if it has her name on it."

"It will be. Everything she bakes is amazing. The cake won't be an exception."

"I know that. You know that. Doesn't take her stress away." She dried her hands on a dish towel and came over to look up at him.

He leaned down to kiss her cheek. "Thank you. For me and for her. I... thank you."

"I'm happy to do it." Then it was her turn to shoo him away, so he went to see if he could sneak a kiss from his girl before grabbing some pizza for himself and getting back to work.

CHAPTER 13

She had just waved the women on their way and poured herself a glass of wine when Noah's truck rumbled up the driveway to the back porch. She'd parked her car in the garage to make room for the van Karli's agent planned to send in the morning to pick up the cookies. On her way to the couch, she paused in the dining room doorway. Covered in neatly stacked boxes, her grandmother's old dining room table was barely visible. The group of women who'd come to her aid delivered as promised and more.

Noah understated their willingness to work, their capability, and their kindness. At the side table, she fingered a sheet of stickers that bore her new, utterly gorgeous logo. In simple, yet beautiful script two words arched over a stunning sketch of her baked goods. *Grace Farm.*

Yet another gift from Noah's friends.

Mind buzzing with cookie flavors and cake decorating details, she had pretty much forgotten she needed an updated logo. Marcy hadn't forgotten, though, and mentioned she wished there had been time to design something.

Cara then brought Addie a glass of tea. Patting the girl on the head, she'd advised, "Get to it. Surely you have a sketchbook in Leigh's car?"

The beautiful young girl's eyes grew wide and as pale as bright full moons. Sylvie barely heard her whispered, "What?"

Leigh replied, "Yes. I'm pretty sure she does. Her backpack is in the backseat. She never leaves home without it." She pointed her thumb in the direction of the front door. "Hop to it, girlie. Sylvie needs something pretty and simple for the business."

Addie shook her head, disbelieving. "Me?"

"Yes, you're our resident artist. You're up."

Addie blinked. "You want *me* to draw something for Sylvie?"

Leigh rolled her eyes. "Yes. *You*." She shrugged. "Something country and bakery like. Yummy and pretty."

Sylvie didn't know how to react at the time. Did they really expect her to put a child's drawing on the favors they were working so hard on? Addie was sweet, and she didn't doubt the girl could draw something nice, but business-worthy?

"Sylvie?" Marcy chimed in, "Do you still have those pale green labels?"

"I do. We only used a few for Kristy's baby shower."

"Sweet! I've got an app on my phone that'll let me resize the image. We can have something printed out in no time." Marcy smiled at Addie. "Show us what you've got, kiddo."

Addie, who looked like she'd seen a ghost, mumbled something like *sure* then went out to retrieve her bag.

A few seconds after the door shut behind Addie, Cara had looked to Sylvie. "She really is very talented, I promise. You're in for a treat."

Sylvie managed an unsteady *okay* before she went to answer the oven timer that beeped at her. She had been fully prepared to let her baked goods speak for themselves until, about forty minutes later, Marcy called for her to come to the dining room where she'd just finished prepping boxes and cutting ribbon.

Three sheets of paper lay in front of Addie. She hadn't looked up as she spoke softly. "I wasn't sure what you'd like, so I made three. If you don't like them, it's okay. You won't hurt my feelings." Her tone said that was anything but the truth. Sylvie planned to proclaim them all beautiful, no matter what they looked like. At least until she actually looked at the sketches.

Her breath caught. "Oh my god, Addie."

"It's okay, really. Cara and Leigh are always so good to me. They... like, actually care about me, so they like my drawings. They do the nice grownup things that good families are supposed to do. You don't have to pick one."

Sylvie looked closer. Although all three were stunning—downright spectacular— one stood out. Her heart stuttered each time she looked at it. "Sweetheart, they're all gorgeous. Seriously. I love them all." She pointed to her favorite. "But this one? It really grabs me by the throat. I can't put my finger on why, but... I have to have this one. You put a lot of effort into it. I'll pay you for it."

Addie looked up with big, startled eyes. "*Pay* me? You don't have to pay me. My pictures have always been gifts."

Sylvie looked down at the image of a plate piled high with cookies and a big, triple layer, slice of cake. She had no idea how the child managed to make something as simple as a pencil drawing look so utterly appetizing. Mouthwatering. The bonus? The bouquet of wildflowers lying beside the plate, bundled with a trail of intricate lace ribbon. The lace looked three dimensional, so much so, she wanted to run her fingers over it to see if it felt as real as it looked. Her head snapped up to look at the blonde hair of a little girl who wouldn't meet her gaze.

"Addie, sweetheart, look at me." Her throat clutched when she noticed the tension in the girl's shoulders. After a heavy moment, Addie looked up. Sylvie saw the pale blue eyes of a child who lived a life a hundred times harder than any adult should have to. "Where did you get the idea for this one?" She pointed to her favorite.

"Um, I copied the flowers from one of your pictures. Are you mad? I thought the picture of the bride on the fireplace was pretty, so I copied her flowers."

Sylvie's belly pitched as she realized why the image looked so familiar. "Mad? No. Not at all. That is my mother's wedding picture. My family didn't have much money when she got married, so she made her own bouquet from wildflowers and flowers from my grandmother's garden. You captured them beautifully."

"You're not upset because I used them? I was trying to decide what to draw, and I just thought they were really pretty. That they might make a pretty design. You really like them?"

"I do. I love them all, but this one is absolutely perfect. I can't wait to show it off."

Addie's only response was a shy smile.

"What's your favorite cookie?" God, why hadn't she thought of it herself? Such a simple and pretty tribute to her mother.

The girl smiled a real smile. "I love them all, but sugar cookies are my favorite."

"I'm sending you home with a big box of cookies all for yourself. When you get married someday, your wedding cookies and cake are on the house. Deal?"

"Deal." Happiness lit the girl's expression.

Leigh chose that moment to walk in. She went straight to the daughter that hadn't been born to her, but that anyone with half a heart could see had become every bit as dear. "Rick will nix that deal before you can spit on your palms. Make them a graduation or birthday present. He says she's not allowed to date until she's thirty. Let me see what you came up with, girlie."

Sylvie slid the drawings over so she could get a closer look. Leigh pointed to Sylvie's favorite. "You did this one first didn't you?"

Sylvie spoke, ready to stand up for Addie if need be. "It's my favorite. She incorporated my mother's bridal bouquet."

Addie nodded. "Yes. I made that one first. Then the other two, just in case she didn't like the first one."

"I can tell. These are really good, but you really put your heart into this one, didn't you?"

"The flowers were pretty and wild. They just seemed special." She'd leaned into Leigh when she kissed of top of her head.

"Child, one of these days you're going to figure out exactly how much talent you have. Then heaven help us all."

Addie grinned big and bright.

"Hey." Noah spoke from behind her pulling her back to the present. "You're still standing, I see. Everything go okay?"

She turned to smile at him and gestured to the piles of boxes. "They're all finished and absolutely amazing. The cake is baked and covered in crumb coat. All I have to do tomorrow is put on the final layer of icing, assemble it, and add the flowers Karli sent over."

Noah blinked. "Crumb coat? Why do you coat it in crumbs?"

"No, silly. It's a baker thing. It's a coat of icing used to seal the crumbs in, so they don't muck up the final icing layer."

"Ah. Kick-ass baker speak. I'll leave the fancy terms to you and stick to taste-testing. Speaking of, there aren't any leftovers, are there?" He shot her a sheepish grin.

She walked past him to the kitchen. "I might have saved a little something for the man who gave me this amazing kitchen and found me the best help imaginable."

Noah leaned his shoulder against the doorframe as he watched her. "He sounds like a good guy. Where did you find him?"

"Believe it or not, in a trashy bar called the Thirsty Beaver." She picked up a storage container and removed the lid then held it out to him. "It's really going to work, isn't it?"

"Yes, it is." He grabbed a cookie without looking to see which flavor he selected.

"Are the barn and meadow going to work okay? I really want Karli's day to be special. I wish I'd had more time to help."

He shook his head. "That's right, you haven't seen it yet."

"Seen the barn? No, the baking has pretty much taken over my life the past couple of days."

He took her hand. "Let's go."

"Go where? It's after ten."

Without answering, he drew her outside. While she waited on the porch, he shut up the house then escorted her to the passenger side of his truck. "Hop up."

Curious, she did as he instructed. He backed out, turned onto the main road, and drove the half mile to the driveway closest to the barn.

She looked up at him as he turned the ignition off. "You could have driven through the meadow. The ceremony will be on the far side of the barn, closer to the lake. It wouldn't hurt anything."

"Yeah. Karli's mother and soon to be sister-in-law were talking. They thought the big oak tree might make a good backdrop for some of the wedding photos. I figured it would be best not to markup that area with tire tracks, if it can be helped."

"Oh. It's been here longer than the Smiths have. My great-grandfather wouldn't let them cut it down when they cleared the meadow. He said the old man deserved better than spending its eternal life as a coffee table. They're right. I never thought of it, but it could make for some amazing photos. Especially with the fall colors..." With the discovery of possibilities came excitement. "Her hair! Oh, that'll be downright lovely. All the long, lovely red hair, with the fall backdrop and a gorgeous dress? I hope they found her a good photographer."

He parked then came around to the other side to help her out. Without a word, he drew her to follow him to the main doors. He looked up thoughtfully for a moment then drew her back from the doors about thirty feet or so. "Stay here a moment." He disappeared into the shadowed interior of the barn. A moment later, the golden glow of light shone from every point inside the barn, spilling into the night. Next to the barn, more lights illuminated haybales arranged in a half circle around an unlit firepit.

Noah's dark form, silhouetted against the backdrop of gold, made its way back to her. Even carved from shadows, his strength made her mouth water. Unknowingly, he moved in a powerful, graceful way that made something hitch beneath her breastbone.

Somehow, he added even more to everything he'd already given her. She met him halfway. "It's the most beautiful thing I've ever seen, Noah. I can't believe how amazing it looks. And they, you, accomplished it all in such a short amount of time." She took in the old rafters dripping with light. "Did they buy every strand of fairy lights in Kentucky?"

"Probably, and then some. I know several expedited online orders were placed. Karli's father said they debated about whether or not to make a daytrip to a wholesale place in Tennessee for even more. Let's go inside."

"Noah, I think I could stand out here and just stare all night. It's so much more than I expected. Karli must be thrilled."

He took her hand in his. "I think she will be. She hasn't seen it in the past few days."

"Really? Wait. Marcy said that she had to let the little details go and focus on being happy. I'm glad."

While she chattered, Noah ushered her inside. "The florist is scheduled to arrive at 4:30 to finish decorating. With the cool temperature, we didn't want to leave anything to chance."

"Cool weather? Out here, there's an equal chance deer could decide to make a snack out of something. Oh! The bars! You weren't kidding, they really did go all out." They'd constructed something that looked as though it belonged in an old saloon.

"Rich, her oldest brother, was quite upset that there wasn't time to give it a more thorough sanding and more polish but, overall, everyone is pleased."

"Maybe I should think about having something like it constructed for future events."

"No need."

His simple words hurt her in a way she hadn't expected. Did he think she wouldn't need it? She could wait, because he might be right.

"I mean later, maybe in the next two to three years, or whenever things are going better."

"I mean that there's no need for you to build something like it because this one *is* yours. All of it is. Well, everything except for the rented tables and chairs they'll be setting up first thing in the morning."

She leaned a hand on the bar to brace herself. "What do you mean this is all mine?"

"When they were joking about drawing straws to see who would get stuck with cleanup and dismantling everything after the event, I told them we'd take care of it. I then negotiated for the bars, lights, and dancefloor."

A dancefloor. She couldn't hardly process it all. "Negotiated? What's the price?" It didn't really matter, did it? She had no extra funds, no matter how great the bargain.

He grinned. "On the understanding that we'll handle post event cleanup and offer them a discount on future events."

"That's it?" It was all too simple and utterly amazing.

"Yeah. I know it all looks shiny and new now. It'll look great on camera, but there's still a good deal of work that should be done. We'll get to it. Karli's father seemed relieved to have one less chore to take care of. Her oldest brother was simply thrilled that she would have a country wedding fit for a Nashville star." Noah grinned. "I'm not going to repeat what the youngest brother said about the first wedding venue. Trust me, they're a happy bunch."

Her first thought was to argue. Again, to insist that he was doing too much. He was too good of a guy, pretty much as perfect as a man could be, but she realized it would be a waste of her breath.

"Thank you. Thank you for everything." She placed her hands on his shoulders.

"You're welcome." He took her mouth with his in a gentle kiss. Warmth suffused her in an easy blush, chasing away the chilled night air.

Without hesitation, she took him in, then gave back, letting herself be absorbed by his heat. The soft warmth grew, intensified, until the golden glow burst enveloping them both. Bathed in the heat of skyrocketing passion, she reveled in his touch and the world fell away. Solid, steady hands anchored her close as arousal swept through, burning away everything that wasn't her Noah.

He groaned into their kiss, the rough vibrations in the muscles of his chest tingling against her palms. Dizzy, euphoric, she needed him more than she needed air in her lungs. She broke her mouth from his to ask one thing. "Noah, exactly how sturdy is that bar?"

He blinked at her question. Then his kiss swollen lips smiled. "Sturdy enough." He took her hand in his and drew her in for another kiss. The moment the soft heat of his mouth touched hers, a blaring siren split the air, ripping it in two. The perfect silence of their night fractured into a million shards as she whipped around in confusion.

"What the hell is that? What's wrong?" The sound was coming from the direction of her house.

With one hand, he reached for his pocket. With the other, he squeezed hers. "Sorry, sweetheart. Someone just tried to break into your house. Damn it." With a hard set to his mouth, he looked down at the phone he'd pulled from his pocket. "C'mon. James will be here in a couple of minutes. Let's go meet him."

With her heart racing, she let him lead her in a jog toward his truck.

~

Anger and frustration bit at Noah as he parked. Just because he wasn't surprised by the downturn of events, didn't mean he liked them. Hell, he'd half expected someone would show. Sylvie unintentionally parked her car out of sight. His had been gone for all of thirty minutes while they'd been down at the barn. Up until that point, at least one of their vehicles remained always visible. He just hated that they'd been almost within reach and had gotten away.

Sylvie sucked in a gasp. "Noah! The cookies. I mean, I know a thief wouldn't want them. It's not like they can pawn them but... what if? I have to check and make sure everything is there."

He had his hand around her wrist before she could bolt from his truck. "They'll be okay." Heaven help them all if he was wrong, but as he scanned the shadowed landscape, he knew anything inside that house should be secure. "It will only take James a few more minutes to get here. We can wait that long."

"Then why did you drive so fast to get up here?" He could all but feel the worry, fear and frustration emanating from her in the darkness as she stared at the lights shining from her house. She hadn't been wrong—his tires had chirped, burning rubber when he'd pulled out onto the blacktop.

"I knew it was a long shot, but I hoped to catch them in the act. The moment the lights came on and the siren sounded, anyone with half a brain cell would have fled." He thought he might have glimpsed a brief flicker of taillights disappearing around the next bend but with Sylvie beside him, he couldn't follow. And they'd gone in the direction opposite in which James would come. He was tempted to tell James and have him follow. No question— with that car of his, he could catch up. But he didn't want to subject Sylvie to anymore stress, especially on the eve of the wedding after she'd been on her feet, working herself to the bone.

"He'll be here soon then we'll go in to doublecheck everything. Whoever it was, they didn't have time to do more than try to open a window."

When her voice trembled, he wanted to choke whoever had done this. "You're sure?"

He squeezed her hand. "I'm certain. We'll go in as soon as Holloway gets here. Then you can rest easy."

Her voice turned speculative as she turned to look at him. "Why don't you seem surprised? Or worried?" Her eyes shifted to the driveway when headlights swept across the yard.

"C'mon. That's our backup." He got out and pulled her across the bench seat to exit his door. His knowledge that their surroundings should be safe was outweighed by the need to keep her within arm's length.

Alert and all business, James walked up. When he spotted Sylvie, he smiled. "Madam." He bowed as if greeting royalty. "Your fantastic hero has arrived." Then he winked.

When Sylvie smiled weakly, Noah felt a small measure of relief.

"Thank you for driving out here. I almost hate to say it, but hopefully it's a waste of your time. Noah's certain that whoever set off the alarm is long gone. The alarms made enough noise to wake the dead two counties over, though something's telling me he hasn't shared the entire story." When she pierced him with her lovely gaze, he held firm.

James shocked question broke her focus, but it didn't save him any trouble. "You used the audible alarm instead of trying to catch them in the act?"

"I did. We couldn't take any chances, not with the work she's done for tomorrow."

In the porchlight, he saw the moment realization struck in Sylvie's eyes. He'd tried to keep as many details to himself to spare her any guilt she might conjure, but she'd been able to read between the lines.

"You could have caught them if it hadn't been for my baking." Her shoulders slumped.

"Better to be safe than sorry. We still might get lucky and see something on the cameras. Whoever they are, they're not very bright. We'll catch them and get this figured out so you can get your life back on track." He took her chin in his fingers, feeling silk against his callouses. "I promise. It won't be long now." He didn't tell her Calvin had to be getting desperate. Or that, more than likely, so was whoever he'd gotten into trouble with. While desperation made people careless, it also made them more dangerous. His primary focus remained keeping her safe until they screwed up. "Let's go. James will look around outside and we'll go over the inside. I know you won't relax until you see for yourself that everything is just as you left it." He couldn't blame her. It probably felt as though the weight of her future rested on those cookies.

While her kitchen skills made her a queen, he hoped that with time and a little nudge she would see that she was capable of even more. "We'll go make sure everything is ready for yours and Karli's big day."

CHAPTER 14

Sylvie wore a navy wrap dress and flats for her walk down to the barn. As she twisted her hair into a simple up-do, she argued with herself over whether or not to go down to the wedding. If she did go, then at what point and in what capacity should she go?

The venue was hers, even though this all came about at the last minute, so she still felt it was at least partially her responsibility to supervise. She'd been down early to deliver and add the final touches to the cake, but she should be there to lend a hand with any last-minute issues. Karli, Cole, and their families were all a casual and friendly lot. They'd probably expect her to be there. No one would be standing at an imaginary gate checking attendees for their printed invitations.

But as she added earrings and a bracelet, a small voice reminded her she hadn't actually been invited. She'd just decided she'd go in an official capacity and slipped into her shoes when her cell dinged on the dresser. She glanced down to see that it was a text from Marcy. *Where are you? Everything looks AMAZING! Get down here!*

Leave it to a good friend to plow right through one's doubts and get to the heart of the matter. *On my way in five minutes.*

Hurry. You won't believe this crowd. You should be down here schmoozing. Seriously.

She stopped herself from sending yet another reply. The ceremony down at the bridge would start soon. It wasn't the time to rub elbows. All eyes would and should be focused on Karli and Cole. There would be time to talk with Marcy at the reception.

The thought of the place where her great-grandparents started their marriage hosting other couples sent a wave of warm sentiment through her. They would have delighted in sharing the magic.

She made sure she'd set her phone to silent mode, tucked it into her purse and went down the stairs. She was looking down to zip her bag when she ran into Noah. He gently gripped her shoulders. "There you are. Are you ready to walk down?"

Oh. Dear. Lord. As his mouthwatering scent registered, her barely functioning brain struggled to find an appropriate response. His hair was still slightly damp from the shower and looked as though he'd just run his hands through it. A crisp forest green dress shirt and a coffee colored sport jacket covered that warm wall of muscle. Her gaze caught on the base of his throat, where the top two buttons remained undone.

She imagined tasting the flesh there and running her tongue up the expanse. Suddenly Karli's wedding didn't seem all that important.

"Sylvie?" His rough grumble registered, barely penetrating her lust-fueled stupor.

"Uh, yeah." She shook her head, trying to get her wits together. "I think I'm as ready as I'll ever be." She couldn't help herself. Her thoughts escaped from behind the lips keeping them prisoner. "You look good enough to eat, Mr. Ramsey. Consider me impressed."

And turned on.

He shifted and tugged at his collar awkwardly, which made him even more attractive. When he grinned sheepishly? A lovely blush, far more powerful than lust, swept through her. "Thanks." He stepped close and swept his palm up the side of her neck, stopping just below her ear. His feather-soft kiss on her mouth made her thankful she held onto the strength of his body.

"I could say the same about you, Ms. Sylvia Grace Smith." He pressed another sweet kiss against her lips.

"Huh?" She blinked.

"You look good enough to eat." He whispered the words into her ear, sending ripples of heat through her.

To keep from fanning her face, she held tighter to his waist.

"Come on. You've worked hard for this. You deserve to see the show." He took her hand in one of his and pulled her to the door. Before they left the house, he set the alarm and locked up.

She let him lead her across the meadow. "I wish I'd had time to help more. I really didn't have much to do with the actual wedding, but today is all about Karli. I really hope everything turns out well for her and Cole."

"Barring any last-minute catastrophes, it should. Her family worked hard on this. She has, too. A couple of days ago, when her family arrived with a team of tractors to mow the lower meadow by the bridge, I made the mistake of thinking the smallest driver was one of her brothers. As a team, they tackled the overgrown grass like a well-trained army. When they stopped by the barn afterward, I realized my mistake. Karli arrived with her father and drove one of the tractors herself. When they left, she waved farewell like a princess in a carriage before hopping into one of the trucks. They were willing to put in the work needed to get things done. Her agent has been determined to make sure nothing stands in the way of Karli's stardom and poured her all into the business side of things. You've worked your tail off. It will all come together."

He was right. Everyone did their part and more. "Yeah, it will. Thank you."

He took her hand and kissed her knuckles as they crossed through the break in the trees. Light filtered through the brightly colored leaves, bathing the world in a golden glow. Releasing a contented sigh, Sylvie listened to the peace of her woods. Muted murmurs of a crowd eagerly waiting for a show but attempting to be civil carried through the field. She smiled as excitement replaced the worry she carried for far too long.

A moment later, they came out on the far side and took in the view. They managed to transform her farm into a scene straight out of a storybook...or a country music video. Leading up to the bridge, row upon row of precisely arranged white chairs held small sprays of cream flowers, each seat decorated with a white slipcover and a sage green ribbon. A wide, matching green runner marked the path Karli would walk from the barn, down through the center of the chairs.

They'd arrived in the nick of time. Cole waited at the mouth of the bridge for his bride. Noah pulled Sylvie to the back row of chairs, where they took seats next to each other. She could just see Karli's mother in the front row, already dabbing her eyes with a handkerchief. Marcy sat in the row behind her with her own parents. An elderly gentleman held the hand of pretty older woman and gestured to the seats beside them. Smiling, Sylvie nodded and shifted closer to Noah to give the couple as much room as possible.

The little gray-haired woman leaned across the gentleman toward Sylvie. "Sorry we're late. We underestimated how long it would take us to get here. It's beautiful though. I'm so glad that the weather is pretty today."

"It is. I think you made it just in time." Sylvie whispered back. "You're fine. We just got here ourselves."

The man patted his own knee. "These old bones don't work as

well as they used to, but they still get me where I need to go. I'm Jack, Cole's great-uncle, and this is my wife, Rose."

Noah reached across Sylvie to shake the man's hand. "I'm Noah and this is Sylvie. This is her farm."

Rose gasped. "Oh, honey. It's just lovely. Do you have weddings here often?"

"Not yet, but I'm considering opening for business."

"Dear, you should. I can't tell you how many weddings Jack and I have been to in the forty-nine years we've been married, but I can say this is by far the prettiest one I've ever seen."

"Thank you." A violin began playing a soft tune and the low murmurs went silent with anticipation. Every head turned as Karli's bridesmaids gracefully made their way down the aisle. Five women total for Karli's bridal party, each dressed in varying gown styles, yet all with the same shade of navy and accented by sage ribbon. When Sylvie turned to get a better look, Noah eased her into his side. Without hesitation, she rested against him. He took her hand, and she wove her fingers into his. Amid all the beauty surrounding her, one thing stood out.

Jack and Rose—the elderly couple held hands, much in the same way she and Noah did. The strength in those thin, knobby hands might have weakened over forty-nine years of marriage, but she liked to think the fierceness of their love far outweighed whatever physical power they'd lost.

Two cameramen unobtrusively lingered in corners of the seating area. She marveled at how seamlessly they blended with the guests, all waiting for their first glimpse of Karli. The moment the last bridesmaid stepped into place, the wedding march began to play.

Karli stepped into view. As she linked her arm with her father's and beamed, Sylvie thought she heard the crowd release a soft collective sigh.

~

A cool breeze brushed his face, chilling the sweat dotting his brow. He wiped it away with his shirtsleeve as he paced the dark parking lot. Water gently lapped against the nearby slip. Dry leaves rustled overhead, whispering and hissing at his misfortune.

"I've *tried*. I can't get in there. She's got some guy staying with her now. He dogs her every step. I don't get it—she was a good lay, but not *that* good. A guy that big? He must have a huge sweet tooth or something."

Sylvia was supposed to be a means to an end—they all were. Sure, she might have treated him better than any other mark he'd suckered, but still. He really hadn't been upset over the loss.

Just a means to an end.

That farm of hers? That was the true loss. *So many possibilities and all of them profitable.*

The man who started all his trouble spoke through the cell phone pressed to his ear. "They have to leave eventually, and they're not glued to each other, for fuck's sake. Get in, get it, and get out. It's not that hard."

"It's impossible tonight. Hell, there must be hundreds of people just a few yards away." The barn glowed as bright as Christmas, the Fourth of July, and a concert all rolled into one. He'd rolled down his window as he drove by and heard music and laughter even from the distance.

"Stop exaggerating and making excuses. You always were a piss-poor liar."

"I'm not kidding. Looks like there's a wedding or something going on." He leaned against his car and took a deep breath. He scrubbed his palm over his face then resumed pacing while he waited.

After a long pause on the line, the seemingly innocuous voice spoke. "Listen, you wanted to run with the big boys. We let you in. Now you have to fulfill your end of the deal."

More accurately, they'd lured him in with bait he couldn't

refuse. *Money.* He clenched his fist. He walked the razor's edge and didn't need to upset the balance by pissing them off.

"I'm *trying.* It's not my fault she shacked up with this new guy virtually overnight."

"It's not? Seems to me, if you'd kept her satisfied, maybe we wouldn't be in this mess to begin with. Clearly this new guy has something to offer that you didn't. Look, I'm through making excuses for you. One way or another, you've got to deliver. If you can't get it, then you can pay back the entire loan, including the interest."

A knowing sneer colored the caller's voice as he added, "That shouldn't be a problem. Am I wrong?"

They knew he didn't have the money. They were there when he lost the first half. When he'd gone back and attempted to recoup his losses, he'd been alone. *Keyword: Attempted.* He only ended up deeper in the hole.

Calvin learned the hard way—when you play the bigger games, the loss hurt that much more.

"Look, I'm taking a big risk here, much bigger than anyone else. You swear that if I get what you want, my debt will be cleared? Every cent?" He still had a little bit of Sylvie's money stashed. He'd take it and disappear. Maybe go to a sunny retirement community near the beach and find a rich, gullible, little old lady to fleece.

"I admit it was a pretty smart move. You keep up your end; we'll uphold ours. You have my word." Calvin ignored the chills skating down his spine and took the words to heart. There wasn't any other choice. "We'll take care of the big guy. You just make sure you stay nearby."

∼

Utter and complete exhaustion weighted Sylvie's every step toward home.

But fatigue didn't have a chance against the joy sparkling and bubbling in her veins like champagne. Lighter than air, she walked over the clouds through the meadow. If she hadn't been ready to drop like a stone into bed, she might have flipped a few cartwheels over her yard as the house came into view. She couldn't remember the last time she'd been so happy. Karli glowed with an unmatched radiant beauty. The wedding ceremony, absolute perfection, would hold beautiful memories for everyone who'd attended. Not a single a dry eye remained as everyone watched spellbound as she joined her smiling groom.

Immediately after the ceremony, the guests—who had all been invited to bring comfortable walking shoes—wandered down to the lake while the photographers snapped a few pictures of the wedding party.

They timed the photos under the old oak to be taken at sunset, and Mother Nature hadn't disappointed. As if honored to be included in the young woman's big day, the blue sky exploded into a backdrop of purples, reds, and pinks. Karli's long train of white lace floated like mist against the green grass. The enormous tree, branches heavy with golden leaves ready to drop, set against her glorious riot of red curls and the vivid sunset were what wedding dreams were made of.

The caterers worked double time in the barn to setup dinner beneath the golden glow of fairy lights. They ensured that, after a long day of travel and wedding preparation, no guest went hungry. The barn—*her* barn—overflowed with light, music, laughter, and love. Sylvie wished her great-grandfather could have seen it all. He would have been over the moon. Her great-grandmother would have only noticed imaginary dollar signs over the happy guests' heads.

In their own ways, they would have loved every moment of it. Sylvie just wished she could share it with them all.

Karli's mother sought her out afterward and thanked her profusely. "All a mother wants for her daughter on her wedding day is for her to be happy. I haven't had more than a couple of minutes to talk with her, but my Karli is glowing with happiness. Thank you for giving this to my baby."

Karli's father simply removed his arm from around his wife's shoulders to pull Sylvie into a bone-crushing hug then kissed the top of her head. She'd been just as moved by his hug as by the kind words from Karli's mother.

Marcy introduced her to so many people, her poor brain swam with an overload of faces and information. A mix of family, friends and music industry people attended the wedding, and many passed Sylvie business cards with inquiries about possible events. One couple—a cousin of Cole's and his fiancée—tried to give her a deposit right then and there for their wedding in the coming spring. She promised they could have first pick of dates, and she agreed to meet with them to finalize everything next Saturday.

Karli's upcoming record producer wanted to plan a party for her daughter's first baby shower—her first grandchild, so the woman wanted to "go all out," because she intended to invite a huge crowd. The sweet elderly couple from the ceremony wanted to discuss holding their fiftieth wedding anniversary party at the barn. Rose wanted to renew their vows in a pretty dress down at the bridge while Jack wanted to sit at a big table to visit with their entire family at one time. He explained that—with six children and their spouses, fifteen grandchildren, some of whom would bring dates and spouses, plus three great-grandchildren—they rarely got to see everyone at once. He wanted them *all* together, gathered at one table for a nice meal.

When she'd asked what kind of meal he had in mind, Jack remarked he didn't care if it was pizza, fried chicken, or hot dogs. He just wanted them all together. Sylvie decided then and there— she would move heaven and earth to make it happen for the couple. Besides, she could make some damn good fried chicken.

She'd stopped throughout the evening to take notes using an

app on her phone. What started out as a short list grew into a mountain of tasks she couldn't wait to tackle.

Restrooms needed to be a priority. Karli's agent had the studio hire out for luxury mobile models, fit for royalty and parked behind the big barn. They'd worked well, but Sylvie couldn't expect the same level of planning from her future clients. Brides needed a large, well-lit dressing room to get ready. If they kept it simple, they could use that area as a preparation space for whatever other events might come later. Definitely a big well-equipped kitchen—either in the big barn or the smaller one. Heat and air. They'd been lucky, the beautiful weather held, so they only needed a few large outdoor heaters to keep the chill at bay, during the reception. Still, again, she'd need to provide better for future guests.

The list went on and on. Every millimeter of it excited her.

She couldn't wait to share it all with Noah, but she couldn't help but feel that, the moment she went inside, her dream would come to an end. It might be silly, but she couldn't help the feeling. Despite her exhaustion, she let her feet carry her to the front porch instead of inside. With a long sigh, she sat on the swing that hung there for as long as she could remember.

Just a few more minutes before I turn into a pumpkin.

As she gave the first little push, she marveled over the swing's silence. *Yet another thing Noah fixed.* Was there anything the man hadn't improved? Tightened or straightened or oiled? She smiled. Her mother would've adored him. Brody might even have grudgingly accepted him. She missed them both so much, but somewhere along the way, because of the weight of her grief, she'd lost herself.

Neither of them would want that for her. In truth, they'd absolutely hate it.

"I should have a little time yet. I found something to compare to. I'll send it before I go back down to the reception." Noah's voice drifted through the window behind her. "I think half the state of Kentucky is at the party. By the looks and the sound of things, it may run until dawn."

Does the man ever rest? His dedication put a monk's to shame.

"As far as I can tell, it went well. Happy people everywhere. Music, drinks, food. Sylvie looked almost as blissful as the bride. I consider that a slam dunk."

The familiar warm blush washed through her. She hated that dawn would arrive before too long. She wished she could sit and swing, hugging her happiness tight for... Well, forever.

"No. I agree. I've watched the video a hundred times. Even with his face obscured by the hat bill, that's not Calvin. Too tall. Too fit. Whoever it was, they move like they know how to be quiet. Confident and focused. He kept his head down at all times. Definitely not a nervous weasel."

Noah paused, and ice skittered down Sylvie's back. They were talking about the most recent break in attempt. They had to be.

"If I didn't know better, I'd think it was the brother."

Sylvie blinked. Calvin didn't have a brother. The happy warmth in her blood chilled, making the cool night air abrasive where it had been refreshing only moments before. *Maybe I didn't hear that right?*

Noah continued talking, with no clue she eavesdropped from so nearby. "Something doesn't add up. I know this sounds crazy, but I don't think the guy in the government databases is the same man from Sylvie's family pictures. He checks off the boxes—right height, eye color, hair, age...it all fits. The driver's license picture looks similar, but it's simply not the same man."

What in the world? Her heart stopped right along with the motion of the swing. The muscles in her legs turned to stone.

"I *can't* ask her. If she knew we were digging this deep into his background, she'd have a fit. She's unflinchingly loyal. It's as admirable as it is frustrating."

Slowly, as if lights switched on room by room in her mind, his words began to penetrate the fog of shock. Noah still thought

Brody was responsible for the break in. Indignation struck, straightening her spine. *I told him that wasn't possible!* Somehow, they had done far more than run a basic background check on her brother anyway.

She always figured her brother might be some sort of special forces soldier or endured intense training, like with the FBI or something. If so, and their snooping got him in trouble, she'd strangle them all. No amount of WD-40 and squeak-proofing her house would save Noah from her wrath.

"Can you get anything from the license plate?" Her fists clenched as she waited through the brief pause in the one-sided conversation. "Okay. Hopefully the partial will be enough."

Not sure she could take anymore, she walked to the door, ready to yank it open and barge in.

But then his next words hit her square in the face. "I still have the knife James found. No, you're right. It's not concrete proof he was here, but what are the chances something with his name engraved on it has been outside all this time and just happens to be found yards away from the house the day after her break in? I'm holding out a miniscule wisp of hope we can clear him, so she'll never know I thought he was part of this mess. It will kill her if he's a part of it. Yeah, this *is* something she may not be able to forgive me for."

Shocked and hurt, she took a moment to process his words then shook her head. It was all too crazy.

Noah's voice continued, it's familiar rumble somehow foreign sounding. "There has to be a lot of value in the farm. What if he's trying to scare her into selling or something? Hell, the place is huge. He could've hidden almost anything here, and she'd never know, especially considering how busy she's been lately."

On his next pause, she steadied herself with a deep breath before she twisted the doorknob. "The only thing I can't figure out is how Calvin is connected. I agree. We're still missing big pieces of the puzzle. Sounds good. Thanks, Rick."

How can he? Fiery anger blasted through her until she felt as though she could incinerate the door with one shot from her palm. Fierce and wicked, her fury boiled, urging her to annihilate the male in her home like a demon princess from a horror movie.

He lied. He'd investigated her brother against her wishes. He planned to continue hiding his investigations from her until the end of time, if possible. Not to mention the very worst blow—he hadn't trusted her. All painful arrows to the chest, but the last one struck home, hitting her in the heart.

With her pulse rocketing, the beat like a fist fighting to get free of her chest, and her vision red with anger, she fought for some semblance of calm. She came up dry. The fury burned white-hot, boiling over in a cascade of lava which engulfed her.

The anger hardened into an impenetrable shell.

Instead of tearing through the house like a banshee, screaming and blasting everything in her path, she opened the door and entered with her head held high.

As she softly closed the door behind her, she found Noah seated on the floor in front of the bookcase nearest the fireplace. In his lap, one of her old photo albums lay open.

"I'll talk to you later." He disconnected his call and greeted her softly. "Hey."

"Hey." She was quite proud of herself, since no flames spit out of her mouth when she'd opened it. "Did you find a suitable picture?"

He closed the open album and returned it to the shelf. "Sylvie…"

She had to give him one thing. He didn't even blink or feign confusion. A small, very miniscule part of her wanted to feel bad when his shoulders slumped.

"If you haven't sent a picture of Brody yet, don't bother, and I mean that with every fiber of my being. This house and everything in it, attached to it or surrounding it, on *my* one hundred and twenty acres, belong to me or my brother."

Noah stood. "Sylvie, I'm only worried about your safety. That has and will always come first. I won't settle for anything else. I'm sorry to hurt you, truly, but I need you alive more than I need you to love me."

His use of the word love hit her like a punch to the gut, knocking the air from her lungs. Incapable of speech, she turned her back on him and continued upstairs. Without stopping, she went to the corner of her room where he'd set two gym bags. She stuffed them both with his things then carried both bags back out the door. From the top step, she tossed one bag down to the floor. She wished she could have felt some sort of satisfaction when it landed with a loud thump a few feet shy of the front door. Taking the miss as some sort of Olympic failure she hefted the second bag to her shoulder and pitched it harder. It flew across space until it smacked her door dead center. It bounced to the floor, where it landed close to the first bag.

She turned on her heel, giving him her back. She wasn't sure she could look at him without exploding. Or crying. It took all of her willpower to voice her demand without screaming or yelling.

Firmly, calmly she instructed him. "Get out. No argument. No pretty words. No more lies. Get *out* of my house."

Once she'd closed the door behind her, she released a long, ragged breath. Staring at the ceiling, she focused on locking it all down. She could keep every thought, every emotion, barred from entry. The blank, white canvas stared back at her silent and wary.

Time for bed. It had been a long, long day. She couldn't make it on her feet another minute. Staring into the mirror, she brushed out her hair then removed her jewelry. *Back to square one.*

She'd done it all on her own before. *I can do it again.*

But, as she stared at her reflection, it wasn't the loss of his help she mourned. Not the loss of a man but *the* man. The loss of Noah made her heart tremble.

The warmth of his chest beneath her palms. His subtle smile. His quiet chuckle.

No amount of hard work or success could make up for the little things, for those were what she mourned.

He wanted to raise his fist to the sky, to rail against the unjustness of it all, but he couldn't. He knew the moment would come. He'd hoped like hell it could be prevented, but ultimately knew better. Stuck between a rock and a hard place. *I can't accomplish anything with Sylvie tonight.* He didn't want to cause her anymore distress, and he'd burned his bridge. There'd be no rebuilding it, not even for him, a man who prided himself on his ability to repair even the most damaged of things.

The best he could hope for was she'd be safe and an end to her nightmare. Despite knowing a good number of people remained in the meadow, and James lived so nearby, he couldn't make himself leave her alone.

He activated the security system, grabbed his bags, and closed up. Maybe, once morning came, he could talk her into letting one of the other guys stay with her. He scanned the quiet darkness. Faint chatter resonated from down by the barn. A steady stream of traffic flowed down the main road, leaving the party behind.

His lodging options were the porch or his truck. He sighed.

The truck it is.

CHAPTER 15

I will not feel guilty. I will not feel guilty. Sylvie chanted the mantra over and over again as she poured a second cup of coffee into her favorite travel mug. Groggy, exhausted, and still utterly wiped, she'd spent every bit of her willpower to get out of bed. Her cell buzzed repeatedly from the nightstand, nagging at her to get up. One glance revealed a number of messages—all congratulatory—about the day before.

As she forced herself to trudge down to the coffee pot, she vowed to play a bigger role next time. When she made it to the bottom of the stairs, she'd slowed, half fearing a pair of long legs would hang over the end of her couch. But, no, brawny limbs didn't dangle off the arm of her furniture. The gym bags she thrown from the first floor were gone. She'd reminded herself she wanted him to leave then promised herself a piece of leftover cake to go with her coffee.

While the coffeemaker gurgled, she found something for her headache. *Three hours of sleep will be enough.* Stumbling back through the front room, blinking past the morning sunlight burning through the windows, she'd stopped. Through a gap in the sheer curtains, she spied a large gray truck parked in her yard.

Noah.

"Damn it." Unable to stop herself, she walked to the window to take a closer look. His form, head lolled back against the headrest, filled the cab. If she'd hadn't known better, she might have thought he'd died there. He looked utterly miserable.

But she *did* know better. He was too damn stubborn to expire from her wrath.

And strong. He was so darn strong.

She sighed and stomped back up the stairs to retrieve her robe.

Lid secured on her travel mug, she shook out a couple of Ibuprofen for herself then stomped out to the truck.

He awoke as she opened the front door then straightened and rubbed his neck. Through one squinted eye, he peered at her as he stretched. "Hey."

She glared then thrust the mug and bottle to him. "I told you to leave."

Something like hurt passed over his features.

She did *not* want to run her fingernails through his morning scruff. *Absolutely not.*

"I know. I will in a little bit. I'm not leaving you unprotected. James will be by in a little bit. He was already out for the day when I texted him a little bit ago."

Hands on her hips, she huffed. "That's not necessary. You still don't know anyone wants to hurt me. Later today, I'll sit down to actually try to figure out what Calvin's doing or hiding." She shrugged. "Maybe I'll search through the house. He's hidden something and I just haven't found it yet."

"I have a nasty feeling. I don't think it's that simple. I learned the hard way not to ignore my instincts."

The pain in those gorgeous green eyes of his made her feel about two inches tall. He'd suffered so much. He gave so much.

And he only asked for her safety in return.

"You can't leave me in the dark. What if your snooping put Brody in some sort of danger? He's a good man, Noah."

"Sylvie, the video from just the other night shows a man that matches his body type. I can't tell you how badly I want to be able to clear him of suspicion."

I will not soften. I will not weaken. She turned her back on him and walked away. "I cannot and will not tolerate lies. They've caused me to much pain. I still want you gone."

"I know. As soon as James gets here, I'll leave. Pieces are starting to fall into place. We'll get this figured out then I'll be out of your hair."

She wished she could feel proud of herself as she walked away.

Once the front door closed, he cursed. He washed down a couple of the orange pills with coffee then checked the security app on his phone. It would have alerted him of any activity, but he couldn't let it out of his reach. He just couldn't.

The situation continued to draw her ever deeper, growing too complex by the day. Clearly, more than one player wanted something Sylvie had.

He'd give anything to know what it was.

He hated that he hurt her in the process of keeping her safe, but he couldn't bend. To say his guilt and frustration irritated him would be an understatement. Deep down, he knew he wouldn't be able to keep Sylvie in the dark.

His phone rang, and he frowned when he saw it was his mother. "Mom? What's going on?" Like him, she was an early riser, but it wasn't like her to call first thing in the morning. He waited through a hesitant pause and hoped everything was okay.

It wasn't.

"Noah?" Her voice sounded unusually shaky and hesitant. He sat up straight, instinct bringing him fully alert. "I...I was just in a car accident. Someone...the truck? It came from out of nowhere and hit me. I mean, it hit my car, and then it drove away. I was headed to Sunday breakfast with the girls and...he just drove away."

"Are you okay?" *Shit. Shit. Shit.* He pulled the keys out of the cupholder and started the ignition. His first instinct was to throw the truck into gear and tear out of there.

But he forced himself to take a steadying breath. His mother was an adult. She raised two hard-headed children while working multiple jobs. He didn't need to hold her hand. She'd be fine. He willed it to be so. He listened to the commotion in the background and tried to figure out what was going on. After a couple of worrying beats with no response, he repeated his question. "Mom, are you okay? Has anyone called the police?"

"I...yes. The police and an ambulance are here. I think I'm okay, but the paramedic is insisting I go with them to the hospital. My leg and ribs on the side where he hit me hurt. A lot. They say I should go in for x-rays. Um. I tried to stand to talk to the police officer, but I can't."

"Do what the paramedic tells you. Go with them. As soon as you know which hospital, text me. I'll meet you there. Okay? *Promise* me."

"Okay." When her voice trembled, he gripped the steering wheel so tightly, his knuckles turned white. "I really think I'm fine, Noah. It's probably just a bunch of bruising."

He hoped she was right, but he didn't like the way she sounded. Yes, his mother was sweet, but never, ever shaky and frail.

"Hopefully, and you're probably right, but I don't care. We're not taking any chances with you. Get looked over. For once, please, just do as I say." He stared at the house in front of him. His first thought was to take Sylvie with him, but he wasn't sure he'd be able to provide the security she needed. His attention would be splintered between his mother and Sylvie's safety. It wouldn't be wise or fair to either one of them.

Thankfully, for once, his strong-willed mother listened. "Okay. I guess it's better to be safe than sorry."

"Absolutely. Text me with the hospital name. I'll be there as soon as I can." The moment they disconnected, he called Sylvie and prayed she'd answer.

Shockingly, she did. "Noah, I'm getting in the shower. Leave me alone. I don't want to hear it. Goodbye." The finality in her *goodbye* wasn't something he'd likely ever be able to accept.

"Wait! Don't hang up. Mom just called. She was in an accident, I think a hit and run. I have to go to her. No idea how long it will take me."

"Oh no." Her tone softened. "Is she okay? I'll throw on clothes and be right out."

Damn, how he hated leaving her. "I think so, but the ambulance is taking her to the hospital. I don't like the timing of her accident. I want you to stay here. James should arrive before too long. I'll tell him to hurry. Make sure the alarm is set before you get in the shower."

"I set it after I brought out the coffee. Go see to your mom." When her voice trembled, his throat grew tight with emotion. I hope she's okay. Really."

A million things he wanted to say, yet no time to say even a single one of them. Even if the situation didn't require his immediate action, he wasn't sure she would listen anyway. "Thanks. Please be careful. Just stay put until James gets here."

"I won't leave the house. I have a mountain of things to do here and will stay under lock and key. Don't split your concern between me and your mother—she needs you, and I'm fine. I know you'll worry, so I'm promising you I'll be here. Drive safe."

Warring emotions frustrated him. Relief because she cooperated, yes, and the bonus—Sylvie was speaking to him.

But he couldn't stomach the finality in her tone.

The moment the call disconnected, he dialed James. The moment the call connected, he said, "Listen, Mom was just in a car accident. They're taking her to the hospital in an ambulance. I'm on my way, I have to go make sure she's okay. But that means I have to leave Sylvie for longer than I like." *That's an understatement.*

"Shit. Is your mom okay?"

"She sounded okay, maybe a little shaky, but her left side is injured. Paramedics talked her into the ambulance."

He pulled out of the driveway and barely resisted the urge to pull his hair out with one hand while he drove with the other. "It sounds like a hit and run. I didn't get many details."

"Okay. Do what you need to do to take care of her. I'll get to Sylvie's as soon as I can."

"Thanks. She promised to stay inside with the security system activated. Hopefully, she won't change her mind. I just hate that she's so far out." His stomach clenched and he pressed his foot harder on the gas pedal.

Torn two directions, both women he loved most in the world needing him, but he knew he had to go to his mother. He hoped Sylvie would remain safe in the meantime...

Freshly showered and dressed, Sylvie sat down at her computer to crunch some numbers. For the first time in ages, she actually looked forward to the chore. By no means had her troubles disappeared overnight, but she found it virtually impossible to see the glass as anything other than half-full after the prior night's success.

Not to mention the big chunk carved out of her debt. It hadn't been erased but—even if she kept a small amount of the proceeds from the wedding to invest back into the business—she earned more than enough to keep the creditors off her back for a while.

Maybe even forever, if I'm careful.

With a smile, she propped her elbow on the table then rested her chin on it. The sound of a car door shutting startled her out of her daydreams. Indecision hit, because she still hadn't decided if she should invite James in or make him wait outside.

She didn't mind him hanging out inside—but she worried he'd take the opportunity to help Noah's case. Before she got to the door, though, rapid footsteps thudded on her porch. "Sylvie! Let me in. I need to talk to you."

Calvin.

She froze. Should she pretend she wasn't home? She could confront him, ask for answers. Though, Noah would lose his mind if she did. She hadn't moved her car, so it sat parked in the garage. Noah's truck was gone. If she remained silent, maybe he'd think she wasn't home.

She winced when a heavy fist pounded on the door.

Still and silent, she waited. After a moment, the doorknob wiggled. Braced, she prepared for confrontation if he decided to use the key he'd apparently stolen to her home...until she remembered Noah changed her locks since Calvin let himself in without her knowledge.

After a moment, his steps moved away from the door and off the porch. Just when she thought she might be lucky, and he'd decided to leave, he shouted at the backdoor. "Damn it, Sylvie! Your car's in the garage. I know your guard dog is gone, so just let me in. I need to talk to you." Unsurprisingly, a scraping sound near doorknob proved he tried to use his old key. "I'm not going to hurt you. Seriously, let me in for two or three minutes then you'll never have to see me again."

He's not going away until he gets what he wants. Tired of the dark veil of whatever trouble he'd gotten himself into shrouding her life, she struggled with the temptation to open the door. She'd like nothing more than to throw it open, barge through, and lay into him.

She didn't even need answers any longer. She just wanted him and his terrible mess gone from her life and memory for good.

Even if his problems inadvertently brought me Noah, who all but exhausted himself to help me time and again.

Noah put her first at every turn.

She placed her hand on the doorknob as she battled indecision. She couldn't do it. The same man—the one who worked a dozen minor miracles for her—would lose his mind if she opened the door to anyone other than James. To open it to Calvin? She hadn't known Noah long, but she suspected when he met his breaking point and lost his temper, it wasn't a pretty sight.

She turned her back on the door and grabbed her phone. Calvin's footsteps retreated from the porch, but no relief surged at the sound. A text from James informed her he was on his way, but he'd hit a traffic snag before hitting the town's outskirts. She hated to make him worry over something as simple as Calvin's normal idiocy. She could handle the situation on her own.

Shouting started at the front door, and she didn't even flinch. "Sylvie! My life is on the line here. I know you hate me, and I guess you're entitled to that, but I *have* to get something out of the house."

She called through the front window, "Go away and take your trouble with you. I'm not letting you in. You're wasting your time and your breath. A friend of mine will be here very soon."

"Sylvie, it's not my fault. Really. They conned me, I swear it. Now I'm the one who's in trouble."

"Gee, funny how that works. You didn't think twice about doing the same to me. Go away." Her nails bit into her palms as she fisted her hands in frustration at the whole situation.

"Okay." His voice broke. "I'll give you that, I didn't think twice. But I never hurt you. If I don't pay them back, they will *kill* me. I'm not kidding."

"Wrong. You may not have the compassion in you to comprehend it, but you did hurt me, Calvin. What you did hurt me very badly. I'm sorry you're in danger, but you put yourself there. Worse, you dragged me right along beside you. You can't play games with people's lives. Lying and cheating to climb your way to the top of some imaginary mountain is a fool's errand."

The door creaked and something large swished against it. She pictured him leaning his back against the sturdy old wood. "They invited me to the races, to one of the executive boxes. They knew I didn't have that kind of money to bet, so they offered me a loan. It snowballed from there."

His words came as no surprise. *A quick buck. Swimming with the big fish.* Whoever he'd gotten tangled up with knew the way to his heart. He'd been as gullible as she her, really.

"I don't know why you thought it was wise to hang out with whoever these people are, but clearly it hasn't bought you anything but trouble. You should go to the police and report everything, especially if you're in danger."

With a false bravado that made her wonder if he even believed his own words, he tried again. "All I have to do is give them the video. Then they'll erase my debts."

"What video? You know what, don't answer. I don't want to know. All I want is for you to go away. Go. Contact the police."

"There's one more option. Listen, before you get mad. You could sell them your property. They really want it. They'd pay you nicely, then you could move closer to town. Maybe open your little bakery. Bake cookies to your heart's content. Then we'd both be sitting pretty."

"You are insane. I don't even have a response to that. Get. Gone. Since you're still hesitating, I'm calling the police."

"Fine, just let me in to get the video first." His pleas reached an all too desperate level as she pictured him, cartoon style, pulling at the door. She never thought she'd be so grateful for Noah's hard work.

"There's some great stuff on the video. I recorded them killing somebody. They don't want it getting to the police. Look, just let me in for *one* minute. I'll get it and get out. You'll never hear another word from me afterward, I swear it."

"Calvin, you *have* to go to the police. I... I'm sorry you're in danger, but you've done this to yourself. If everything you've said is true, giving them the video won't be the end of it. You're a witness. Do you honestly think they'll be okay with you walking around free? They're not going to take a conman's guarantee."

Of course, now he's sharing his story and trouble with me. Idiot!

"Sylvie, I've thought it all over a million times. Again and again. You're my only option. I should have never involved you, but it's too late now for both of us."

"You're right, you shouldn't have involved me. You told them it's here, didn't you? That's what those two men were looking for the night of the break in."

Something thumped at the door, as if he slapped his palm against it. "Listen to me, damn it! They'll kill me. Don't you have one ounce of care for me in that tiny, cold heart of yours? You always were selfish. I should have known you weren't the one for me."

She couldn't believe his audacity. "You're delusional. I gave *everything* to you, both my heart and money. *You* created this mess. I'm finished talking and listening. If you won't call the police, I will. Leave." On second thought, she should call the police either way. She didn't have anything other than his words to go on, but she believed them. It was too selfish and...Calvin-like for it to be anything other than the truth.

Sadly, she wished she could be surprised because he'd gotten tangled up with scum. But where had he found them? He believed himself to be high-class and wouldn't dare enter a bar like the Thirsty Beaver, let alone go somewhere in the city slums.

She looked at the screen of her phone to call the police. She'd asked him repeatedly to leave, yet he refused. She needed to report his crazy, but likely all too true, story.

Her heart lightened as the crunch of gravel signaled a car pulling into her driveway. James must have arrived quicker than she'd expected, but he was definitely a welcome addition to this mess. At the window, she realized it wasn't James' beloved Chevelle. Instead of the red muscle car, Travis Garrison's silver SUV parked in the bright sunshine.

Though her relief wasn't as great, she still welcomed the appearance of her boss. Surely his presence would be enough to run Calvin off. Her relief mixed with confusion over why Travis appeared was short lived. Someone moved in the passenger seat. When Michael stepped out, her stomach fell and hit the floor.

A black handgun gleamed in his hand. Travis held a similar model, both weapons aimed toward her porch.

She stepped away from the window. Calvin's pleading became downright panicked as he stated his case again. "Sylvie, you *have* to let me in. They're not playing. I need that video."

"Calvin?" A shrinking rabbit hole opened up at her feet, or so it seemed as she stepped closer to the window but remained out of sight. "Who was killed on the video?"

"They killed Charlie. He got too greedy. He intentionally misidentified the trees as high value timber so the Garrisons could launder money through the business."

Charlie? They—Travis and Michael—killed Charlie? Money laundering? Without another thought, her hands flew to the security panel by the door, and she pressed the silent alert button.

"Sylvie? Open up, dear. Otherwise, poor Calvin here gets a bullet right between his prettyboy eyes," Michael called out. "Let me tell you, he has really been a pain in the ass. It wouldn't be a hardship."

Caught. Confused. Scared yet disbelieving. Too many emotions to process and she didn't know what to do. She couldn't let them kill Calvin, but she couldn't imagine any sort of positive outcome if she opened the door.

"Sylvie, don't give them the video! You were right. I'm sorry. They'll kill me the minute they get it." Calvin's voice sounded steady for the first time that day.

AMY J. HAWTHORN

"I don't even know where you hid it, asshole," she muttered under her breath.

"Ow! Sylvie, Travis is holding his gun to my head." Panic returned to his tone. "You gotta open the door."

She didn't think they'd kill him, at least not until they had what they wanted. She gripped the hope close and held her phone tight. They *would* get in the house, one way or another, and she really didn't want to be there when they did.

The moment they retrieved the video, both she and Calvin were dead. She didn't fool herself into thinking she could help him.

Her first impulse screamed for her to run out the back door, to fly as fast and far away from her home as she could.

oah just entered the emergency room waiting area when his phone rang. Frowning, he answered the call from Rick. "Hey, listen. Mom was in a car accident. I can't really talk now, but I'll call back as soon as I make sure she's okay."

She should be. In addition to the text telling him which hospital they transported her to, he'd also received three more telling him not to worry about her. Still, he wouldn't settle until he'd confirmed for himself she was okay. Afterward, he could figure out the mess with her car, then see if the police had any info on who hit her. At the security desk just outside the ER, he asked, "I need to see Margaret Ramsey. She was brought in by ambulance."

"I understand, but listen we have another emergency." Rick's grim tone slowly ground through Noah's worry.

A dour faced guard pointed to the double doors. "Room three." Noah accepted the yellow visitor's badge and waited impatiently for the door to open.

"What kind of emergency?" Gradually, one by one, facts penetrated the wall created by his single-minded concern.

Rick might not have known about the car accident, but the

moment he'd been informed, he would've ended the call to allow Noah to tend to business. Rick would have insisted Noah ask for help if he or his mother needed a single thing.

Rick wouldn't have kept him on the line to talk about something else if it wasn't critical.

With sinking feeling Noah asked, "Rick?"

"Which hospital are you at?"

Noah stared unseeingly at the room numbers over the cubicles as he answered.

"Okay. I'm sending Cara to stay with your mother." Another partial piece of information filtered through. Cara was a nurse. She'd be the perfect person to sit with his mom. She'd understand every bit of medical jargon and know what questions to ask if anything needed to be addressed. Depending on the situation, she could also act as a bodyguard.

"Are you going to get to the point? Tell me why I can't be the one to sit with her." He knew why, even as he asked the question.

Sylvie's in danger.

"Take a minute to see your mom. Tell her Cara is on the way." Rick's grave formality aggravated Noah's frustration.

Noah wanted to growl in frustration. As it would be a waste of time to do anything other than what he'd been told, he opened the curtain to room three. With her head elevated, his mother lay in the hospital bed.

"Noah! There you are. They just drew blood. They're supposed to take me to radiology soon." She smoothed the blanket over her thighs. "I really am all right, like I texted you."

"Hey." He leaned down and kissed her cheek. "I just had to see that for myself. How are your ribs? Don't sugarcoat it," he warned sternly, not for a moment expecting her to listen.

She huffed. He noticed her mussed hair and pale face as she spoke. "They do hurt quite a bit. I'm hoping it's just the muscle soreness settling in." He hated seeing her in a hospital gown instead of one of her usual blouses.

"You promise that you told the doctor about everything that's hurting you?"

"Yes, I already did." She looked as though she would roll her eyes at him next. *Caught between a rock and a hard place.* He wanted to fuss over her and see for himself that she was indeed fine.

But he hadn't forgotten. Rick waited on the line with bad news.

"Listen, I have another emergency. As badly as I hate to do this, I have to leave." Her eyes widened in concern, so he kept talking before she could interrupt. "Cara is coming to stay with you. You do exactly as she says, okay?"

"That's not necessary. You just go on and do whatever you need to do. I'm fine."

He bit back a curse. "Mom, you stay with Cara and do what she says. I'm going to need to concentrate, and the only way I'll be able to do that is if I have your word."

His seriousness penetrated her independence, and she thankfully capitulated. "Okay. I'll listen to Cara. You—" She pointed at him. "Best let me know when you're finished and when you're okay."

"Yes, ma'am." He kissed her cheek in farewell. The moment he'd gotten out of earshot, he put the phone back to his ear. "What's wrong with Sylvie, and where the hell is James?" He practically growled the words even as he jogged back toward his truck.

She'd already activated the alarm and had every confidence that help would arrive soon. *Noah installed it. Of course it works.*

All she had to do was buy herself some time while staying out of sight.

She opened the back door a couple of inches and left it ajar. Then, like a stealthy little mouse on the run, she hurried up the stairs and into Brody's old bedroom. His window faced the field opposite the garage and barns, where she hoped they would expect her to hide. Holding her breath, hoping the window didn't squeak, she pushed up on the lower sash. When it opened with a swish and a quiet groan, she released her breath.

Though loud to her, she was confident they couldn't have heard the window opening. Slowly, she eased outside and onto the roof. She and Brody rarely ventured onto the steeply pitched roof for fear of rolling off, but she didn't need to go far. *Just stay silent and out of sight.* The moment she found a stable spot, she'd send James a message. She could let him know where she hid and warn him not to come until help arrived.

She didn't expect him to actually listen, but she had to try. Holding onto the soffit with a death grip, she scooted a single agonizing inch at a time until she made it to the window's side. There, her bare feet turned awkwardly angled on the shingles, her body all but laying on the roof, she half climbed, half pulled herself into the nook where the outside of the dormer met the roof.

Of course, then she realized she hadn't shut the window behind her.

As she pulled out her phone, she prayed they didn't search upstairs. If she was lucky, they'd see the back door ajar. They'd waste precious time searching for her outside before ever going up the stairs. Maybe enough time for help to arrive.

If not, she managed to back herself into a corner. She doublechecked to make sure her phone was on silent. How did she even word the message? She's decided to start with James, since he was probably the closest. Noah would be with his mother.

Hey? Um. Calvin showed up. So did Michael and Travis from work. Turns out they're really bad guys. Calvin hid video of them killing someone in my house. He owes them a lot of money. I'm hiding on the roof on the side opposite from the barn. I activated the alarm, so help is incoming, but you need to stay away until I tell you it is safe. They have guns.

After she clicked send, she reread the message in frustration. She muttered under her breath, "*Really bad guys?* Jeez, Syl, he's just going to love that."

She probably should've stuck to the basics, but in case something happened to her, the information she provided would be a good starting point when they tried to solve her murder. She laid her head back against the shingles. Closing her eyes, she listened and waited as the breeze cooled her panic sweat to ice.

A moment later, a loud bang practically shook the house. One of the Garrisons kicked her front door in. She sighed. While she'd expected as much, she would've rather they tried the back door before breaking her home into pieces.

Her phone buzzed against her palm. James responded to her message. *Do not come out of hiding for any reason. I'm letting everyone know your location. Be there soon. Are there still only three?*

She wondered if he was crazy. *Only* three? She wasn't sure Calvin truly counted as much of a threat, but still. In her book, even two armed men was two too many.

Yes. Travis and Michael Garrison both have guns. Calvin is more of a hostage. I think they just got inside, but I can't see from here to verify for sure.

The reply came almost instantly. *Do NOT move. No matter what. Police are on the way. Calling Noah now.*

He would be out of his mind with worry. He'd couldn't have done more than said hello and goodbye to his injured mother before having to turn around, if James called him at this point. The last thing he needed, while his mother was in the hospital, was to worry about her on top of it.

Guilt washed through her. She still didn't agree with the way he'd done things, but through it all, everything else over the past couple of weeks had been for her benefit.

Not even the best guys on the planet did that much simply because they were nice.

They did those kinds of things for the people they loved.

She sent another text to James. Before sending it, she deleted it. Noah deserved to hear it from her, not secondhand. *I'm safe. I went out Brody's window. I'm wedged between the window and the roof. I left the back door open to make them think I ran out to the garage. Please be careful.*

Good girl. Be there soon. DO NOT MOVE.

From the back of the house, a few simple words made her blood run cold. "You know what? It doesn't matter. If we can't find that old cell phone with the video, we'll just burn down the house. We'll toss the bodies in and let all the evidence go up in smoke at once." Already tight with tension, her shoulders snapped ruler straight. The muscles in her chest, already aching from her constant alertness, squeezed even harder. "After that knock on the head, Calvin's not going anywhere. I'll get Sylvie out of the garage and see if there's something to start a fire while I'm there. You look through the house. I'm not crazy about those security panels by the doors. We need to stage this and get out quick."

"Agreed." Silence weighed down around her as they went about their tasks, thumps and movements allowing her to track their positions.

All too soon, she heard footsteps cross the back porch. *I thought I could handle this on my own. Noah was right the entire time. I did need him here.*

Knowing he planned to keep his suspicions about Brody to himself still stung, but she had to admit he'd done it because of the man he was. His fierce protectiveness was another of the many traits she loved. He did everything completely and correctly, never cutting corners. Plus, he'd done it all to ensure her safety and happiness.

He put her in the light, never expecting her to share it with him.

When she should, absolutely share the light with him. Always.

Movement and footsteps came from the window beside her. A moment later, Travis craned his neck out toward her. "Hey there, Sylvie. Come on, let's get this show on the road. Time's a'wasting." Caught in a surreal nightmare, she froze.

Her boss aimed his handgun at her, his friendly smile in place like every other day at work.

Numbly, still only half believing what was happening, she shook her head.

No.

"Come on out here. I always liked you, Sylvie, you know that. I don't want to hurt you, but I will."

"Travis! This is crazy. Whatever you're doing, this will break your father's heart. Please don't."

The oddest thing happened then. He laughed. "Sweetheart, who do you think started this business?" His good ol' boy tone shifted to something darker and far scarier. He jerked his head and snapped. "Now."

Out of options, she obeyed, remembering quickly that going down the roof was far scarier than climbing up. She held onto the dormer's soffit with both hands as she inched down into a world that felt as if it had been physically turned on its side. She couldn't imagine how off-balance he must feel with...*only one hand to stabilize himself.*

Her thoughts stuttered, stopped, and realigned. She knew what she had to do. Risky, but far less so than going back inside the house with both desperate Garrison men.

She had so much to look forward to. She wasn't going to go quietly into the next world when everything she wanted was in this one. The home she loved, her dream business. *Noah.*

As she neared the bottom of the window, she took a deep breath. She braced for what she had to do. Awkward, yes, but she had the roof at her back. The majority of Travis's body was outside, with nothing but empty air behind him.

With her bottom to the roof and one foot braced, she raised the other as if to take a step. Travis shifted his focus to something inside the house and offered her the moment she needed. She slammed her foot into his lower abdomen, one swift motion before her own position was compromised. He scrabbled, windmilled with his gun hand, but managed to hold tight to the window with his other hand. Hurrying, taking advantage of his loss of balance, she stood straight. With the corner of her phone, she jammed hard into the back of his palm. He cursed and released his grip on the window. His arms both spun and he wobbled to and fro.

"Travis, we gotta go!" Michael shouted from somewhere in the house. Travis's body swayed forward and then back, a treacherous teeter away from falling. On the backward sway, he thrust his arms forward to grab for the window and the gun fell. With a clatter, it skittered and slid down the roof. His fingers grazed the soffit, nearly righting his position. With a growl and with murderous intent in his eyes, he grabbed her upper arm, squeezing tight.

She jerked it away and pushed his chest in one motion.

A deafening crack split the air. Falling backward as he released her, she wasn't able to halt her momentum. Her head hit the roof —pain reverberated through her skull and stars swirled before her eyes. Dizzy, with her ears ringing, she shook her head to try to clear it. When she opened her eyes, Travis was gone.

It took every drop of Noah's willpower not to yank his earpiece out and throw it through the truck window. The primal male raged against its cage, roaring at him to drive his truck straight up the driveway to the front door then run inside, guns at the ready.

Rick didn't operate Dark Horse that way, though. For good reason, he reminded himself. They observed, gathered intelligence, planned, and made smart moves, even when situations were dire. Their team as a whole was always stronger than a single soldier. Rick knew what he was doing, and that was why they followed his lead.

Knowing Sylvie remained trapped in her home with two murderers desperate to cover up their wrongs was about as bad as things could be.

"Shit!" James whispered through the system. The first to arrive, he intentionally passed the main driveway and parked where the intruders had fled the first night. Once he left the vehicle in position, he'd made his way through the trees before he stopped just shy of the tree's cover. While Rick could see video of the house's interior, they didn't have video surveillance on Sylvie's entire property. It was too large. On the house's southside, James could spot Sylvie.

"What's wrong?"

"Travis just came out the window. He found our girl. How long until law enforcement arrives?"

Noah closed his eyes as he waited for Rick's update. Though he didn't expect it to differ much, not since the last update was only three minutes ago.

"Joe's closest, though this isn't in his jurisdiction. He's off duty and one of us today. He'll be there within five minutes. Local law enforcement shouldn't be far behind him."

Noah pulled in the driveway to the big barn where the reception had been held and continued driving to the trees. There he stopped, checked his weapons, and hopped out. A millisecond after he shut the door, a loud crack echoed through the woods. "Who was that?" Noah barked.

Rick asked cautiously, as if he were afraid of the answer, "Noah?"

"Not me, I swear. My feet just hit the ground in the planned location. James?" *James doesn't have his rifle with him.* The long echo hadn't sounded like a handgun, but like a round fired through the long barrel of a sniper rifle.

"Not me, I swear. Oh hell. Travis is down. Sylvie pushed him, but that shot took him out. She looks okay."

"There's someone else out here?" He hustled through the thin section of forest, his thoughts spinning as fast as his feet. The last thing they needed was an unknown player.

James responded. "Sounds and looks that way."

Noah reached his position, facing the house's north side.

Stunned, Sylvie stared at the empty space where Travis had just been. The air in her lungs fled in one giant rush. She recognized the sound—anyone who lived out in the county would—but what did it mean? She'd just decided to retreat back to her nook when she realized her phone was gone. She must have dropped it during her tussle with Travis.

They knew her location and help would be there soon. She clung to the knowledge with a grip stronger than the one she'd kept on the window soffit.

Her heart almost returned to a near normal speed when movement caught her attention. James hurried across the meadow. With a terrible sense of shrinking time, she inched her way down the roof toward the back of the house.

"Sylvie, damn it. If you weren't already dead, you'd pay for that!" Not sure she wanted to know what angered Michael, she continued on her slippery path, finally reaching the porch roof. With her heart in her throat, she crabwalked over the shifting slopes. On her belly at the very edge, she dangled her feet over into empty air. Taking a deep breath, she closed her eyes and let herself drop. She landed with a hard, clumsy thud, her momentum knocking her to her knees on the ground.

Quietly cursing, James made it to her side. He whispered in her ear "You okay?"

It took everything she had to nod her assent.

"You weren't supposed to come down yet."

"I know, but they're going to set my house on fire."

"Rick's watching the camera footage of the interior. No fire yet." He crushed her to him in a hard, bruising hug then kissed the top of her head. "Noah's coming up behind you. When I give you the all clear, make your way to him. Go as fast as you can, okay?"

Again, she nodded, then concentrated on catching her breath. James crept up the steps and eased the backdoor open. Before he stepped inside, he whispered, "Wait, okay?" Then he vanished inside.

Less than a minute later, James stuck his head out the door and pointed in the direction he'd previously indicated. She didn't hesitate. She spun and ran harder than she ever had in her entire life.

In seconds, she was around the corner, the open meadow in view. Barreling straight toward her, bigger than life, was Noah. Worry dimmed his green eyes. His mouth was tight, a grim soldier instead of her gentle lumberjack. The next thing she knew, she was wrapped in his strong arms, crushed tight against his heaving chest. "Let's go. We gotta get you out of here."

He took her hand in his, ready to draw her away.

"What about James? You can't leave him alone."

"He knows what he's doing. I *won't* leave you alone."

She stopped moving, determined to make him listen. "Yes, you will. Michael and Travis, both—"

"Travis is dead. Someone shot him. James only has to contend with Michael, and he's more than capable of doing so. Let's go."

"Look, I'll go. I promise to do everything you say, but you have to go help James." She took in the hard resolve in his features. "Please, if you go, I… I know he'll be okay. Otherwise…" She shook her head, unable to finish the thought aloud. "I'll never forgive myself if something happens to him. He's done so much for me." She put both palms on his chest. "Not as much as you, of course. No one can ever touch that, but a lot, so please?"

His expression was anything but happy, but he placed his keys in her hand and closed her fingers around them. "You know the drill."

She nodded then whispered, "We need to talk." So many things she wanted to say to him, so much so she worried she wouldn't know where to start.

The hard lines around his mouth softened. "Yes, we do, but we're sitting ducks. Go. Head in the direction of the main barn. You'll run straight into my truck."

She smiled as the most ridiculous thought hit her. "Okay. Will do. Go save *My Fantastic Hero.*"

She winked then did exactly as he'd instructed.

Noah didn't run to the backdoor. He ran straight for Travis Garrison. He intended to verify the man's death for himself. He blocked all thoughts of what could have happened if Travis got a hold of Sylvie.

When he reached the body, it took him little more than a glance to verify that whomever took the shot knew exactly what they were doing. The headshot had done far more damage to Travis than his trip to the ground from the roof. The asshole would never take another breath, that was for damn sure.

Without touching the corpse, he left the crumpled remains where they lay on the ground. He wouldn't tell Sylvie, but he suspected he knew the identity of the mystery sniper. With any luck, they were long gone. If they'd wanted to harm Sylvie, they already would've—ample opportunity while she'd been perched on the roof like a damn bird. If he hadn't realized that, there was no way he would've allowed her to flee on her own.

Surveying the meadow, he verified Sylvie made it to the trees.

Soon, she'd be locked in his truck out of sight. "She's clear," he whispered into his headset, updating James so he'd have one less thing on his mind.

Rick responded, "I'll send Joe straight to her location."

"Thanks."

All business, Rick updated him on the house's occupants. "Looks like Michael's given up on the search. He's headed for the front door. James is closing in behind him through the dining room. Michael carried in a gas can from the garage, but he hasn't done anything with it yet. Go around to the front entrance."

"Copy."

Sylvie glimpsed of Noah's truck through the trees, and a small measure of relief washed through her. With an odd sense of déjà vu, she headed straight for the driver's side. Just when she'd nearly made it through the trees, a large male stepped into her path. A hard arm wrapped around her upper body and he placed his palm over her mouth. She struggled, fought, and wriggled trying to get free.

"Shhh." When she heard his voice, she stopped cold. Tears pricked her eyes. "It's me, Syl. It's okay. You're safe."

She could only stare up at the man she loved so much that it hurt. He'd aged, turning into a world-weary soldier. Long gone was the man-boy she'd idolized. A grim, hard mouth replaced the easy grin she remembered.

"Are you okay, sis?" When she nodded, he cautiously uncovered her mouth, almost as if he wasn't sure if she'd bite his hand off.

"I'm fine. Bruised here and there. Shaken up, but I'll be okay. What's going on?"

"I can't tell you. I just had to make sure you were okay. I'm moving back to town, but you won't see much of me. There will be talk. I'm sorry, it won't be pretty, but I just had to let you know what you hear won't be true."

"Brody..." What could she say? Her heart ached for the boy he'd been and the trials the man likely survived. She wished with everything she had that she could wipe it all away.

Much like the last time they met, he changed the subject. "Is that man the one you want?"

Without hesitation or needing clarification, she answered, "Yes. He is. Noah's the best man I've ever known, beside you."

Her beloved brother frowned. "I'm not a good man, Syl. Really."

She sensed him pulling away and knew he'd leave again. "Bullshit."

"I'll make sure you get back the money Calvin took. The balance on the bank loan was taken care of Friday morning. I'll make sure you get the rest."

Surely, she hadn't heard him right? "What?"

He grinned. "You heard me. If he makes it out of this mess alive, Calvin now owes *me*, not you. I want you happy, Syl." He sighed before asking again, "Noah's really the man you want?"

"Yes, he is." She smiled at the thought. Light shined bright and vivid on visions of her future.

"Okay." In a gesture reminiscent of her big brother of years gone by, he winked. "Then I guess he can live. Get in his truck. Stay safe."

When he tried to release her, she wrapped her arms around his middle and took her turn squeezing tight. "I love you, Brody Allen Smith. I always will, no matter what."

He gave her one hard final hug and kissed the top of her head before heading back the way she'd come.

"Go, now!" Rick gave the order and Noah moved, knowing

without verification James did the same from his position. The moment Rick spotted Michael set his gun down to drag Calvin across the floor via the video feed, he'd seen their opportunity.

Working together, they dropped and restrained him in a matter of seconds. As they dragged him out of the front door, the first police cruiser pulled up the driveway. Joe connected Rick with the local sheriff, so they'd wouldn't be alarmed when they'd arrived to see two men hauling a body across the porch before dumping him unceremoniously in the grass.

They repeated the process with Calvin's limp form, and Noah had a new appreciation for the cameras he'd installed. Recorded proof could easily be provided to help erase any confusion or potential headaches with law enforcement.

He just wanted the whole matter washed away so he could get to Sylvie. When Rick had Joe to bring her back to the house, he would finally be able to relax.

Exhausted, worried about his mother, the unknown shooter, and Sylvie's state of mind, he wasn't sure he was capable of putting up another fight over where he slept.

While waiting on Joe to arrive with Sylvie, he sent Cara a quick text. *All is good here. How is she, really?*

His friend's reply came swift and sweet. *A lot of bruising, and she'll be in pain for a few days, but no fractures or internal bleeding. They'll probably discharge her soon.*

Thanks. I owe you, he replied.

Never. I'll get her home and make sure she's comfortable before I leave.

He counted down the longest five minutes of his life. Finally, Joe MacDonald arrived with Sylvie. Once he saw for himself that she was whole, he could concentrate on the mess surrounding them.

∼

When the last person left, Sylvie realized that the entire day had passed. By the time she'd been questioned by the first round of police, then again when detectives arrived, and more by the state police...she'd lost track as she repeated the same thing over and over. Her head swam with exhaustion. She'd begun to think they would never finish and leave.

Literally moments after the last police car pulled out, she searched the yard for her phone. Of course, then Karli's parents stopped by. They'd been down at the big barn packing up a few decorations from the wedding. When they heard the sirens of arriving patrol cars, they'd worried. Karli's mother fussed over her and her father headed straight to Noah for the "full story."

Before leaving, they'd given her a thank you gift. The framed photo of the meadow and barn, all lit up, utterly beautiful, and... alive—it brought tears to her eyes. As appreciative as she was of their kindness, she admitted to feeling equally happy to see them go. Exhaustion leached into her very bones, those few hours the night before in her own bed insufficient with the activity, adrenaline, and work yesterday.

Noah hadn't been given even that much rest, though, and he'd worked every bit as hard as she had in the past few days.

She owed him so very much. He gave her everything she'd ever wanted without any expectations for himself. An apology was just the beginning—hopefully, *their* beginning. But when she sought him out, he was gone.

The last of day's light faded from the sky as she sent a text to *Her Fantastic Hero.*

Noah woke to the smell of food. Confused, groggy, and out of sorts, he scrubbed his hands over his face and fought for consciousness. He slapped the nightstand until he found the base of the light. Fumbling, he felt his way up to the switch.

Once he clicked it on, he cursed when dim white light filled the room.

His bedroom. For the first time in almost a month, he'd slept in his own bed in his own house. It should have been comfortable. Familiar.

He didn't like it one bit. It lacked the sweet scent he'd grown to love and the warm, soft body he wasn't sure he could live without.

He'd left Sylvie's the moment he'd finished talking to Karli's father—after her parents gifted him with a bottle of bourbon and appreciative hugs. Utterly exhausted and worried he wouldn't be able to have a civil conversation with a rock, let alone the woman he loved, he drove home on autopilot then crashed face first into his bed. Looking at the clock, he estimated he'd slept for almost ten hours. A savory aroma registered in his still groggy brain, so he shook his head to clear his thoughts, but the scent remained.

Why in the world does my house smell like bacon?

The only people with a key and the security code were James and his mother. His mother knew better, as she should be in bed resting. James just…wouldn't. More likely, James would let Noah stew in his own misery through the day then stop by with a case of beer later that evening to commiserate…and possibly plot how to get back in Sylvie's good graces.

Stretching, he cracked his neck and groaned. Once he pried his ass out of bed, he made a quick trip to the restroom. After splashing liberal amounts of cold water over his face, he trudged to the kitchen to investigate the delicious scents. He'd decided the intruder had to be his mother, despite her injuries, because no criminal in their right mind would break in to cook him breakfast.

Eyes squinted and an admonishment ready on his tongue, he rounded the corner to his kitchen then stopped cold.

Sylvie manned the stove, spatula in hand. Over her shoulder, she shot him a shy smile. "Hey. It's almost ready. I would've brought it up to you, but since you're here, have a seat."

Feeling as though he'd stepped into an alternate universe instead of his own kitchen, he couldn't think of anything to do other than what she'd instructed.

She plated his meal then made it to the toaster in time to catch toast the moment it popped up. In two blinks, she buttered the browned bread and added it to the mountain of food on the plate. She set the feast before him then made a second trip into the kitchen. As she moved, her lavender colored dress swished around her calves. The skirt reminded him of the evening they'd spent in her backyard. He'd never forget the warmth of her silken skin under his palms. Unable to resist her simple, yet somehow staggering allure, he admired her sweet curves as she comfortably navigated his space. His home.

What in the world is she doing here?

He didn't want to curse what he hoped was good fortune, but felt lost, so far out of the loop he might not ever find his way back. She returned with a glass of juice and mug of coffee, setting each beside his plate. Once she took a seat across from him, she wove her fingers together on the tabletop. After a glance at his plate, she dropped her gaze to her folded hands before unconsciously nibbling on the corner of her bottom lip as if in thought.

He picked up his fork. "Where's your plate? You have to be hungry, too."

She met his gaze. "I... I don't know. I have a lot on my mind. I need to talk to you first."

"We can talk and eat at the same time. I promise not to banish you from the kitchen if you drop eggs on the floor." He sipped his coffee. Next to finding Sylvie in his home, it might have been the best thing he'd ever been given. *Probably not, but it sure feels like it.*

With a sigh, she returned to the kitchen. When she came back, instead of sitting as she had before, she leaned on the end of the counter, her plate balanced on one hand.

As concerned as he was curious, he didn't know how to help her start the conversation she wanted. If he knew what she planned to say, he could help pave the way, but after the way things ended the other night, he had no idea what she might say or do.

He wanted to take the breakfast as a positive sign, but what if it was only a thank you for coming to her aid when the Garrison's showed? Or her way to cement the ending she'd set in motion the other night?

He didn't want any more gifts of appreciation. He wanted his woman.

She poked at her food for a moment then set her fork on the plate.

His head aching, groggy with fatigue, and with his heart uncertain of its fate, he set his own fork down. He started with the most obvious, and likely the simplest, question. "Did James or Mom let you in?"

"James. I don't think he was too thrilled with getting up early, but he didn't even ask me why. He met me here about an hour ago. I wouldn't dare ask your mom the day after her accident. Is she really going to be okay?"

He softened at the genuine concern in her soft words. "Yeah, she should be. I haven't been by to see her except briefly, but Cara stayed at the hospital in my place. Cara knows her stuff, and she assured me that aside from some ugly bruising and muscle soreness, Mom is okay. She's too stubborn to be anything otherwise."

"That's good. I mean, that she's okay. Although, arguably, stubborn is good, too." She took a bite of her eggs.

He intentionally tilted his head to look at her as if she were crazy. "Stubborn is *good*? Care to explain how?"

She rolled her eyes and took another bite. When she set her plate down so she could put her hands on her lovely hips a sprinkling of relief eased his tension. He suspected she had no idea how well the position showed off her curves. "Sure. How do you think women get things accomplished? By persistence. Dedication."

He held his palm up. "Point taken. Mom is definitely dedicated *and* persistent."

"Are you going to go see her today?"

"Yes. First thing on my list, actually, as soon as I get my head together."

"Did I wake you too early? I was so wrapped up in my world, I didn't pay enough attention to you. I regret that. Between helping with wedding prep, the day of, sleeping in your truck... there's no way you could have slept for more than a few hours in two or three days."

When she came to the table to sit beside him, he remained silent. Waiting.

She continued, "I owe you an apology, probably a few of them, the most important being for how I behaved the other night. I'm still not completely over the Brody deal, but after some thought, I realized he would have done the same thing, if he were in your shoes. Not a single stone unturned. Given the opportunity, he would've torn through your business like a tornado. While I *know* with everything I am that he would never in a million years do anything that might put me in danger, you've never met him. And...I think I know you well enough to know that if someone..." She poked him in the chest. "Anyone you care about is in trouble, you'd pull out all the stops to protect them. I know it because that's what you did for me."

As if with longing, she cupped his jaw in her hand. Her deep, mysterious eyes met his. When she dropped her hand a moment later, he wished she'd return it to its rightful place. On him, stroking his stubble. "Look, I've been wrong before, but I think you care a great deal about me. You've gone above and beyond repeatedly for me over the past couple of weeks, and I'm not sure I can ever repay you. At the very minimum, I do want to thank you."

"You're wrong about one thing." He took both of her hands in his and held on. "I don't merely *care* about you a great deal. I love you, Sylvia Grace. That's why I've done so much for you. I will continue do everything in my power to keep you safe."

Meeting his gaze, she whispered, "I know you would. I love you, too, Noah. Truly and deeply. I know it's all happened so fast, and the last few weeks have been crazy, but I know what's in my heart. I love *you*, Noah Ramsey."

His shoulders raised a little then dropped as if in great relief, which in turn eased her own burden. When he winked, the bubble of light inside her grew. "Eat up, Sylvia Grace. I plan to let mom sleep in before I go fuss over her. You and me, we've got lost time to make up for in the meantime."

She laughed, little bubbles of her happiness escaping with the sound. "We only spent two nights apart."

"Yeah, and that's far too many for me." He stood, extending his hand toward her. "Come on."

She slipped her hand into the his larger, rougher one. The rasp of his callouses sent shivers of anticipation whispering through her. As she followed, she realized she'd happily follow anywhere he led.

He drew her into his room and turned to her with an easy smile. Relief coursed through her, freeing the last remnants of her worry. She stepped into him, wrapping her arms around his neck.

Making the first move, she brushed her lips over his, then happily gave in when he took over, following his lead. It might not be everyone's idea of a happy ever after, but for Sylvie, Noah's arms offered something like salvation.

EPILOGUE

S ylvie pulled the roast from the oven and set it on the counter. She and Noah both remained so busy over the past couple of weeks, so they hadn't been able to spend much time together. That morning, as he'd kissed her goodbye, he'd grumbled over how much he missed her.

The feeling was mutual.

She'd taken his face in both palms. "Can you be home in time for dinner? I'll make it worth your while." She closed her offer with a kiss that should make certain he wouldn't be able to think of much else all day. Then she'd released his mouth, but not him.

He'd pulled her tighter against his hard body not hiding the fact that *all* of him was hard. "What time do you want me?"

She'd grinned. "I want you all the time. Tonight, I'll settle for dinner at six-thirty." She couldn't resist taking another sample from his lips, but he hadn't appeared to mind as he'd let her get her fill.

But, again, they'd had to part ways in order to take care of all the adult things. Rick had called an early meeting for Dark Horse, ensuring everyone could attend before their regular work day. Noah explained how Rick planned to eventually expand Dark

Horse to the point where he needed them all fulltime. Their security business wasn't quite there yet, but she didn't figure it would be long.

Sylvie suspected for a while that they did more than install simple security systems, but whatever it was they did do, she knew they worked on the right side of the fence. Besides, one thing her man excelled at was helping others.

Noah also explained that, due to prior troubles, they developed contacts in the prison and jail systems. Teddy and Michael Garrison got arbitrarily added to their growing list of troublemakers. Calvin clammed up hard and fast the moment he entered police custody. It didn't take a rocket scientist to deduce he was afraid of somebody. Bricks of the Garrison's empire might have fallen, but Teddy was smart. Unraveling the intricate system they'd established to launder money led to more dead ends than useful info or additional suspects.

Sylvie worried their early meeting meant more trouble.

As she'd reminded herself daily, though, her man and his friends could handle anything.

She pulled a loaf of fresh bread from another oven and she heard the crunch of tires over gravel. Her smile blossomed before she realized something wasn't right.

Not the low grumble of Noah's big truck, rather a sound like James' Chevelle. Also, her visitor came all the way up the driveway to the back door much quicker than usual. *Too quick.* She was turning off her ovens when rapid footsteps crossed the porch. She spun as he came through the door.

The muscle car still rumbled as if unhappy waiting on its driver. "Hey love. Noah's been in an accident. We gotta go."

The world tilted around her, leaving her nauseous. She braced a palm on the counter. "What?" It couldn't be. Her Noah was too big, too strong. James had to be mistaken. "How?"

"I didn't see it happen. We were finishing up the framing on the house; he was doing something up on the second story, I think. I don't know, he was high up in the air. We heard a loud crack then he was on the ground."

She asked the question that she needed the answer to most yet dreaded asking. "How bad is it?" She spun around in a circle, looking for her purse and phone. *Extra cabinets on the far wall, where I unloaded groceries.* She doublechecked to make sure the ovens and stovetop were all turned off. "Don't answer yet. Let's go. Talk in the car."

He moved but continued in a nervous ramble. "He was talking when they loaded him into the ambulance, but he sounded a little dazed. The leg injury looks the worst, I think." He grabbed her hand as they went out the door. He locked up as they went out, then ushered her to the passenger door.

Once inside his car, she swiped at her eyes. *Please let him be okay. Please.* She settled in for what would be one of the longest rides she'd ever take.

While James searched for a parking spot, she looked for his room.

Room 8. There it is.

After a mad whirlwind dash to his side, she paused, half-afraid to open the curtain and half desperate to see how he was. She shook off her hesitation and pulled the blue curtain with a jerk of motion. He sat up, blood running down the side of his face, and a mound of gauze wrapped around his head. When he opened his eyes, the pain she saw in his green gaze brought her to tears.

He was the strongest person she knew. For him to hurt so badly... She swallowed back her worry. He didn't need her worry right then. It was her turn to be strong for him. Her turn to take care of all the things.

I've got this. I'll do anything for this man. Surely I can sop up a few tears. She clung to the brave words even if she wasn't sure they were true. "How are you?" She sat in the hard, plastic chair beside his bed.

"I'll be okay, sweetheart. Don't worry." He squeezed her hand.

The doctor chose that moment to arrive. Tall, thin, and gray-haired, he looked as though he'd seen everything over the past six decades. "Mr. Ramsey?"

Noah nodded then winced. "That's me."

"The cat scan of your head came back, and results are negative. No internal bleeding or fractures, but you're displaying signs of a concussion. We'll monitor you for that while you're here. The orthopedic doctor is in surgery now, but she'll come by as soon as she's finished in OR. I think there's a very real probability they'll want to take you to surgery for the fractures we discussed. Is there anything else we can get you to make you more comfortable in the meantime?"

"No, but thanks," Noah answered as if resigned to his fate.

"I'll be in shortly to put those stitches in." He gestured to his own head, as if to clarify where he would be placing the stitches, then he was gone.

As the doctor's update registered piece by piece, Sylvie didn't know whether to feel relief or more worry. "Surgery for your leg?" Those were the only words she could find as she took a closer look. Worried about his pain and the mountain of gauze on his head she hadn't given much thought to the extra-large lump in the sheet below his knee.

Sounding exhausted and pained, he barely opened his eyes when he answered. "The tibia, the bigger bone in the lower leg—it's in four pieces."

She couldn't think of anything to do other than hold his hand and wait.

It hadn't taken long for Sylvie to figure out Noah did not like hospitals. He really didn't like being a patient, either. Once they admitted him to a room on the third floor and gotten him settled, his visitors began arriving.

He'd been pleasant to his mother, but everyone else hadn't fared as well. After he'd kissed her cheek and sent her on her way, he resorted to grunting at everyone instead of speaking.

She and James, the only remaining ones, debated over who would stay the night. Noah rolled his eyes. "Guys, I'm not a child. You can both go sleep in your own beds. I'm fine, and I'm not going anywhere."

She unfolded the guest blanket and claimed the recliner by putting her purse on it. "I know, but give me tonight, okay? I'm not ready to let you out of my sight just yet."

"Not you, too. I swear. I'm a grown man." She turned at the sound of Noah's grumbling and wondered if his latest visitor had any idea how cranky the "grown man" was becoming.

Rick entered the room, but something about his demeanor made her think his worry went beyond Noah's injuries. He looked prepared to deliver bad news, not simply check on his good friend.

When Noah and James spoke at the same time, she sat on the edge of Noah's bed and reached for his hand. "What's wrong?" They cut straight to the point, only cementing her suspicion.

Noah used his arms to sit up straighter in bed. James crossed his arms over his chest and spread his legs as if braced for the worst.

Quick, blunt, as if ripping off a bandage, Rick delivered his news. "Long story short, we got word through one of our contacts inside. Somehow, Teddy Garrison made a connection on the outside. He's spreading word on two fronts. First item? He's offered a very large bounty to anyone who breaks him out. If he sees daylight, someone gets a hefty million-dollar prize. I've passed that information on to the authorities."

Noah bit out a few terse words. "Spit it out. You didn't come out here to tell me that in person. That's bad news, but not doomsday bad."

James quietly waited, ready for whatever was to come.

"He sent a message. He's wants revenge for Travis's death, and there's no convincing him that you're not responsible."

"You've put Sylvie back on surveillance." It wasn't a question but a demand. "She'll stay here with me, but I still want extra protection on her."

"Yes, but part of the message stated he still thinks of Sylvie as a daughter. Wouldn't harm a hair on her head, supposedly, and he plans to let Michael rot for putting her in danger. I've passed on word that, since he's the one that drew her into this mess, Calvin's life is probably at risk."

While Sylvie didn't know what to think or how to react, James got more impatient until he finally spoke. "Get to the punchline."

Rick met Noah eye to eye. "Teddy Garrison is so confident he'll get out of before his trial that he's let it be known wide and far that he wants Nicole Ramsey dead. He'll offer a handsome reward to whoever makes that goal a reality."

It took about a half a second for the meaning of Rick's words to register. When they did, without thought, Sylvie all but jumped on top of Noah. Even with her weight, he already tried to climb out of the bed. "You can't," she pleaded. "You're in no shape to go anywhere."

He gripped her waist as if she weighed nothing and twisted his upper body to set her on her feet. "I'm going," he said with cold finality.

She just swiveled and sat on his lap, putting her weight on his uninjured side. Capturing his jaw with both hands, she used every drop of seriousness she possessed to stare into his tormented gaze. "You *can't*. If you weren't injured, I'd let you go. Baby, you can't even walk to the restroom."

James spoke, "I'm going. Noah, tell me where she's at. I'll leave now. I give you my word, I'll drag her ass back home where we can protect her."

Noah jerked his head from her grasp and pitched his phone against the wall, the impact jarring in the silence as it busted.

Her voice sounded shaky she spoke up, but she admitted something she'd struggled with. "Noah didn't kill Travis. I think it was Brody. I saw him that day. I—"

Noah gripped her shaking hand. "I figured as much. He did it to protect you. By protecting you, he also did me a favor. I'm glad he did what he did. This is on Teddy. No one else is to blame."

"Noah? I need a description. I'll head out now and get what I need on the way." James pulled out his phone, prepared to take notes.

"She's my twin, she looks just like me."

His eyes wide, James wisely stayed silent as he left the room.

A THANK YOU

Thank you for purchasing and reading Sylvie's Salvation. If you have a moment to leave a review I would appreciate it so very much. Without you, the reader, I wouldn't be able to do what I love best.
Thank you!

If you'd like to receive updates on new releases, contests, and whatever randomness I come up with, join my Newsletter at amyjhawthorn.com. I only send updates once a month or on release days. I'd love to have you!

ABOUT THE AUTHOR

About the author

As a teen, International Best Seller, Amy J. Hawthorn, fed her reading appetite with fantasy and horror stories. Then she stumbled upon a pretty book cover—complete with a bare-chested, sword-wielding, Highlander. That Highlander and his author showed her the magic of a Happily-Ever-After.

She has read her way through Kentucky, Arizona, Southern California, and then back home to Kentucky, where she's living out her own Happily-Ever-After. The only person surprised by her Best Seller title? Amy. Her friends and family are laughing and saying I told you so.

Find me on social media!
amyjhawthorn.com
amyjhawthorn@gmail.com

ALSO BY AMY J. HAWTHORN

Protecting Kate: Dark Horse Inc. Book 1

Catching Cara: Dark Horse Inc. Book 2

Finding Leigh: Dark Horse Inc. Book 3

Winter Deception: Dark Horse Allies

More Than a Rescue: Dark Horse Allies

Azrael's Light: Demon Runners of Unearth 1

Sunlight's Kiss: Demon Runners of Unearth 2

Lacey Temptations: Crave 1

A Craving For Two: Crave 2

www.ingramcontent.com/pod-product-compliance
Lightning Source LLC
Chambersburg PA
CBHW050517260626
47157CB00004B/1362